D1534924

Books by Peter De Vries

No But I Saw the Movie
The Tunnel of Love
Comfort Me with Apples
The Mackerel Plaza
The Tents of Wickedness
Through the Fields of Clover
The Blood of the Lamb
Reuben, Reuben
Let Me Count the Ways
The Vale of Laughter
The Cat's Pajamas & Witch's Milk
Mrs. Wallop

Mrs. Wallop

Mrs. Wallop

Peter De Vries

Mrs. Wallop

Little, Brown and Company — Boston — Toronto

LIBRARY OF CONGRESS CATALOG CARD NO. 77-126169

FIRST EDITION

Published simultaneously in Canada
by Little, Brown & Company (Canada) Limited

PRINTED IN THE UNITED STATES OF AMERICA

I

I

one

Ever wake up one fine morning to find yourself a character in a novel? When I heard I was the landlady in Randy Rivers's *Don't Look Now, Medusa*, I naturally hightailed it over to the Appleton library, where they were naturally fresh out, this being the author's home town, buzzing with gossip about his firstborn. So I trotted around the corner to Freitag's book store. I took a copy from the huge local-boy-makes-good display, and after glancing at the jacket, which showed a dark-complected, Cubistic-type woman sitting under the dryer in a beauty parlor, her hair a nest of vipers, began paging through it, a smile of anticipation on my face as I looked for myself, so to speak. For my memories of the days I had Randall Rivers in my rooming house on South Crown Street were happy ones.

My eye picked up a sentence, "Her knuckles were gnarled from a lifetime of penny-pinching," and then something about a woman who "took up where Mrs. Malaprop left off. Her mastery of the dislocated cliché was second to none's (as she would have been the first to say); her misuse of the language brought new color and even dimension to it, particularly in the attempts to stud her conversation with big words . . ." But nothing about me that I could seem to spot just then and there. I was about to buy a copy and take it home when I checked the price. Ouch, six-fifty, which is a lot of money even in these costive times. Better think that over, meantime stealing another peek here, the browsing itself already bringing back the flavor of those happy days four, five years before when I was giving aid and comfort to literary talent.

We always had a pleasant relationship to my way of thinking, reading poetry out loud to one another, or at any rate him not caring a fig who overheard him chanting his own favorites by the yard, often leaving the bathroom door open, and also trying out lines of his own whilst he shaved. You're familiar with writers saying they get their best inspirations when they're shaving? Which probably accounts for the vast amounts of lousy material around these days. (I think you get me.) Well, high on Randy's list of favorites was T. S. Eliot, of whom I'd heard of course but with whom I'm naturally not familiar, except for one poem Randy would intone more times than I could remember, which goes if memory serves:

4

Leave us go then, you and I
When the evening is spread out against the sky
Like a patient etherized upon a table . . .

A figure of speech I can appreciate after some twenty-odd years of nursing.

He would go anywhere he wanted in the house, being very democratic in that regard, always making me feel at home where you normally might not when you suddenly found yourself giving sucker to genius. I never dunned him for the rent, beyond slipping a note under his door to remind him it was due, then past due, then skedaddling on tiptoe downstairs to be waiting in full view in the parlor when he knocked off, thereby giving him ample opportunity to remit in full. I might be paging through a magazine so as not to make it too obvious, or him self-conscious. But the artist has his mind on higher things. All as would reward the tail of my vision was the sight of him plunging down the stairs and through the vestibule, a big and big-footed young man sounding like a whole group leaving the house as he plowed on out the front door and down the porch steps into the street, complaining that April was the cruellest month or the wench was dead, probably having imbibed a little too much, muffler flying and the famous scowl like a cap pulled down over the brow. Describing it in this autobiographical work, he speaks of the hero wearing "the inscrutable glower of a Beardsley foetus," already sensing cause for anger in the world to come, which is a new one on me. In more than two decades of nursing,

5

practical and registered, I have come across every conceivable kind of obstetrical complication, from your placenta previa to your breech delivery, but a Beardsley foetus doesn't seem to ring a bell. As for waiting up for him, forget it. He might not return till the small hours. Forget also "going for a walk" or "taking a constitutional" on the standard human scale. His descriptions of these midnight rambles are well worded, I want to submit. He got around a lot by night, like the angel of the Lord in some of the bloodier sections of the Old Testament, a nocturnal creature stalking the million-legged monster of the city, striving to still the seething torments of his spirit, driven by the lost anonymous generation-drowned ancestral furies brewed in the ferments of his vatted blood, as he tells about it in the book, which as I say is obviously autobiographical. He feared the life to be faced not because it was so great, but because it was so small, shrinking a man far, far below the scale on which in his youthful dreams he saw himself living it. He was cast in a Rabelaisian mold, and society had a nerve asking him to launch in its puny pond the ocean vessel of his spirit. I say bully to that attitude in an age of instant whipped potatoes, ballpoint pens built to last three signatures, and an average of 25 percent of all people undecided in polls asking their opinions on issues vital to the nation at large. A lot of this tended to be laid on with a trowel (as better critics than me have noted) but never mind. It's better than that pernickety kind of style, you know the sort I mean. All fine points, every hair in place, and enough understatement to choke

6

a horse. He was a demigod, lashed by gods. Not bad. Sensing he was a plagued and driven young man I had under my roof, I advised him to seek divine guidance. But I can see where that would cut little ice if your problem is that deities are grinding your bones to a pulp. What good to pray if you have got the entire Pantheon on your back? Classical curses were his portion, as the title indicates.

Now these were the facts as I was to garner them later when I got around to actually reading *Don't Look Now, Medusa*, not then skimming through it hastily at Freitag's. There was some more about the Night Devils, and about prowling the million-footed city and him the only party in it sensing the illimitable and bitter odyssey of man as (well behind in his rent) he plunged alone down the unlistening streets. This stuff was boss. Anybody could spot the genius in it a mile off. But I was looking for little old me, certainly no more egotistical than seeking at last in the blazing ovens of the dawn some semblance of a Self newly forged from the smelted remnants of the old, to hear him tell it like it was.

A line caught my eye, and I flipped back to the page on which my radar had picked it up. "She had a smile like something carved out of a jack-o'-lantern." Who she? I wondered (assuming the characters to be all Appleton, Indiana, folks as rumored). A little farther on I picked up another blip. "She wore her hair in a thick plait on top of her head, where it sat like a coiled adder, a fit trademark and apt metaphor for one ever poised to strike the unwary with her wicked tongue." This seemed to date the story at a period when that kind of hairdo was popular in Appleton as elsewhere, and a lot of us sported it for a while, roughly the period that coincided with his leaving home and moving into the digs with me so he could get some work done. One of those rages that die down as fast as they spring up. Well, on with the search for the landlady of 312 South Crown Street. A few pages farther along we were still with Mrs. Hallowe'en apparently, or back to her: "The caricature smile perfectly expressed the caricature of solicitude behind it. She positively foraged for the misfortunes she could then emotionally revel in appeasing; calamity was her meat; she glutted on trouble of any kind, provided it was not her own." Well, we've all known that sort, haven't we, and this one sounded like bad news all right. I flipped through a whole bunch of pages and Buster was still piling it on this same customer, a "Mrs. Lusk" in the book. "One of those dragons of respectability in which American small towns especially abound. Devils quoting Scripture all!" Amen! "As for sex, her husband found a clamshell between those legs." How would you like to be married to that type? "An ample bosom — of pure granite." In other words nobody you'd care to have in for a bite to eat followed by an evening of chitchat. A real platter of nettles.

I might of continued combing the cast of characters for our widow of Crown Street, not only renting a few rooms to selected lodgers when her husband passed away but also taking in a little needlework to tide her over a period when an ailment of her own forced her to suspend her nursing temporarily, had I not picked up a blip from another direction. My radar told me to raise my eyes and get a load of somebody perusing *me* from across the counter. It was not, as I had feared, a clerk come to remind me that browsing was all very well but this was hardly the library. It was Cora Frawley, the news behind the news, a Meddlesome Matty of the first order. He's been fired, she didn't make Radcliffe. Sports and weather in a moment. She wore a faint smirk as she glanced first at the book as I half laid it back on the counter, then at me.

"Well, Emma Wallop. How are you, Emma?"

"Fine, Cora. And you?"

"Fine." She came around. "I understand there are some pretty acid portraits in that. People are blushing all over town."

"Especially those who were left out. Anybody who is anybody is in it, I hear."

"They say the Rivers family are in a state about what he said about them. Especially the mother. She's prostrate, to hear them tell it. Not been out of the house since the book was published, and swears she never will. The shades are drawn. She's taken to her bed and has turned her face to the wall. They say it will kill her."

"It killed Stella when the other boy was arrested for marijuana, and it killed her again when her only daughter married a Jew — the only stable member the family has got if you ask me. Of course she's got nine lives for reasons we all know." It was irritation with Cora that made me pooh-pooh a story I later learned was quite true, with no exaggeration or embroidery by anybody. I was going off half-cocked in a manner typical of Cora's effect on people. But I continued, "I can make a wild guess. Stella Rivers has spent her life trying to pass for a Wasp, as they call us, after being lucky enough to marry one. Now Randy's spilled the beans about her origins being quite otherwise. Of course that's off the top of my head. Have you read it?"

"No," Cora said, "I find I don't have much time for light reading any more. I came in to buy this," and get a load of her, waggling an anthology of Oriental wisdom the size of second base. You can have that branch of human thought. I suppose it's a bald spot of mine, but there it is. Cora Frawley would be following that intellectual fashion, yogi and all. Some years back I had an arthritis, a woman I tried my best to keep on the medications prescribed and in bed where she belonged, but she embraced Zen Buddhism as the road to mind-body health, and insisted on her yogi exercises to the last. We finally had to rush her to the hospital locked in the lotus position. But getting back to my own feeling about all this Oriental wisdom now in vogue, especially Chinese proverbs, is that they *sound* profound at the time you hear them, mentally very filling so to speak, but they don't stick to your ribs. An hour later I'm hungry for another Chinese aphorism. And the astrology it's all often mixed up with, as it was in the case of Cora Frawley. Astrology is the bunk, as any Capricorn with Mercury in his third house knows. That's the planet that gives us intelligence and skepticism, you know. Certainly enough to see through the folderol and fiddle-faddle. Well, anyway.

"How's Ralph?" I asked, to get her off the subject before she could get on it — giving her a chance to brag about her son being also an expression of my own Western Christianity. Not that there wasn't a little game in it for me: seeing how long it took her to tell me where Ralph was flying to — London or Paris or Rome or whatever. Ralph was beginning to look more and more like he could do it without a plane, but then that could happen to anybody. I wouldn't sit in judgment there, or mock. We all liked him as a boy. Bright, talented, clearly headed for success. You could see him in New York, one of those chaps in gabardine suits who will give you a buzz. Don't call him, he'll call you? But hold it. Just a minute. What's this feeling for fabrics, this highly developed color sense, to say nothing of walking on the balls of our feet, sort of floating along? It's certainly something on the increase. Gotten so it almost makes no sense to ask in the maternity ward, "What is it, a boy or a girl?" The question will just have to wait. Eighteen, twenty years.

"Oh, Ralph," she said with a broad smile, and smoothing down the collar of my coat out of insecurity. "Mike and I spent a couple of weeks in New York recently, and saw him of course. He's fine. He's doing the sets for a light farce. Just a piece of inconsequential fluff, but Ralph says it's amusing for what it is. Then when he's finished with that he's going to spend the summer on the Continent."

"Which one?"

"What?"

"Which continent?"

"Well, he'll fly to Amsterdam, actually, do Holland by

car, and then tour the wine regions of France. As many as he can tuck in. He has to be back toward the end of the summer to start work on another show scheduled for a winter opening. He's in constant demand as a scenery and costume designer."

"It could happen to anybody."

"Of course he can get you tickets to anything. We saw three plays in the time we were there. Oh, and we went to the opera."

"Grand or light?"

"It was a production of *Madame Butterfly*, with a fabulous Cio-Cio-San. Ralph would love to do an opera sometime."

I knew I was pulling the bung on a subject dear to her, and why not? I gave the woman credit for not letting his alien way of life diminish her pride in his accomplishments. I heard her out for a few minutes more, insisted on equal time for my own boy, Osgood, who lives in New York just as much as Ralph, then beat a quick retreat. I had long ago put *Don't Look Now, Medusa* down again, and I left the store while she was still in it, so she could see me not buying the book with her own eyes.

My curiosity now had got fixed on something else. The title. Who was Medusa and what was the significance in this case? Instinct told me Medusa would be a figure in classical mythology, which I could probably look up in the big Webster's unabridged in the reference room in the library, to which I accordingly returned. As I made for the dictionary I saw that Milly Gordon, the assistant li-

brarian, was on duty at the reference room desk. Another
Nosy Parker. As I turned the pages, I could sense the
wheels of her mind grinding: What would anybody as ig-
norant as Emma Wallop be doing looking up a word in the
dictionary?

"Anything I can help you with, Emma?"

This is the kind of ploy they call it that's all the more
irritating for its politely helpful surface. It packs an invitation to expose the ignorance you're trying to correct, and a
chance for the asker to display her knowledge by remedy-
ing it for you. Well, two can play at that game I thought.
I quickly cased a couple of pages for the biggest word I
could find, and lit on a beauty. There it laid, like a long,
fat, juicy worm.

"Yes. 'Isoagglutination,'" I sang over. "That's what I
was looking up, Milly. Any idea what it means?"

"I think you'll find it in there," she said, looking over
her half-glasses and pointing at the dictionary I was deep
in the heart of.

"Thanks, Milly. I thought as much." Whoso diggeth a
pit shall fall therein.

There is a medusa which is a type of jellyfish, but I
doubted that was the connection here. The mythological
creature obviously referred to in the title was "one of
three sister Gorgons, whose heads were covered with
snakes and whose glance turned the beholder to stone."
Or 2 (l.c.) "a dreadful woman."

All these vexations got me out of the mood to read the
book, and I certainly had no intention of putting my name

13

on the waiting list at the library, for everyone there to see. When Stella Rivers kept her promise never to leave the house again, until she left this world, why, you lost some of your eagerness to see what kind of job the author may of done on you. We buried her a year after pub date, whether a victim of natural causes or "literary matricide" makes no difference now. Neither do any of the reservations I had about her in life. She was a valuable and respected citizen of Appleton. Active in worthy causes, a fine church soprano, and, if I may say so, a great parallel parker. I have seen her backwhip her Cadillac into spaces a truck driver might take pride in. She had climbed to her place in the sun out of humble origins, as we shall see. Gone now was that example which was nothing if not exemplary — gone with the wind. All these things combined to sour me on *Don't Look Now, Medusa,* which gradually slipped out of my mind. I forgot about it for some time. For several years to be exact. By then it had gotten itself salted down as a kind of modern classic, especially among the young people. The whole keg of nails was suddenly reopened for me when, one afternoon in late spring, I overheard some of our local college students talking about it in Lamson's drug store.

"That landlady, I wonder if she's still around," one of them said. "I'd certainly love to talk to her!"

Well! I had been in the dulldrums for some time, everything going, oh, not wrong so much as just flat. The salt was losing its savor. You can imagine how those words made me prick my ears up. I leaned closer to listen.

14

There were six or seven of these kids roosting along the coffee counter there at Lamson's. They took up all the stools, and I was standing behind one of them, a girl in a sweater and slacks of mattress-ticking stripes, waiting for a place to become vacant. She was sitting next to the speaker, a reedy rather good-looking boy with long yellow hair. They were dawdling over coffee and cigarettes at a rate that indicated a long wait. Well, I reminded myself, you can't blame all our young people for the behavior of most of them, and these didn't look like the kind who carry their chewing gum in their navel as a protest against bourgeois values. Which is at least something. I shifted my weight from one foot to the other, and my bundles to another arm. The girl in the mattress-ticking pants lit a cigarette from the butt of another, then still another from that. By this time the book was available in cheap reprints. She was snapping her thumb against the pages of a frazzled paperback as she talked.

"Do you think she's still around here anywhere?" she said. "She must be a pretty spotty banana by now."

"Tuck Walters said someone told him she was. Where would you begin to find out where to locate her, and if she has anything to say? Who'd know?"

A lot more water had run over the dam since the original publication of *Medusa*, as the scholars called it for short. Positive Rivers, the father, passed away before the book came out; the mother soon after; the younger brother, an aspiring painter, disappeared after his release from prison following the marijuana conviction and nobody knew a thing about his whereabouts; and the sister, now a Mrs. Feldman, lived in Oregon and washed her hands of the whole matter, declining to answer any questions about Randy — in whom interest was now running at a fever pitch. He had become a kind of legend in his lifetime, both because of the rage of the book and his steadfast refusal to give interviews, receive pilgrims or even answer their letters. He hid out like a bandit wanted for something. All this of course only doubles the curiosity about a celebrity. Whether he knew it and played that game, or guilt over what he had done to his family had made him take a vow of silence and even embrace a sort of monastic life, or a mixture of the two plus an honest reticence about his work was behind it all, nobody could say. But anybody could guess. Six months of availability to the press and the whole mystery-man boom might collapse. Or maybe not. Who knew? At any rate, and whatever his motive, you couldn't get a word out of him edgewise. He clammed up absolutely while the rumors swirled around his name like the waters in a riptide. Anybody with a crumb of information about him was now fair game for the chase. Anything I hadn't suspected about that before I could pick up in a twinkling right here eavesdropping on these scholars. I was, now, a chapter in the life of Randall Rivers. I was a legitimate object of literary research. It would be only a question of time before they ran me down, and I would either have to speak up or head for the tall timbers myself. Because it was also plain that the scholars here were interested in me as a real-life, not a fictional, character

— the landlady Rivers lived with, not portrayed in the novel. One of them, the towheaded boy, was doing a term paper on him that he wanted to "hop up with a little scuttlebutt."

"Where could I find that woman?" he said.

"You're looking right at her," I said.

Of course they hadn't been, but they did now, swiveling about as one on the stools.

Well, waters in a riptide is good. They boiled around me with their questions, all talking at once and offering me every seat in the place. It was from the middle one that I held court, answering their queries as best I could. Thick and fast they flew.

"Is it true that he wrote off the top of the refrigerator?"

"He never had kitchen privileges. None of my guests did, since they were only roomers, not boarders. I was not that impoverished. Yes?"

"Did he salivate when he composed, as they say? You know, drool?"

"What he did in the privacy of his quarters was his own business. I never tried to regulate my guests' personal lives. I felt that was their own affair. They were all adult, they knew what they were doing."

"Did he sleep diagonally in the bed, because he's so tall?"

"I'm sure he did, as we all do, from time to time. We all change positions a hundred times in a night, eventually hitting all that there are. Yes? I believe this young man has his hand up."

17

"How many drafts did he write?"

"Enough to satisfy himself he had reached the finished version, is all I can say there. I'm sure that varies among writers, and for each writer at different times. I've heard Randy speak of fussing with a paragraph for a week, and of hammering out a chapter in a day, when it seemed to write itself. Randy would say writing is one-tenth inspiration and nine-tenths desperation. But why all this interest in the technical aspects of writing?" I asked with a laugh. "Hoping to become writers yourselves?"

They laughed and confessed, most of them, harboring that ambition.

My own credentials in that area are hardly in order I realize. The reader will notice something my boy Osgood once said about my grammar both written and spoken. That it is not consistent. Now it's right, now wrong, then again wrong in a fresh way. Well I quoted a line from a poet named Cummings, a taste for whom my boy got from Randy, who played recordings of him reading his own stuff on a phonograph in his room. He the one whose poems look like they been fished out of a bowl of alphabet soup? Never mind. I can still hear that beautiful voice coming out of Randy's phonograph. "Who pays any attention to the syntax of things will never wholly kiss you." Once the needle got stuck in a crack in the record and downstairs I heard, "tax of things will never, tax of things will never," over and over again. Randy was dosing a bout of the flu at the time with a liquid diet, as you may be sure, and when I finally climbed up the stairs to his room he was sprawled out on the bed, an empty bottle on the table beside him. "Oh, *there* you are," he said, sitting up glassy-eyed. He pointed a finger at me, as though wanting to share with me the discovery of my whereabouts. And as for my spelling, my son in a somewhat more filial mood called that "nothing if not Dionysian." Of course I am in over my head with all this, but how else are you going to learn to swim? The purpose of art itself is to get man a cut above himself. Leastways it's how I look at it.

So I then asked the scholars why Rivers was such an idol among the young, why *Don't Look Now, Medusa* was their Bible.

"I think it's because he speaks to our generation about yours," the girl in the mattress-ticking pants said. "Though of course he belongs to neither, really. He falls between the two. Maybe that's why he can do it. Being neither, he's both, sort of. But as for the writing itself, what's especially so gripping is his gift for characterization. The way he brings people to life."

"Not in the case of his mother," I said. "He killed her."

"Well, I was thinking more of their vividness on the printed page."

By now it was obvious that I could not discuss this intelligently until I had corrected something you have undoubtedly guessed. I must read the book, not just dip into it. I therefore told the scholars I had no more time just then, but that if they would let me finish my coffee and then some more shopping I had to do, I would grant them an interview in the very near future. We even set a date, a week from the following Sunday afternoon. I figured that would give me ample time to do my homework. They trooped out in a chorus of excited thanks and I hotfooted it once more for Freitag's, this time the paperback section, where naturally a good supply of *Medusas* was on display.

Lo and behold if history didn't repeat itself in the form of one of those minor coincidences life is always dishing up to us. Cora Frawley was in the store again, browsing at the nearby greeting card counter.

I kept the swivel rack the *Medusas* were on between us as long as I could, circling now clockwise, now counterclockwise, as she herself orbited the card counter. I certainly didn't want her to see me looking for myself *again*, in what was now a minor *classic*. I peeked around the side of the swivel rack and watched her. She was apparently looking for a Get Well card, probably one that didn't tell the sick party to drop dead or jump in the lake or something else in the current insulting vein, because she shook her head and put one back in the slot and picked up another. I was trapped there. I couldn't move out of my shelter without running the risk of being seen, with no guarantee of remaining concealed even there when she turned to leave, because she'd have to pass the swivel rack to do so. Which she did, clutching without much pleasure her ultimate selection. I ducked to the right to keep out of view, but the motion caught her eye. She got a glimpse of my face and said, "Emma Wallop!" with all the false enthusiasm of two women who can't stand each other. My own situation was now as follows. I had a copy of *Medusa* in my hand, at a side of the rack away from the main supply of this title. I tried hastily to jam it back into one of the pockets where I stood, any one, but they were all full-up, so in the split second remaining to me while she hove around toward me I simply dropped it into a paper bag of previous purchases I was carrying, like a shoplifter. That's Cora Frawley for you. Then grabbing another book at random I went to meet her, singing out in turn, "Why, Cora Frawley, how are you? How's tricks?"

It's wrong to say we dislike each other. We dislike seeing each other, because we feel uneasy and self-conscious in one another's presence, for reasons neither of us could explain. We all have acquaintances like that. So do you in all likelihood. Overcompensating is I think the way they describe the exaggerated manner with which people try to cover up in such cases.

"We just had a letter from Ralph in which he mentions seeing Osgood," she said, with too broad a smile, and again laying the hand on my shoulder out of insecurity. My son kept so little in touch with me, off there in New York, I might very well have said, "Oh? How is Osgood?" But with a mother's natural pride I lied, "Yes, he wrote me he saw Ralph." I mentioned having enjoyed her son's sets for a production of something at our local summer theatre some months before, which was neither truth nor lie, his stage designs being something I can take or leave. Or say I'm not equipped to judge. They are the kind that are

21

called imaginative by the critics because half of them is missing — you can see through the walls and there are no doors, only a general framework like in an unfinished house — whereas if they are all there they are jumped on for being over-explicit. I tell you I've had it. I'm fed up, to here. If you're the same, why not run down to Gatlinburg, Tennessee, for a couple weeks' vacation among the mountain folk. It will do you a world of good. Nobody there has ever heard of the human condition, being too busy hewing wood and drawing water, marrying, giving birth and dying to of done so. These thoughts went through my mind then as Cora rambled on about her children, because she comes from mountain stock, this sturdy woman, so the folk songs her daughter, Toby, sings have been come by honestly. Toby is little mentioned. She too went to New York and there as far as I can make out ran foul of some Achilles heel, who in the end didn't marry her, is all I'll say. I honestly hated to think of Cora not having any grandchildren — having to be satisfied with what she keeps calling grand children, which in their respective ways both Ralph and Toby are. You *watch* a woman like that talk as much as listen to her, and I tried to generate within myself as much sympathy as I could for this acquaintance who says "women our age" when she's fifty-seven and you're forty-nine, noticing the coarsened complexion and the heavily upholstered arms and the silk scarf of the sort we knot and fluff around our throat when our skin is strictly speaking no longer skin-tight. But how that chin could wag. Cora's renown in Appleton goes back a long way, in fact to the days when she was a crack debater on the local high school team. I never went to high school, but I use to hear about her and see her picture in the paper. Of course that really does go back. In that era they were probably debating subjects like, "Resolved, that the United States should get out of Oklahoma."

She seemed to be taking the affirmative of some proposition now, the New Freedom. With her Ralph sleeping with every Tom, Dick and Harry, and I do mean just that, there was nothing for her to do *but* go along with it. A lecture on the post-Sputnik sex morality was the last thing I needed just now, so at the first pause I shot in, "Osgood has had a play running on Off Broadway for five months."

"Oh, really? Then that must all of developed since Ralph ran into him about three weeks ago."

And the tile teeth. Square things like Scrabble counters. Get at them with a Brillo pad and some Ajax you wanted to write anonymously in a letter signed "Charitable." What issued between them was generally square too. Appleton certainly has its share of small-town characters for a place of only 48,000. She had on pearl eardrops and a string of pearls. I'm partial to the old tapioca myself, but not in broad daylight in that quantity.

"Maybe some day Ralph and he will get together on a production," she went on. "Who knows? I'm glad Ozzie is getting along with his writing. Does he maybe have something in that?"

I suddenly note a gesture she's picked up from her Ralph. Birds of that feather do it all the time. They'll point to something, like a darling pin of yours they're admiring, touch it with a finger and instantly draw back, as though it's hot. I'm not lampooning the type here. I would not be putrid in this area — as we shall see, I think you'll agree. And I'm not criticizing the woman. I'm simply noting the way she touched the paperback in my hand.

It was the first real look I got myself at what I had snatched up. It turned out to be an anthology of new writing, which gave me a chance to say how I kept looking for Osgood's things because he was so lax about letting me know when he had something published. Which gave Cora a chance to bet he was an Aries, who were like that, and then to exclaim that she wanted my opinion of a shirt in the window of a nearby store, which she was thinking of sending Ralph for his birthday. "Come on, if you're leaving anyway," she said, steering me toward the front desk where old Mr. Freitag sat smiling behind the cash register. What else could I do? I paid for the one book and walked out with the other in my shopping bag, like a common thief. People are awful. This human nature is shabby stuff, as you may know from introspection. That, at any rate, was Cora Frawley for you, in terms of her effect on other people, and the counter-behavior, you might say, to which she drove them. It turned out I liked the plaid shirt in question, though what else could I say, and she thanked me and we bad each other goodbye, and home I went, to curl up with *Don't Look Now, Medusa.*

I settled down with it after dinner, a Coke at my elbow and my stocking feet up on an ottoman. I now fully in-

24

tended to read this book straight through from beginning to end, without skipping and without skipping around. But I found the opening chapter slow going. Endless descriptions of all of the hero's immediate ancestors, a lusty lot who were all larger than life, even when laid out at the local undertaking parlor. I like a story that moves right along. I began to skip pages, finally several at a time. Then a sentence caught my eye: "She had a laugh like the clapboards being ripped off the side of a house." This is the kind of writing I like. Plenty of sock, plenty of zing. I let out a guffaw you could hear to the city limits. I took a swig from my Coke, still smiling as I set it down again and returned to the book.

I found my place and read on, with the same relish. But hold it. Just a minute here please. Who is it that possesses this horse laugh? None other than our landlady, Mrs. Lusk. In real life a certain Mrs. Wallop? All right. No offense. All in good fun is all in good fun. Now that I had located the character they said was me, I sat back to enjoy the description of her in full. And it turned out that what I had got snatches of riffling through the book that first time in Freitag's, with no shock of recognition whatever, applied to her. Plus any number of worse libels culminating in a little piece of character assassination about her narrow-mindedness and provincialism ending in the sentence: "In short, nothing alien was human to Mrs. Lusk."

I drew back my arm to throw this particular piece of literature across the room, but stayed myself with an, "Upupup. Hold it. Let's not tar ourself with the same brush, shall we? Let's be fair where he wasn't. Let's consider the source. To understand all is to forgive all — remember? Let's consider the source and maybe go even beyond that to his origins, to see if we can get some light shed on what makes an ingrate tick." All right, then. Here we go.

His mother was a Slobkin. The Slobkins were third-generation foreigners whose grandfather came over from somewhere in central Europe in the middle of the nineteenth-century, or perhaps great-grandfather, making them fourth-generation, at any rate bundling his family into steerage for the voyage to the land of the free. I do not intend to go into his bloodlines here, or make a point of the matter save insofar as it might explain his conduct. So anyway, after a generation or two as blacksmiths and construction gangsters they managed to get over to the right side of the tracks. Not by much, the sparks from passing locomotives coming in through the kitchen windows, but the right side. From there the later Slobkins could spread out and begin their long uphill climb along the trolley line to the Crown Street section and the better element. We could only wish them well as we watched them make their way, on all fours it sometimes seemed, to the maple-shaded porches of rambling white houses such as my grandfather's, which passed to my father and where I grew up, and into which I later moved with my husband of eight years, when both my parents had gone.

Stella Slobkin was a few years younger than me when I first saw her working as a waitress at the Golden Ox. She was quite a dish, with a bonfire of red hair and great rolling hips with the power of the very tides in them. She had quite a prow too, making for many a joke from masculine diners about waterwings on backwards and the like of that, but never mind. She knew the hand nature had dealt her and the tricks she could take if she played it right. She wasn't long on brains, but what she lacked in intelligence she more than made up for in promiscuity. Or so they said. But she wisely drew the line on anybody really worth hooking — such as Positive Rivers, of *The* Riverses. He was one of the crowd of fast young blades who hung out at the Golden Ox. He fell madly in love with her. Head over heels. It was a blind, unreasoning passion, which I think is great in this day of canned hams, built-in obsolescence (so that you better trade your car in every two years if you don't want to wind up on the parkway grass waiting to be rescued), and the kind of status-seeking that includes petty fears of marrying beneath you — which was the cry set up by Positive's horrified family. To no avail, them with their stucco house with seven acres, where they gave parties with themes and served the above-mentioned hams, which are no longer smoked at all but chemically cured. For it was in those rosy fakes that the Rivers family made their money and got their name. I mean the Chicago Rivers, of which our Appleton branch was a shirttail connection and in whose reflected glow they gave themselves what airs they could and cut such a social figure as they were able.

Anyway, our flaming hunky had the last laugh on the rest of we girls. (And speaking of laughs, *there* was a goose-honk.) The next thing we knew the girl of whom it was said the boys all worshiped the ground she laid on was going down the middle aisle toward marriage with Positive Rivers, and a home out in East Hills, and benefit teas among the pinky-lifters sitting around clucking about young girls of whom it was said the boys all worshiped the ground she laid on. In one dramatic leap she had left us all behind, there in our once-choice Crown Street section, now decaying under the influx of construction gangsters who had made it as cement contractors, chiropractors, and filling stations issuing green stamps for premiums the cost of which is added onto the price of the original merchandise.

The big blow for me fell when my husband died and I was forced to take in selected lodgers. I never got into serving meals, as I wanted to get back to nursing as soon as my back allowed it. One of my first tenants was young Randy Rivers, who turned up one day with a suitcase and a portable typewriter, his brow dark with the famous frown and even then talking about ceasing upon the midnight with no pain and what have you. No Meddlesome Matty, I never pried into why a boy would want to leave home while remaining in his home town. He just said he needed a place to write, and taking the room was no more than the equivalent of renting an office to pursue your profession, as many writers did — reeling off a number of examples of which the only one that comes to mind just now is Oscar Wilde, who apparently couldn't concentrate with a woman around the house neither. That didn't explain our hero's moving

28

out to eat and sleep too, but I didn't press the matter, glad to have the ten dollars a week. How often he went back home for a square meal as a change from restaurant fare, or just to visit, I wouldn't know. His parents only called on him once, just to give his new digs the once-over. Maybe they disinherited him, which was why he so often fell behind in his rent. Stella Slobkin Rivers didn't recognize me, or gave no sign that she did, as we passed on the stairs with a nod. Now stout and matronly, the beautiful red hair worn in a tiara braid something like my own auburn mop, with a glittering comb in it, she probably thought she was slumming. Positive Rivers looked very handsome and distinguished with his gray hair and pinstripe suit and kid gloves he kept on in the house. His own financial position was a little rickety then, thanks to some shady deals involving local real estate development stock, so if he had married beneath him, so had Stella Slobkin, so they were even.

Thus the origins of the artist presuming to look down his nose at his fellow men.

The main gouge job on this "Mrs. Lusk" embodiment of the fair sex seemed to be a psychological analysis of her do-gooding, which I will simply reprint here without interruption.

"In Mrs. Lusk the town had an oxymoronic epitome of more of the occluded contradictions of sweet-sour, kind-cruel, prurient-prudish, neighborly-misanthrope, love-hate, dove-serpent than it might have seemed possible for nature to scramble in one human being. She enjoyed vast repute as one 'always there in a pinch,' but even some of the objects of her mercies must have sensed the sinister appetites these ministrations slaked. In the guise of an angel she circled the city like a vulture, descending by instinct on any house calamity struck, with that relish of another's misfortunes that is all too sadly human but exists as an unappeasable fever in a few, usually women. No rumor of illness reached her but her ear was cocked for the wail of the ambulance; no ambulance went moaning down the hill to the hospital but she began to watch for the hearse to ascend it, her harpy feathers ruffed impatiently for the consolatory swoop.

"For if the bedside was her green room, the funeral parlor was her true stage. There she burst into full bloom, one of those Bacchantes of mourning, those orgiasts of grief who can disrupt a burial service with their carrying on (as a too risible theatre-goer may disrupt a comedy with his laughter). There was to every death in Middleburg the dénouement when, after a decent interval, Lolly Lusk could tie on her bonnet and set out for the bereaved home, there to enact with calm joy the ritual of Going Through Things. She preferred consoling widows, as she did nursing men — a male struck down being the source of her deepest emotional reverberations. She knew exactly where to take old clothes, her antenna leading her straight to the houses where destitution made them most welcome.

"When not ministering to sickness she was fighting vice. Vice is a noun that has curiously little resemblance in meaning to its adjective. People with vices are often not in the least vicious, while those without them frequently are. This stainless woman gossiped viciously. She took special pleasure in slurring the proprietor of a roadhouse on the edge of town, in whose upper rooms she hopefully hinted ladies were obtainable for a price. Proof that they were would have fulfilled one of the fondest dreams of this fine churchwoman. Her own husband could have supplied it. For as an escape from the meagre appeasements to be found within that clamshell —"

Here I did sit bolt upright and hurl the book across the room as hard as I could. It struck the far wall with such force it broke in two. I immediately picked up the paperback of current writings, *New Voices* it was called, and began a short story. An allegory of guilt in our time, it was about a man who drove a car with blood in the crankcase, instead of oil. Everybody did, but this particular gink, this one motorist, would sit at the wheel with his straw hat tilted at a jaunty angle and a cigar jutting out of one corner of his mouth, tooling his family through Sunday traffic to a beach picnic, thinking nothing of the fact that his automobile was operating on human plasm, and the filling-station attendant either as he said, "I think she'll take a quart," holding his thumbnail on the dipstick to show where the level was, and blithely oblivious to our common human betrayal as he trotted off to get a can of the wherewithal which was stacked outside on the racks. I tell you I've really had it. I've had it up to here. I took this volume and also heaved it at the wall, where it dropped beside its mate. And there I left them lay, both of them, for over a week, only picking them up in the process of tidying the house for the young scholars, whom I was receiving the next day. I had promised to grant them an interview you will remember. That meant I still hadn't done my homework on *Don't Look Now, Medusa*, but ish kabibble. It was me they were coming to see, not T. Randall Rivers. Him and his peccable prose, his warped view of human nature. Driving through a strange town one summer's night I stopped my car before a funeral home on a sudden impulse to pay my respects to someone laid out there whose official circle of acquaintances seemed to be all lounging and laughing on the front steps. He was as alone in the parlor as I had a hunch I'd find him. I stood beside the casket a moment, to pay a little anonymous tribute to its occupant. He was a tall, rather cadaverous-looking man in his late fifties I should judge. I signed the nearly empty guest book and went out, shouldering my way through "mourners" now trading funny stories as they smoked their cigars. I did not judge them too harshly. I simply cite the incident as another example of the importance of keeping our sense of proportion. Only man is vile, sure. But man isn't only vile.

Well, we would see.

two

As youngsters they were not an unusual assortment for the day, with the Hallowe'en look that made you expect to hear "Trick or treat" when you answered the door. One kid went around in a bandmaster's jacket because his parents give him false values, another wore what seemed like a train conductor's coat. The girl in the mattress-ticking pants was there, pulled way down on her hips to de-womanize herself as much as possible, but of course the youthful feminine bloom always comes through. There was one very cute small girl with granny glasses. And get the walk, a regular Renault, the motor's in back. Most had long hair, most of it washed, and in some cases probably ironed. I could even smell soap. I think most of these anti-establish-ment yaks don't care if they really aren't grubby, as long as they look grubby. This baker's dozen milled around me like a freshly laundered herd.

It is now three o'clock of a Sunday afternoon in mid-April. I get the Cokes and cookies I have ready in the kitchen, we sit down, one or two pull out notebooks and pencils, and the catechism is on.

"Was he such a hypochondriac?"

"I have seen him put on his cap to poke his head out of the window to yell down at some children making too much noise in the street. But here's an odd thing. People who are deathly scared of drafts will think nothing of walking around in rain and windstorms. Maybe we feel more vulnerable inside. Anyway, it's part of the contradictoriness of human nature. But in general, the artist can be quite a baby. Nobody knows what notorious babies they are. Yes?"

"You probably knew him around town as a boy, I mean before he took a room here. Can you tell us anything about that? Like did he have a nickname that you know of? Things like that."

"Well, I had a nickname for him, kidding him about all the weight he was putting on, because he could certainly pack it away. 'I'm going to call you the Crisco Kid,' I said. 'You're fat in the can.' All in good fun, you see. Yes? This young man over here."

"Do you know if there was ever a time when he was called by his first name — Tom, or Thomas?"

"Well, now there's an interesting thing. Revealing about a person. Anybody who'll go to work and part his name on the side is someone who tends to give himself airs.

34

Your F. Scott Fitzgerald I gather was a social snob. Of course Randy must of been called Tom at first. It was his first name, the name his parents gave him and intended him to have. But no. They were origins he was trying to live down, so T. Randall it must be. It's a flossy kind of thing to do that tells a lot about a person. I believe the young lady there has a question," I said, pointing to the girl in the striped slacks who had her hand up.

"Is it true that he could only write on yellow paper?"

"Well, we all have our little quirks and crotchets. I like to eat prunes on a train. I'll bet most of you flying youngsters have never ridden on a train, I mean overnight, a trip of some consequence. Let me tell you what you're missing. Rocked to sleep in the berth overnight, then breakfast in the diner with the scenery going by in solid comfort, the cattle grazing in the fields, the little towns gliding past your window. Now of all meals breakfast is my favorite, and so it is on the train. How I love that first taste of chilled prunes, and then washed down with good strong hot coffee. Of course it isn't the prunes as such. They're only symbolic. Of taste sensations that wake you up, and starting a new day and all. The boy over there. I believe you had your hand up?"

"Do you think he had a sense of mission? I mean about the future importance of his work, even before he had written a line, or at least had anything published."

"I would say that he had few doubts about himself, but when you say sense of mission I'm afraid it's me who will have to ask the questions, in all modesty. What do you mean by a sense of mission? Of what?"

We got on the nature of his work for a while, and the pilgrims said what they liked about it was the honesty embodied in his very ambivalence — about life, about people. It was modern in its fidelity to the truth, which is that there is no truth in an absolute sense that we can fully and finally grasp. "He has a certain elusive quality," one of them said.

"Yes, they couldn't locate him when his mother died," I said. "He was traveling somewhere, no one knew where, so they buried her without him. But at least he had contributed his bit to the funeral up to then."

"Well, the story is that he was in Palestine at the time."

"Going for walks on Lake Galilee I have no doubt. Confident that when they bury *him* it'll only be for three days."

The pilgrims laughed and said it wasn't his fault that we all deified him at the moment, especially the young people. Those fads didn't last, they emphasized, there was always somebody new they would boom next year. A writer was in today and out tomorrow with the campus crowds. Rivers was now required reading, which was the first step to the skids. Most of this from the boy in the bandmaster's tunic, who sounded like a smart apple to me. "I shall watch his career with interest," I assured them.

Now more questions about working habits. For their benefit I dilated at some length on Randy's methods, and as I went on, giving myself my head, it became a kind of ramble down memory lane for me as well, the whole tone and feel of those days coming back to me in a rush. He worked long and hard, and at the end of the day his face

36

showed it, not sagging into lines so much as cracking into them, like granite, his black forelock half dangling into the deep brown eyes with their still faraway look, not quite back from the land of make-believe. For pastime he use to like to tinker with things, though I noticed that if given a choice he preferred repairing objects on which he could use a hammer. He mended his own shoes, of which he had several sturdy pairs for walking. Sometimes I'd take him up hot cocoa or tea when I heard the typewriter stop and the other thudding begin, for from below, the ceiling was like a summer sky rumbling with thunder. Once I offered to read some of my husband's poetry aloud to him.

Frank never fancied it was anything much, just verse to relax with himself after a long day of floor finishing, "getting it right" with the rotary sander or so. He was not one of your Attic poets as they call them, scribbling great art in a garret. From the little of that he read he could sense that writers today were going in for pessimism and denial. Well, he would be a Yea-sayer, writing poetry that frankly rejoiced in life and reveled in nature. In fact he frankly modeled it on college cheers — "yells" of thanks and appreciation for the beauties all around us. One for example goes:

> *Flowers, flowers, rah rah rah!*
> *You've smelled 'em with your noses*
> *So let's hear it for the roses,*
> *Roses, roses, sis boom bah!*

I read that one and a few more in a similar vein to Randy Rivers that evening. But the scowl on his face and the racket he made hammering the shoe he was fixing both grew in intensity. He evidently needed more pepping up after a hard day than I had suspected when I brought in the cocoa and the notebook containing the poems my husband left behind. When he began muttering to himself through my reading and his own pounding I knew I had my work cut out for me if I was going to cheer our Buster up this night.

I pulled out another stop. I demonstrated how my husband use to read his own stuff, with commentary, at church socials and Golden Age Clubs and the like — actually becoming a cheerleader as the audience joined in chanting the verses from mimeographed copies handed out to them. While, as I say, it laid no claims to being great poetry, or even poetry at all if it came to that, it did have one virtue generally not possessed by the stuff that is. It was not obscure. There was no mistaking the author's meaning, as I emphasized to the one I was trying to perk up with this little entertainment. Before whom, and despite his still hammering away, I now took my cheerleader stance. I crouched down at one end of the room and worked my way across to the other, in front of him, as though he were a cheering section, with the "locomotive yell" on which this particular number was based. I began my "choochoo" effects very slowly, gradually picking up speed toward a climax delivered at the top of my lungs. All the while his hammering went into a kind of creshendo too, the rhythms building crazily against each other, almost like in a mixed-media technique, a wedding of two forms. Talk about clearing out your liver. I remember the strange glow that came into his face, like something about to explode. This one was for fruits and vegetables.

> *Two four six eight*
> *What is there to celebrate?*
> *Fruits! Vegetables!*
> *Rah rah rah!*
> *So let's hear it for the merits*
> *Of cantaloupes and carrots.*
> *Don't clobber your guts*
> *With ifs and buts*
> *Just give a big hand*
> *For the fat of the land,*
> *Fruits and vegetables yeah!*

He flung the hammer and the shoe both into the open closet and went out for one of his walks. He thanked me warmly and, murmuring some apology about not having had anything to eat since breakfast and thinking he would stop for a bite of dinner on the way, went out the front door and "down the unheeding streets." Everybody turning to rubber at him as usual. Not excepting myself who watched from the front window, shaking my head. What a price to pay for genius. Being cast in a heroic mold was no picnic either.

Rutabaga, rutabaga, diddledy um bang!

He returned a little while after midnight, by no means a long night prowl for him. I could hear him from my bed as he put out the lights and came upstairs to his own. We were alone in the house those days. I had not yet found a suitable tenant for the one other room now available since my nineteen-year-old son, Osgood, had dropped out of Appleton and gone East to seek his fortune. He lives in New York, his hair a dark contrast to his pale skin and light blue eyes.

All through this long account to the pilgrims I was getting vibrations from Miss Striped Slacks. You know how Rubinstein keeps saying in interviews how he picks out one person in the audience the minute he steps out on the stage, a young woman, an old man, and plays to that person. I found myself talking to her, and thinking of her when looking elsewhere. It was the oddest thing. I had a hunch her heart wasn't in those casual hipster slacks and denim shirts; that once away from her peers, I believe you call them, she would put up that mane with a jeweled comb, and stand in silk frocks before a full-length mirror, with high heels for a little extra height. She lived in Evanston, Illinois, where I gathered her father was a top commuter, and for the last month of this her last year at Appleton was rooming with the Renault, who lived here and whose parents were traveling in Peru. They were ruin buffs. I was sure that as the years went by she would be increasingly one of those individuals who prune themselves on their social standing, their more money, their status. In that Dresden figurine face and those cool watching and waiting China-blue eyes methought I could see mirrored already the unarrived lover, who must woo her not with a face as handsome as hers, never mind that so much, but with money, or talent, or both. Class she had to offer, and class she wanted in return. Had I a crazy hunch that when she left it would not be the last I saw of her? They were far from out the door yet. The Renault had a question, the one with the motor behind, often pacing a bit to display same.

"It's said that you can't expect a good artist to be a good citizen too," she said, serious behind the steel-rimmed granny specs. "Observing him at close range like this, almost living domestically with him you might say, would you have any comment about his relations in general with other people, or his attitude toward them?" Here the towheaded boy who was writing the term paper, and wanted some biographical material on the subject, chimed in. "That's something I wanted to ask too," he said, settling a notepad on his knee. "In effect he told his family to go to hell. Did he tell the rest of the world that too? Where does the responsibility end of the creative person who is paying other dues to society than the standard ones most people pay?"

I smiled, setting down the glass of Coke from which I had paused to wet my whistle. It hadn't taken me long to recall an incident that illustrated this point. "I'm glad you asked that question," I said. "Let me answer it by suggesting shouldn't we turn it around to ask where the artist's *irresponsibility* ought to end. Where the freedom from the obligation to be a good citizen is no excuse for being a shabby one. Then paint a little picture for you, the

41

artist not at home, but among his fellow men, downtown, on Main Street."

It is a Saturday morning in early October. At one end of this long business block stands our hero. At the other is his objective for the morning — Folsom's liquor store. In between lie half a dozen charity booths like gun emplacements, to be slipped past and around with all the stealth of a one-man patrol unit if we are to make it to Folsom's without serious loss of funds. Yes, a row of dogooders whom we ought to observe at close range if we are to portray them accurately, though not too close for comfort. One of them happens to be his landlady, able to report the scene for the benefit of biographers because she witnessed it from midway the block where she is manning the Osteomyelitis booth.

Well! Caution and stealth must be the order of the day. He saunters on the right to within a few feet of the first enemy emplacement — some refugee relief or a local scholarship fund where the volunteers are shaking their cans. Suddenly he remembers something he must get in the drug store across the street. Over he pops, darting among the cars, hauls himself up short in the doorway as he apparently realizes he has forgotten what it is he needed. Window-shops a moment, moseys on down that side until he nears the next danger zone. Red Cross, March of Dimes, whatever. Can he contribute to that perhaps? No, unfortunately all his assets are tied up in cash at the moment, so it's back across the street to the other side again. We're moving right along now, swinging our arms like a solid

42

citizen glad to be among his humble kind, just plain folks again, but oops, what's this? Arthritis? Society for the prevention of something? Another fast thirty-degree angle to the other side on this zig-zag, the important thing of which is not to zig when you should of zagged. Then the reverse again, because there looming up is Freitag's where the P.T.A. is selling books on a profit-split arrangement with the proprietor. So we skedaddle back again, pretty nimble for a Crisco Kid, and this time the pickings are slim too. The best choice of store to window-shop at being a ladies' footwear. So we admire the pumps and wedgies for a while, whistling innocently as though this makes sense that doesn't appear on the surface. Then moving right along again, but watch it, what's this? The Osteo booth run by that famous penny pincher we are portraying in that book we're writing? We don't seem to recognize her this morning, for we cross again, stand gazing a moment with complete absorption at some rakes and trash incinerators set out on the sidewalk, and then one more bound and we're scuttling into that haven, the liquor store. We've made it without a financial scratch. We chat with our vintner, very neighborly really, buy a quart of booze, and repeat the obstacle course in reverse, perhaps stopping in the cheese store to pick up an Edam for snacks. Then home with our purchases, striding along at a brisk clip, glad to be alive among our fellow citizens, stooping as though out of a lifetime of ducking original beams, and leaning a little to the left to compensate for torque.

So there you have it — a Home Town in a Town of

Homes. Culturally-speaking-wise Appleton is probably no great shakes, except for producing an occasional writer gifted at depicting it. Though leaving out what a generous-hearted community it is, with a philanthropic record of collecting, that is to say giving, *far more than the per capita average for the country, according to figures recently released.*

"Of course," I said, in the silence that followed my story, "there are always exceptions."

Now for the Big Question I knew would come.

The Renault brought her hands together in an eager little clap. "Kwee see his room? Oh, please," she squealed through the general hubbub which this request set off. "Please kwee see his old room?"

I rose and trooped up the stairs, the scholars at my heels.

"I haven't kept it exactly as it was, though I'm still vacuuming cracker crumbs out of the corners. In all fairness, I brought him lots of those snacks myself." A couple of the boys at the tail end seemed to be complaining that they hadn't been told all they wanted to know about "the drafts." I turned at the landing, which I had now reached, and said, "You mean the ones he wrote or the ones he was afraid to sit in?"

"The ones he wrote," the towheaded boy said. "How many would you say he did on the average, before he was satisfied he had the finished version?"

I answered from the head of the stairs, along which my audience was now distributed from the top very nearly to the bottom.

44

"That varies among artists, and with each artist from page to page," I told the sea of upturned faces, "like I said at Lamson's drug store. The true workman knows himself when he's got it right. His own instincts must tell him. That's true of every craft. My husband was in floors, as I've said, and to his dying day his worry was to 'get it right' on every job, because for every job it was different. Sanding and finishing was one thing for the original oak boards at Mrs. Dalton's renovated farmhouse, another for a split-level in a spanking new subdivision. Till God called him home he said you never stopped learning the fine points of your trade. How you had to know to a gnat's eyebrow how many 'cuts' a floor needed in being sanded down, what thickness of sandpaper to wrap around the drum of the rotary. You could feel it, feel it in your bones right through the rumble of the electric power machine if you were cutting too deep or not deep enough. In the finish you were taking off before refinishing. You can rub down too fine as well as too coarse, don't forget it. Like once he sanded an oak floor down to so smooth a surface it wouldn't take the stain — a condition he sometimes had to correct for others who called him in as a consultant after making the same mistake themselves. The way you'd call a doctor in on a play that's in trouble out of town. How do you correct such a situation you ask. My husband would wet the floor down, because when it dries again it leaves just enough roughness of texture to drink in the stain and retain it. So there's the moral that applies equally to the writing many of you want to go into: you can polish it too

45

much, just as well as not enough. So it's so slick and perfect a reader just slides over it. No purchase. Give him something to grab him now and then, a common term, a little roughness here and there. Once you've got it sanded right you can finish it right, but get that right too. So get it right. And don't preach. Writers are too inclined to do that. I went to see *Hamlet* at the college here once, and there's a lot of preaching in that. I don't know how familiar you are with the play, but there's a scene with the players where the main character tells them he doesn't know too much about the theatre, other people's opinions in that area are high above his, but he's no sooner done so than he's telling them all how to act and what not, do it trippingly on the tongue, suit the action to the word, and so on. So even Shakespeare didn't get that right. I had a sander here recently re-doing my floor, and sitting around chatting with him and one thing and another, I told him everything I've just told you, by way of praising his occupation. And do you know what he said? He said, 'Lady, you're going to drive me into another line of work.' Imagine that. Things were sticky between us as a result, and come lunchtime he said he went out for lunch, though I knew perfectly well he had his lunch with him. He got in his truck and bounced off on one of the longest lunch hours I ever see a workman take. After an hour and a half I was so upset I went out myself. I did some shopping, and my feet killing me, I dropped into a movie down the street here for a bit. There were very few people in it, and from the back I looked over and saw somebody a few rows ahead who looked vaguely familiar. It was the floor sander, slouched down in his seat eating popcorn. He left before I did, and when I got home there he was, trundling his rotary around the floor of my living room. Right down there where you were. I said nothing then, or when he come back the next week to stain, but gave him a look when I handed him the check. But how would a novelist pin a character like that down? How's that for human behavior? Or for artistic temperament? A regular prima donna."

A hush fell over them when I finished. You could hear a pin drop. They gazed up at me in rapt attention, awe in their upturned faces. I turned and said quietly, "Now we can go into the room."

I pushed open the door of what I must say I never expected would become a museum. (How much could I rent it for now?) I had dusted it in full anticipation of this request, of course, once I had agreed to grant them an interview. Good thing they had asked all their questions, for they were speechless now. Pilgrimage is good. They wandered around the room in a trance, touching the desk where he sat, the old brass bedstead where he slept. One girl opened the closet door and looked inside, like a woman who was thinking of renting the place and wanted to see whether it had adequate space. "What did you think of the book?" she asked with her head well inside it. She had made the question general, not coming out point-blank to inquire what I thought of Mrs. Lusk. None of the scholars seemed to be looking directly at me. "I haven't read the whole book through," I said, saving us all embarrassment with the same evasive courtesy, "but the characters I have come to seem to me very vivid and colorful, though maybe on an exaggerated scale."

The girl came out of the closet nodding. "Mmm. That's his special genius of course, Rabelaisian extremes. And his weakness too, because they sometimes get into caricature. Anyway, all his mistakes are big mistakes."

"Oh, I don't know. He makes some little ones too," I said, coming to his defense. "Quite a few. He has this Mrs. Lusk keeping the soil in her raspberry patch 'as acid as herself,' whereas in fact it matters very little to raspberries whether the soil is acid or alkaline, as she herself knows. She would not waste her money feeding it aluminum sulphate. And he has a couple walking along the beach of Lake Michigan at low tide! Lakes don't have tides. Only oceans."

"Well, it's like Shakespeare giving Bohemia a seaport. Even geniuses make booboos. I'm not saying Rivers is in the same class, but he is a major writer."

There are a lot of lousy major writers around, as we all know, but I didn't see any point in pursuing the matter there. In any case the conversation suddenly took an unexpected turn.

The girl of whom I remained so obsessively aware had despite this fact said next to nothing since entering the house. Now she threw in something that I must say come out of left field.

"I was interested in what you said about his never giving to any worthy causes. That's why it would be odd if there's really any truth to the rumor that he's going to break down at long last and give a lecture for the benefit of something in town here. Muscular Dystrophy I believe. Or maybe perfectly natural, a sort of atonement for all his sins."

"That'll be the day," I said with a skeptical laugh. "Every new program chairman of every organization in town has been trying to snare him for years. Where did you hear this?"

"A friend of ours in town here whose aunt is chairman or something of the charity. A Mrs. Tatum?"

"That's Muscular Dystrophy. Well, if Lizzie Tatum has him bagged for a speech, she's got something on him," I answered with a laugh in which they all joined.

We closed more or less on that note. They completed their rounds of the shrine, then said they had taken up enough of my time, thanked me profusely, and left. I watched from the window as they piled back into the two cars in which they had come, dropping the lace curtain only after they turned the corner and vanished from sight. I hated to see them go.

The scuttlebutt they had left turned out to be true. T. Randall Rivers was coming back to his birthplace in the fall, to deliver his one and only public lecture. If anyone could snare him for such a benefit it was Lizzie Tatum, who knew him. Still it was a feather in her cap. I heard it was definite from Milly Gordon, who was leaving the library after work just as I was passing it, one afternoon in late August. We fell in together for a block or two.

"We got the posters in today for the Rivers lecture,"

she said. "He's coming in early October. Did you know about it?"

"Yes. Well, that's fine. That'll be a sellout."

We ambled along in silence through the balmy afternoon for some moments. Milly remained noncommittal. I knew her opinion of Rivers was moderate — she didn't think he was the greatest thing since feet. Still I sensed an undercurrent of excitement in her, and also that she might be playing a little cat-and-mouse with me.

"Strange, after all these years of everybody trying to land him for every cause in town, and drawing blanks," she said. "Mrs. Tatum knows him, but not that much better than some of the others who've been after him. I don't know why he's particularly interested in Muscular Dystrophy, but it's good he is."

"Yes . . . Of course we don't know whether he's for or against it, but it's good he's interested."

"Well, I turn here. I expect I'll see you at the lecture, if not before, Emma?"

"I'll be there with bells on," I said.

three

The lecture was held in the Presbyterian church (where I exchanged vows with poor Frank) which was good for two reasons. First, it was large enough to accommodate the overflow crowd — that is, the surplus was relatively small and comfortably favored by speakers set up in the basement where they were herded when the auditorium proper filled up. Second, the platform was only a foot or two off the floor, not away up at traditional pulpit height, which gave the feeling of hearing a speech rather than a sermon. Thus when, whether by reason of having fortified himself too well beforehand or nervous distraction or a combination of the two, the speaker walked off the edge of it in mid-sentence and pitched forward on his face, he had only a short distance to fall.

Our party of ten arrived at five to eight, a good half-hour before the time set for the lecture, but the church was already three-quarters full then. We had been to one of the pre-event dinners that are part of these charity affairs everywhere I guess, ours at Cora Frawley's. We made quite a stir as we entered, thanks mainly to Cora's outfit. It was one of those one-piece overall-type jump suits such as are worn by garage mechanics and fashionable women, all the rage just then in New York. I wouldn't run the garment down by any means. They are eminently practical and I'm sure comfortable, and Cora's was an all-white silk and lace number in which she looked stunning to say the least, but it gives you something of a start to see your hostess greet you at the door looking like your friendly Mobil dealer. All she needed was her name in script across the breast pocket. "Fill 'er up," I said at one point during cocktails, handing her my empty gin-and-tonic glass for replenishment. Nobody laughed, especially Cora. Except for my escort.

My escort was old Will Gerstenslager, three years widowed, one of those lawyers who are a standard fixture in every town. I mean he's a family lawyer, like a family doctor. He greets everything with that adenoidal chuckle of his, as he did now this implication that you were helling it up by having a second drink with a hostess in a jump suit. I had always been fond of Bubbles Gerstenslager, but never felt friendly enough toward her to ask her how she stood that adenoidal chuckle of Will's all these years and that Bay Rum he uses.

Knowing I wouldn't be seated with him at dinner, I took advantage of cocktails to huddle in a corner with him and swap such gossip as we had accumulated since last together. I told him how miffed Lizzie Tatum was that she couldn't spear the lion as a house guest, and didn't even know the name of the motel he was holed in at, thus losing any satisfaction in keeping it a secret. He told me that Milly Gordon had come in to make her will because she was going into the hospital for a completely minor operation. Milly is in her fifties now, and beginning to get her fibroids. Then it was Will who told me how Cora had finally "made" the menu at Wolff's delicatessen. Wolff has a line of two and-three-decker sandwiches named after local lights, like those in Reuben's in New York where they are named after notables of stage and screen whose favorite combinations of ingredients they are. An honor society of ham and cheese and pickles and coldslaw. One had at long last been added to Wolff's menu called "the Cora Frawley," Will told me. "Mostly tongue, I take it," I said. That's the way she was. Will gave his adenoidal chuckle and said, "That's rich. I'll dine out on that." "Not here," I whispered, shushing him with a right to the ribs.

By eight-thirty the church was packed. By a quarter to nine there was still no speaker. People kept turning their heads to the back doors through which he would supposedly be ushered. It got to be ten to nine, five to. Then there was the long-awaited stir at the rear vestibule — the front of the church of course, but the rear of the auditorium. Every head craned around as a collective sound

53

agitated the crowd like a gust of wind rustling the forest. The doors swung inward and there was His Nibs, led in triumph down the aisle between the two women who had bagged him at long last, Lizzie Tatum and her program chairman, the latter so full of hanging ribbons that she looked like a diploma he was going to be awarded. It was that juxtaposition I think they call it, together with the fancy that he was handcuffed to his captors, that suddenly made something pop in my mind like a spark snapping off a burning log.

As he passed our pew, looking neither to the right nor the left, wearing the dark inscrutable scowl, I remembered something that had tantalized me when reading phrases in the book about Mrs. Lusk the landlady's "captives," for the patients she nursed, the prostrate "prisoners of her mercies." The teasing association surfaced now. I had it as he was marched past. Of course. It was those newspaper photographs under the familiar caption "Held in Slaying." It was the Slobkin aspect. Something in the dark smoldering slightly cockeyed gaze of those murky characters seen manacled to dicks in the tabloid halftones was what leaped to mind at the sight of this "catch" tramping along between the women who had caught him at last — one of the Ten Most Wanted celebrities.

Some said Randy Rivers's coming back to Appleton was a form of pennants. God knows he had done enough to enough people. Just exactly why he had broken down and consented after all these years of being adamant was hard to say, maybe even for him. Such a tangle of desires and motivations are we all that half the time we don't know ourselves why we're doing things. But you bought the atonement theory the minute you saw what agonies public speaking held for him. He rose, on being introduced by Lizzie Tatum, and wobbled toward the pulpit like a Christian facing lions, not the other way around. He mopped his brow and took a gulp of water the audience could hear even before he had uttered a line. The manuscript rattled audibly when he drew it from his bosom, and his hands shook visibly as he flattened it down upon the lectern. He cleared his throat and began in a high dry voice far from his normal register as I remembered it:

"The traditional novel often concerned itself with heroes seeking what was once called the Good Life. It was a moral quest. Today heroes, or anti-heroes if you prefer, are bent on a search not for moral meaning but for any kind of meaning at all, even the barest kind of relative intellectual certainty, the faintest sense of sheer minimal autobiographical pattern, or — the last-ditch existential consolation prize — the *illusion* of meaning while life lasts. There is no destination, only a journey . . ."

Once under way it seemed to go better, but not much. You supposed he moved around from behind the pulpit more to give himself the illusion of relaxation than because he was relaxed. Of course carrying the manuscript with him to read from, with his head necessarily down in order to keep his eyes glued to it, which is a great aid in not watching where you're going, especially in a state of nervous distraction not really helped by a few quick ones before going on. He gestured freely with his unoccupied hand, again perhaps to affect platform ease and thereby generate it. No ease was generated in us though, who watched in spellbound anxiety as he strolled around. The suspense was terrific. Would he walk off the edge?

"This moral vacuum is reflected, curiously enough, in the passing of the villain." Here he stepped back and we drew a sigh of relief. There were one or two nervous titters. It's certainly a different way of holding an audience in your grip, having them hang on your every step rather than your every word. He sauntered around to the back of the pulpit, stopped for another swig of water, and continued the semi-circles he more or less kept describing.

"For it was the villain who helped polarize the moral elements into the conventional black-and-white, good-and-evil opposition that was once a human staple. An elderly lady recently complained to me that she missed the villain. Where has he gone? What has happened to him? . . ."

Here I leaned toward Will Gerstenslager, sitting beside me, and whispered, "With the heroes they give us, who needs villains?"

This produced more than the adenoidal chortle. It had the effect of putting him in stitches, so that I had to give him another right to the ribs with my elbow. That only made it worse. Head down, he sat like a boy creating a disturbance in church — which of course this was. I gave him another warning nudge, smiling myself, which he returned, and that gave *me* the giggles. It was probably a kind of hysterical release from the tension we were undergoing. It became uncontrollable. Never have I been unable to stop laughing so hard, never have I nearly busted such a gut. We were soon both shaking with laughter. Several people turned to glare. Among the faces I recognized one or two garbage-gathering Slobkins, shirttail kin of the speaker he was probably hiding out from as much as from hostesses, and it was the sight of them that brought me up short. There was more drama going on on the stage anyway.

"I recently reread *Heart of Darkness* soon after attending a production of *Waiting for Godot*, and was struck by a curious common thread linking these two vastly dissimilar works. The theme of both is search, the search for someone who will Speak, who has the gift of the Word, but in the one case it is active while in the other it is passive. Beckett's dusty vagabonds wait on the edge of nowhere for someone who will bring them answers, while Marlow penetrates the wilderness in quest of that one the rumors of whose eloquence . . ."

How best to describe exactly the way he walked on off that platform — and into our hearts — forever? In a way his last step was a kind of goose-step, that of a soldier so blindly intent on his drill that he marches right on over the edge of a cliff he doesn't see. But I think maybe the idea of a figure coming out of one of those old tower clocks striking midnight conveys the picture a little better. Except that instead of turning stiffly around and going back in, as a clock statue does, he kept right on, his left foot continuing out into space, pausing there a moment at the end of a rigidly thrust-out leg, and then going down, to find nothing there. It's a little like the way we all do when we think we've negotiated the last step at the bottom of a staircase, only there's one more there. And at the same time just the reverse of course, which is little comfort if you're going to take a spill. "Godot by his failure to appear deposits a harsh truth," he was saying, "but Marlow takes back to mad Kurtz's poor fiancée a healing lie, the analgesic herb of human—" He toppled forward with the same mechanical continuation of his walking rhythm, with a kind of dreamy, or eerie grace, a long ballet kind of step that calls to mind a little of Buster Keaton's in those silent comedies that were so full of gymnastic shenanigans, gave half a turn in mid-air as he tried to recover his balance, hung in space in a long moment of serene astonishment which we all shared, and sprawled out on the floor.

We all sat glued to our seats for a moment, hypnotized. Then one or two in the first rows sprang forward to see what they could do. They seemed to be trying to help him to his feet, a poor piece of first aid, and impossible anyway, as he was a dead weight. It was hardly a question of upending the man so he could finish his spiel. What followed was the chaos that results when there is nobody to take hold in an emergency. Cries of "Doctor! Is there a doctor in the house?" went unanswered. I noticed several people turn to look inquiringly at me. That was when I jumped to my feet and darted down the aisle. Always glad to be of service, I made my way as fast as I could through what was suddenly an impeding melée, elbowing, shouldering and shoving a path through honored guests, the morbidly curious, what seemed now hordes of garbage-gathering Slobkins, one or two quite demented looking, and rotten Mayor Pfannkuch's official party which appeared in time to choke the last few feet of my passage. But when they saw me they gave way, and there were cries of, "It's Emma Wallop! Back everybody, let Emma at him!"

The place was of course thick with students, some with notebooks still in hand and even pencils poised. One knelt beside the speaker, ready to dash down any possible last words. What floated into my mind, as I got down on the floor across from him, was rather quotations from the favorite authors Randy use to read aloud to me in the old days on South Crown Street, or anyhow not care if I crept up to listen, unbeknownst to him, as he read or recited them to himself, up there in his room. An exit more in keeping with their words could not be imagined. He had gone gentle into that good night. He had ceased to be before his pen had gleaned his teeming brain. There was always our beloved Eliot:

> I should of been a pair of ragged claws
> Scuttling across the floors of silent seas.

Well, maybe next time around, in his next incarnation. And Faulkner! How I shall never forget him intoning the lines from *Sanctuary*, reaching me clearly through his bedroom door up to which I had stealthily, in the preceding moments, snuck: "Removed, cauterized out of the old and tragic flank of the world." He was removed as removed could be, now, at last. He had ceased upon the midnight with no pain, and a good two hours to spare. He had made it to the river Sticks.

But hold it. Just a minute. What's this normal pulse here, respiration steady? Something's wrong here, everything seems to be in order. Color healthy, apart from maybe a little too rosy, limbs relaxed. No muscular tension of any sort. A faint suggestion of a smile, even, on the lips. I open a closed eye with my thumb, then the other. Dilation of the pupils not marked — but the whites definitely bloodshot. So we have been preparing for this lecture for three days. A sniff confirms the diagnosis. In plain terms any layman can understand: Stinko.

He has been lying more or less on his side, his head cradled on an arm. When I roll him onto his back he exhales a low moan, like a loose note squeezed out of an accordion.

"Randy. Randy, do you have any pain, distress or discomfort?"

Another groan, that sounds affirmative.

"Where? Can you tell me?"

He points to his body.

"Can you be a little more specific?"

The again raised hand flops to rest on his midriff.

"Is it a pain? A sharp pain? Do you have any breathing difficulty?"

He worked his mouth in a series of mumbles, swinging his tongue across his lips. His eyes fluttered open, and seemed to widen with alarm at the ring of faces bent over him. "Whassa mah . . .?" he muttered thickly.

One of the committeewomen thrust her way into the circle.

60

"What do you think, Emma?"

"I believe I know what it is, but I'd like a second opinion. In any case that does it for tonight, and I think he should be hospitalized for observation." I climbed to my feet. "Will! Will Gerstenslager?"

"Over here, Em."

"There's a phone in the basement. Call Hanson's ambulance, and then Doc Wilson, Nathan or Pickett, in that order till you catch one in who can meet us at the hospital. Oh, and Will, tell Hanson never mind calling for a cop to meet him here. Plenty of us to help carry, and we can get an orderly at the other end. I see no need for any emergency treatment en route. Hanson's number is 266-0758. Have you got that?"

"266-0758," Will repeated as he ran for the back stairs, like a football player with a caught pass.

I turned my attention to getting onlookers back so the patient could get some air, and to loosening his clothes for the same purpose, tucking the fallen manuscript into his coat pocket. Hanson was there in five minutes, and inside of another five we were in the ambulance, heading for the hospital with the siren going. I sat in the chair beside the stretcher on which he lay, snug as a bug. I smiled down at him.

"Well, Randy, here we are. Do you recognize your old —?" I bent closer, my attention caught by a goose egg that had developed on his head. I rattled off a string of questions aimed at determining the nature and extent of this contusion.

"When did Columbus discover America?"

61

"Whuh?"

"Columbus, when did he discover America? What year? Quick. What year did he sail the ocean blue?" I said, giving him a hint with the old schoolday rhyme. "Sailed — the — ocean blue."

"Fourteen hundred ninety-two."

"Good. Who was our first President? The father of his country, praise God he can't see the shape it's in now."

"Washington."

"Who freed the slaves?"

"Lincoln."

"Who wrote *Evangeline?*"

"Oh, my God," he groaned, his eyes rolling away from my face after what seemed a vain attempt to place me in the half light. "Why are you asking me all this?"

"You struck your head on something in falling. We're always concerned about the possibility of concussion in those cases, and so we ask questions that will gauge a patient's mental alertness, as well as keep him awake. Who am I?"

He rolled his head on the pillow again, with a defeated little moan. He didn't want to play any more games, was what his muttered reply sounded like, though I couldn't make it out. I must keep his spirits up with an amusing story.

"I once nursed an elderly woman with a concussion — I'm a nurse, so that's one clue who I am, Randy Rivers — a woman who fell into her son-in-law's pool. On the way to the hospital, this was in the doctor's car, the doctor kept asking her these questions, for the reasons I've explained.

Who, or what, was Tippecanoe? The Bill of Rights, the Eighteenth Amendment, who won the War of 1812, the Punic Wars, what hill did Teddy Roosevelt charge up or down? Who was Savonarola? One thing and another. Well, the old woman — she later died it developed — There, there, lie down, you mustn't disturb yourself. The poor old woman kept shaking her head at everything, and finally began to cry. She couldn't answer *one* of the questions. This made the doctor, a Harvard man, look very serious and shake his head gravely. 'It doesn't look good to me,' he told the daughter to one side. 'I don't like the looks of this at all. She's not half there. She doesn't seem to know *anything*.' Then the daughter broke in and said, 'But, Doctor, she never has. Mother doesn't know the answers to any of these things anyway. She never finished the fourth grade.' Isn't that funny? Isn't that an amusing story, Randy Rivers?"

He threw the covers back and tried to climb out of the stretcher. "Let me out of here!" I pushed him back down, using all the force I could muster, and threatening to have Mr. Hanson stop at the police station we were about to pass and get an officer or two to help us apply restraint. That quieted him, and he laid still for a while, gazing out the window and trying to identify what we shot past with the siren going, or so I supposed.

"Who said, 'Go west, young man.'?"

"Horace Greeley."

"That's right. I think we can rule out a concussion. How's that pain in your tum?"

"Why?" he said, gazing up at me with great sheep's eyes.

"Oh, none of my beeswax, is that what we're trying to say? Well, it is my beeswax, we make it that when we're conscientious with a patient. We want to rule out everything we can. Acute indigestion, gall bladder attack, appendix — ruptured or otherwise — an ulcer kicking up. It could be any one of these things. It could be an atypical coronary. There's no end of things we could be taking somebody to the hospital for, to rule out."

"What's an atypical coronary?" he asked, quite stricken now.

"One with unorthodox symptoms, that's all. You were pointing to your tum as though there was some distress there, and you know what we say in medicine when it comes to symptoms. 'The stomach is the biggest liar in the anatomy.' "

Moving right along, we're now bowling past the library, the familiar building unchanged for the most part since the days as a little boy when he took books out, dreaming perhaps of the time when his own books would adorn the shelves. As indeed they now did.

"That was a splendid lecture you nearly gave," I said with a smile. "We could all see what an ordeal public speaking is for you, so this may be nothing more than a complete nervous collapse. We're all the more grateful to you considering the trouble it is, and tickled pink to have you back. Especially me. I'm going to do all in my power. I've issued orders to have the three best doctors in town meet us at the other end. If they're all out or unavailable, I know I can get old Doc Sturtevant. He's perfectly O.K. after his stroke, hardly uses a cane at all to walk with, and even has a few good operations left in him if it comes to that. Here's an amusing story they tell on Doc Sturtevant, to pass the time till we get — Where are we? Mile or two. Steady. Easy there." I related the story through a steady flow of bleating protests, so that I had to raise my voice to be heard. I saw that I was going to have to work harder than I had suspected to perk this one up with a little humor — double the dosage so to speak. "Surgeons are always leaving things behind after an operation, as you know. I mean inside the patient, so that they have to be taken back to the hospital and opened up again. To recover a sponge, or some gauze bandage, or even a pair of forceps I once heard of. That's quite a grotto down in there that things can get lost or mislaid in. Well, Doc Sturtevant had old Abraham Wills in at the age of eighty-seven for some rather drastic intestinal repairs. Wills stood it very well for somebody that old. But after he got home he started finding lengths of bandage coming out of him, prompting him once to exclaim from the bathroom, 'Jesus Christ, what am I, a kite or something? With all this tail?' They took him back to remove the roll of gauze, but the point is, *that's how reliable Doc Sturtevant is.* He'll make good. I learned a lot from him, on the many cases of his I worked. I'll sum him up in a word. He'll give you anything but sympathy. I learned that principle from him. Sympathy is the worst thing you can give a patient, especially if it's serious. It'll scare the daylights out of them, where a matter-of-fact and even gruff word will reassure them. I can still hear him telling me that rule. 'Give them anything but sympathy, Emma.' He's just been appointed town coroner. No better proof of a man's reliability could be asked."

His head begins to rock violently from side to side, alternately catching and losing sight of the mother-bird he is struggling to recognize in the intermittent flashes of street-light from the new cloverleaf underpass through which we shriek at top speed. She lays a hand on the coverlets, which his hands are independently trying to pick to shreds. "Do you know me now? Your old Mrs. Wallop?" His head continues to shake in the negative, "No, I don't," or in protest, "No, it can't be," or in simple resignation: "This is the end."

"Let me out of here. I've got to get out of here." Wild clawing at the sheets again, the eyeballs now rolling like a stricken horse's.

"Right. Because here we are at the hospital."

"Aren't you just a practical nurse?"

There are those who will tell you they don't come any more practical. Dependability in a pinch was bred into me from earliest girlhood, when my sickly father always chose me to nurse him, though I was the youngest of three sisters. It was me he wanted to fetch his medicine, his food and drink, his newspapers and magazines, and even his bedpan. Talk about nepotism. But the efficiency cultivated in me then and through all the later years has stood me in good stead in getting a patient admitted and comfortably settled with a minimum of fuss. This one was in the emergency room and strapped onto a table for a cardiogram before Doc Nathan arrived, and he was there in ten minutes more.

He stood over the cardiograph, watching it, a short, intent figure with a stubble of black hair like a wire brush, and almost as much on the dark gills which always needed a shave by noon. He shook his head as the stylus scribbled out its message. "I don't see anything —" I called him over with a "Shh!" and a jerk of my head toward the door. "This is a very nervous patient," I whispered, drawing him into the corridor. "Don't let him see and overhear you like that. I think we should take the routine blood and urine samples and so on, and keep him for observation at least overnight."

Doc Nathan shrugged. "You'll find an alcohol level, is about my guess, but if you think he should be put to bed overnight for safety sake, why, I'll order it. It's simple enough now that he's here."

"And order a sedative. Or better yet give him a hypo yourself right now. He's starting up again. Listen to that. I've heard coyotes on the lone prairie, but this — You're not going to get any accurate readings out of him tonight. Listen to him tuning up."

That's how we got poor Randy into bed in 417. He was drowsy by the time we got the samples out of him and Doc Nathan had taken his temp and blood pressure (which was a little high) and palpated him some, and practically asleep before we got him between the sheets. Once sure the sandman had him, I hurried downstairs to meet the press.

The lobby was swarming with reporters from ours and surrounding papers, local radio people, audience members who had chased the ambulance, and the inevitable morbidly curious. Lizzie Tatum was there, pacing agitatedly in her own mechanic's outfit. They all swept toward me with such a babel of questions that I had to get around behind a table and rap for silence. I issued a formal statement to the effect that the patient was resting comfortably upstairs, that he was undergoing tests which would take an undetermined period of time, and that I hoped to have another medical bulletin for them sometime the next afternoon.

"What would be your opinion is the trouble?" a reporter from the Appleton *Messenger* asked.

"I wouldn't want to give a judgment there until the tests were complete. We don't like to say there's something seriously wrong when it's merely guesswork. We like to be sure. Yes?"

A chunky little man in salami-colored tweeds said, "It might as well be admitted straight out that there's a rumor Mr. Rivers had had something to drink before he went on. Would you care to comment on that?"

"I wouldn't say there's any evidence of that, though I can't help adding I couldn't imagine anybody making a speech without fortifying himself a little. I needed one just to come down here and face you boys," I answered, and they all laughed, knowing it was a joke to fend off a question nobody had a right either to ask, or, considering the circumstances, to ignore. It seemed a nice way out of it. Tact.

68

"I'd be tempted to guess he's suffering from acute nervous fatigue brought on by overwork, but I'm not speaking medically, and it's strictly off the record. Maybe a little rest is all he needs, but that's up to his doctor to say once he's made a diagnosis. You'll have your full communiqué then."

"How long do you think he'll be here?"

"That I do not feel free to divulge at this time, even as a personal conjecture. Now I think this young man over here is popping with a question."

A blond fellow with heavy mustaches and side-whiskers had been huddling with the chap in the salami-colored suit and Lizzie Tatum both. The nature and fruit of that whispered conference was evident when he said: "If it turns out, as we all hope and pray, to be nothing serious, the matter of the lecture itself remains unresolved. Lots of people have paid admission tonight without hearing more than a third of it, if that. How can they get their money's worth if Mr. Rivers can't give them a raincheck, assuming he can't? Mr. Jarvis here of the *Messenger* would like to reprint it in full, as would some of the other papers. We at the radio station would love to have Mr. Rivers read it for a broadcast, as soon as he's well enough of course. Would you convey that suggestion to Mr. Rivers, for us and Mrs. Tatum?"

"I certainly will, and I'll urge him to do it. He might even do a bedside broadcast, if and when he's up to it, naturally. These things should all sort themselves out in a day or two, during which we'll keep in touch. I might say that I've been favored with a glimpse of that lecture,

69

and it goes on to say some things that very much need saying. He goes into the whole despair bit, the whole existentialist thing, in a bang-up way. We all have a treat in store for us, if those of us close to him can manage to persuade him to do that broadcast. I think that's all for now. Thank you, and good night."

Will Gerstenslager came shouldering and wigwagging through the mob to rescue me. I was glad to see him. He took me for some coffee to a nearby restaurant, then immediately back to the hospital and my patient. As I went up, alone, in the automatic elevator, I reflected to myself on what an art form the news conference really was, what skill and knack it took to field questions from media men, experiencing fresh admiration for other people who had to do it too, like Nixon and Johnson.

Randy was sleeping like a child. I made sure he was comfy, had a word with the floor nurse, and settled myself in the armchair beside the bed, turning up my toes on a straight-back. I soon dropped off, with a delicious little wriggle of pleasure in a job well done, of satisfaction in a role that was important, however humble, and a high heart for the morrow.

"So you're going into a far country, and disappear from the knowledge of men."

It is morning. Bright sunlight slants across the bed on which, cranked up, he eats his breakfast. With a gusto it's a pleasure to watch, for one who has by now had hers in the restaurant downstairs. He gobbles the bacon strips in his fingers, slathers jam on the toast, washes it down with drafts of the good hot coffee. I slowly pace across the foot-end of the bed, after a questioning glance shot at me from his bent head.

"It's what you said in your sleep. I heard you clearly enough, and me only half out of mine. I forgot you talk in your sleep. I sat up, Randy, straining to catch every word — like a scholar caught without his notebook. I didn't get every word, but I got the gist, and that was it. You're going into a far country and disappear from the knowledge of men. You'll go to Poland, what's more, and there learn to write better in Polish than somebody else did in English. Who? Obviously some Pole, Conrad somebody I thought. Who he? Oh, none of my beeswax again, I see. All right. But, and this seemed to be the point, you'd be one up on him, because you'd be plucking from a lousy ukulele — check me and see if this can be what you mumbled — you'd be plucking from a lousy ukulele, music he had a violin to draw out of. Comparing the two languages I suppose, and I agree with you, though I've never tried to talk Polish. Well, if you think you've got troubles, wanting only to be let strut your stuff, if you think you've got a hard row to hoe, listen to this. The last time I was in this hospital it was on this floor, maybe even this very room. That's no matter. The case was a prostrate. In for removal, and not an old man either, by any manner of means. Because you can get your prostrate acting up at any age. In fact I was wondering last night if . . . But never mind that now. Next door — to the prostrate — was someone I knew personally, in bad shape I could tell from the minister who was in to call on him. An Episcopalian priest famous for not visiting patients till rigor mortis was setting in. Little more toast and jelly? Okie doke, but we've got to build our strength up. I chatted with him in the hall on his way out, this priest, and he asked me whether my prostrate would like a look-in and maybe a little bedside prayer. 'No,' I told him, 'I've already asked him about all that, and he says he's a confirmed atheist.' Well, this priest, who was famous for his dry humor, he nodded, thinking it over kind of, sucking in his cheeks in that way you knew a witticism was coming. 'A confirmed atheist, eh?' he said, in the dry foxy way he had. 'I wonder — ahem — I wonder who confirmed him.' "

T. Randall Rivers shoved his tray away with a violence that almost knocked it off the table, and the table and all to the floor. "On what charge am I being held here?"

"That's the stuff! Crack jokes! It's our sense of humor that sees us through! Let's not harbor under the delusion that anything else does."

"Where are my clothes? Give me my pants and coat and so on."

"We'll wait for the tests, and then see."

"I insist on my right to make a phone call. Aren't you allowed that single phone call here?"

"There's a telephone right there. Do you think I cut the wires, like Peter Lorre? It's right there at your side. Who are you going to call?"

"My lawyer."

"Great. Keep it up. I honestly like to hear a patient crack jokes. It's two strikes in his favor. Seriously though, Randy, who are you going to call? Doc Nathan, who's due here on his rounds in a couple of hours anyway? And he'll tell you the same thing I do, which is simply to wait till we get the results. After all you're here for observation. It isn't as though it'll be weeks, or even days. Just a matter of hours."

"How many?"

I shrugged. "Forty-eight, seventy-two . . . Look, I know how you feel." I stood with my hands on the foot-end of the bed, looking at him straight and earnestly. "I know what you're thinking. 'I've failed. I've made a mess of it. My one return home, and I blow it.' "

He turned his head from my gaze, with a look on his face so woebegone my heart went out to him. I experienced a certain alarm, a professional anxiety, bred of experience. Many's the recovery I've seen retarded by dejection and defeat; many a patient, indeed, slip into irreversible decline because he had lost the will to live. This one looked a likely candidate for that. I clapped my hands brightly and came around to the side of the bed.

"Now look. You can lie there and lick your wounds and nurse your humiliation, finally slinking out of town with your tail between your legs. Or you can pin up your hair, pull yourself together, and save the situation by delivering the goods yet."

He gazed up at me with the mournful sheep's eyes that melted my soul. "How?"

73

"Broadcast the lecture. Over our radio station. There's been some talk of it, and so I'll make the suggestion official, with a strong recommendation in favor. Holy Toledo, it might even be better, because then everybody can hear you, at least who wants to. You could even do it from your bed here. The station'd be tickled to death to pipe a mike in here, live, or get it on a tape. No trouble at all."

His face brightened like a cloudy sky pierced by the sun. "Do you think I could?"

"Of course! I've already hinted as much to the press, and now if it's O.K. with you I'll issue an official communiqué. Along with a bulletin saying something about 'acute nervous exhaustion brought on by overwork' or something of the sort they're always saying about actors who collapse on the set or wind up in the sanatarium."

He looked away again, shaking his head, not in protest but in simple amazement, at developments that beat the band, at solutions he hadn't dreamed. Not that they could be realized without a little sweat and strain.

"I need a drink," he said.

"You'll get one. I'll bring you a bottle this afternoon."

He darted me a sidelong look, suspecting a trick. "You're not treating me as an adult in my own right, are you? Because nothing is more infuriating than that. That isn't your little game, is it?"

"No. Everybody knows patients have liquor smuggled in, though not usually by nurses. It's strictly against the rule. But you have to know when to break a rule. I'll sneak a little nip in for you this afternoon — if you behave."

I kept him incommunicado by getting Doc Nathan to seal off buttinskies with a No Calls or Callers order at the desk (without which Randy himself saw he'd be in a state of telephone siege at best). His condition was rated Fair to any newsmen, pilgrims or Paul Prys. I checked him out at the Riverside Motel, paying his bill for which I knew I'd be reimbursed by somebody later, and took his luggage home with me. There I changed into something comfortable (I had all this time been in evening wear, though nothing like as stylish as ground-crew rigs).

When I returned to the hospital just after lunch, I could see right away we were some better. The brow wore its dark indecipherable scowl as it bent over a crossword puzzle in a magazine someone had given him — now put by with a start. "Where's my drink?"

"I'll see what I can do." I rummaged in my bag and brought out a plain household bottle into which I had poured some of the Old Crow found among his effects at the motel. "Ah, what have we here? Something for the occasion." I poured a generous belt into a beaker, added water from the sink tap and gave it to him. "The reason I'm putting it in a beaker instead of your glass is that in case somebody should walk in and see you drinking it we can say it's a urine specimen." I poked my head into the hall to make sure the coast was clear. "All right. Ready and — go!"

I held the press conference downstairs in the lobby as promised, where I was able to announce that Mr. Rivers would deliver the lecture over WRLZ from his room the next afternoon, when the complete text would also simultaneously appear in the Appleton *Messenger*. I got him through all that with a couple more snorts and a Dexamyl bummed off one of the nurses. All that behind us, I got him back into bed, and, standing again at the foot-end, said, "Randy, I've seen the results of those tests, and I don't like the looks of it."

"But Doctor Nathan said they were all negative."

"Yes — thereby completely lacking in the word of warning you sorely need. You'll think you're ship-shape, everything is O.K., and you'll go right back to your old ways and not take a lesson from the episode itself. You'll go right on undermining your health and land back here or someplace even worse in real trouble. You need a rest, to take it easy for a while, charge your batteries. You broke down and came back — though it turned out you came back and broke down. Why? You've been in a state of emotional and physical turmoil only a period of rest and relaxation will get you out of. A period of spiritual inventory. To say nothing of waking up those sluggish bowels. You won't rest unless you're made to — you'll go right back to undermining your health, bodily and mental."

"Anyway, getting out of here is next on the docket."

"Yes — on one condition. That you're put on probation, and remanded to my custody."

He looked at me open-mouthed, and laughed. I did too. It was a joke, but only in the choice of words. The intention was serious, and he saw it. "What the hell do you mean?" he said.

"Come back to 312 Crown Street. For a while."

76

There were several expressions on his face, amalgamated into the multiple expression actors use when they are going to say, "You mean —?" But I had already said what I meant. I pressed on, taking advantage of his flabbergastation, if there is such a word.

"Besides a rest, you need a period of revisiting the old place *at your leisure*, to take stock, sift things out, get your bearings, or whatever way you want to put it. Why did you come here at long last? The lecture wasn't the only reason, though you may of thought you were paying some dues that way. No, you felt a need to return to your roots. Now that you have, do the sensible thing and stay. The house is empty. There'd be nobody in it but us. You could have all the quiet and seclusion you wanted."

"Well, I was thinking of sticking around for a bit," he said, looking away with the kind of guilty expression people wear when there really is no question of guilt. "Prowl around some of my old haunts . . ."

"You'll be at no liberty to do so if you check in at some motel or hotel, because they'll smoke you out and drive you from one to the other, till they drive you out of town, mission unaccomplished. The only solution that makes any sense is mine. Nobody'd ever think of looking for you there."

He sprang out of bed and began pacing the floor, echo of them restless wanderings on which he had so often gone and would go again. He churned about the furniture in his absurd and libelous nightgown, his great bare feet spanking the bare floor. He chewed on the butt of an extinct black cigar, working it from one side of his mouth to the other. Anybody could see he was excited. "Jesus Christ, it may just be the ticket. It may just be crazy enough to make the right kind of sense right now. I may even get some work done. God knows I haven't everywhere else I've tried to hole in. Where are you going?"

I was on my way down to tell the ever-lurking reporters and hangers-on that he had given them the slip, that he had gone out the back door and been whisked away to an undisclosed destination. It was all I was at liberty to say now. And then, the minute they were gone, to whisk him away to one — the house on Crown Street that was the last place they'd ever look because it was right under everybody's nose. After dressing and giving me the check to pay his bill with, he climbed into my old Buick that I had waiting at a side exit I knew about, and before we knew it we were pulling into the driveway at 312 Crown. I made him stretch right out in bed and have some hot tea and cake, which I took up to him. The climb up that staircase was harder than in the old days!

"There," I said, watching from the same armchair in which he had himself so often sat, all those years ago that were both only yesterday and a whole nother existence. "Isn't this nice? Just like old times. Here you are, not only in Appleton, but back in your old room. So you see? You *can* go home again."

four

It was all right being a buffer between the Randall Rivers watchers and himself, and no point in denying that I enjoyed the role. But it was soon evident that I needed a buffer of my own, so they wouldn't all be on the telephone or the front porch trying to pry out of me where his hideaway was, *at* the hideaway itself. I had no trouble deputizing the right person for that. Will Gerstenslager. I'd refer the curious to him, and when *he* said he didn't know anything, brother, you believed it. Because a resemblance to Mortimer Snerd, the ventriloquist's dumbbell, has been noted by more than one person clapping an eye on our Will. This whole ruse to throw everyone off the scent entailed their constantly descending on his law office, but I had no qualms about injecting a little life into that mausoleum. They even began tailing Will, both on foot and by car. One night he picked me up to take me out to dinner, and sure enough, we could see another car following ours, with three or four people in it. They turned every corner we did, no doubt hoping we'd lead them to the prize, who was back at the house curled up with a good book or watching television, not in a cave on the outskirts waiting for the ravens to feed him. Will chuckled, loving every minute of a hugger-mugger that made him feel like a gangster. The chase petered out at restaurant called Spinelli's that was anticlimax for me too.

His devotion to it was unexplainable unless on the ground that he liked Italian food well but not wisely. I had catfood Bolognese, which I don't remember how it was designated on the menu, if I ever heard, as letting Will do the ordering like a man of the world was part of dining out with him. Though he needs a course in remedial eating. We washed our food down with a bottle of Chianti he said was robust, which you had to be too to negotiate it. "These wines should be drunk young," he said. "Preferably under forty," I said, "when you can take it." "You seem glum tonight, Emma," he said. "This will loosen your tongue." And a few teeth too, thought I. Spinelli stopped by, bowing from the barrel that was once a waist, to ask how everything was. "Couldn't be better," I said, not perjuring myself one bit.

People thickening up send out the same warning signals to you as those wasting away — like Will's mother who was ninety-one and, wasting away or not, would live to be as old as the lama in *Lost Horizons*, two hundred and some, not high on my list of priorities, but then. Randy was supposedly watching it on Million Dollar Movie right now. I drew my coffee to me and said, "Will, I'm going to sell that stock of mine you're keeping in your safe for me, and live a little."

"Emma, you'll do no such thing." This was a little game we periodically played, a ritual in which he always enjoyed holding up his end. "Those shares have doubled three times since Frank left them to you, and God knows how many more times they'll increase in value before you get to the old age you said you'd let me mind them for you till." At that stage I'd probably have to get in touch with him by séance, but I let it pass, listening with half an ear to Will's part of the scenario. "You may think you can pry those securities away from me, but I double-dog dare you to try."

I'd never had any intention of cashing in on this lucky buy of Frank's, but now the vague notion teased my fancy that maybe I should do so and blossom out, travel around the world and what not, before I actually *did* hit the winter for which Will kept insisting I was saving these nuts. I remembered how Bubbles Gerstenslager with her little knowledge of the stock market apparently realized Bailey Instruments might be my IBM, and at the time she was still alive there weren't nearly so many of these electronic breakthroughs and laser developments important to this small but growing conglomerate. How much was that original nest egg of twenty-two thousand dollars worth now? Will wouldn't say, only drop hints. "Forty thousand? A hundred thousand? Fifty thousand?" he twitted me with my own questions. "Anyhow, a nifty little dowery to bring to any marriage you might care to ginger up those sunset years with," he chortled wickedly, and leaned back and set fire to a cigar the size of a chair splat.

I watched smoke issue from his middle nostril. This business of not wearing your specs out of vanity will get you some interesting special effects while half blinding you. There he was, a blurred little roasted apple of a face, grinning in duplicate. He was two faces. He had four ears, four lips, four eyes (or eight if you counted his own cheaters), but only three nostrils — the middle, best-defined one being the duplicate of the left superimposed upon the real right. A genuine Picasso. He was what the boys use to look like when you open your eyes while kissing them. It was even time to change the seeing glasses I had in my *bag*. And I remembered the two or three kids among the scholars at my house who wore granny glasses. I toyed with the idea of switching to them for my next pair, since the frames were probably a lot lighter than the horn-rims I now had, but discarded it. I was too old for granny glasses. How does that grab you? Oh, things can be so complex!

". . . finds he needs someone," Will was saying, with his suggestive grin. Was the man trying to work up a canoodle? He wore the reprobate air he always did when talking about marriage, as though getting married at our age was like living together without doing so when you were young. It was indecent. It would "be a blast," would "set the town on its ear," and so on. "A man needs a woman, there's no doubt about that," he said. "All my socks have got holes in them."

"Cut your toenails," I said. "It's a lot less trouble than getting married, for everybody concerned, and it wouldn't kill your mother."

He laughed and shook his head, as though this brittle dialogue sure beat the band. "Imagine getting this every morning at breakfast," he said into his expresso cup. He liked to live it up, and prided himself on everyone's knowing that Will Gerstenslager was a man who did so. He traded in his Pontiac every two years whether it needed it or not, ran down to Miami every once in a while, and always carried a few raisins in his coat pocket to nibble on in court no matter what the Puritans thought. He gestured at a woman in a bright red dress who was on her way to the can. "That's Lolly Wainwright," he told me, as though I was seeing life. "She's had three husbands and is looking for a fourth."

"In the Ladies'?" I said. "I hope she finds him, if that's what she wants this time around."

He shook his head again, chuckling: we were the limit. Then he turned sober. "But if I could find the right woman, I'd marry her like that." He snapped his fingers. The waiter trotted over in response. "Nothing. I was just . . ."

We got home to find a rather bazaar development.

Randy had solemnly agreed to remain upstairs in his quarters, except for a possible snack in the kitchen or to watch television in a back room next to it. He could have the run of the house for all of me, but he ought not to void all this conspiracy we were up to by walking or sitting near windows with the shades raised. As we drew to a stop in Will's car I saw a shadow on the drawn parlor shade, and thought I caught a glimpse of another. As I climbed out I remembered a song about two silhouettes in the dark. No, that was two cigarettes. But there was a song about silhouettes . . .

As I trudged up the broad plank steps leading to home, trailed by my adenoidal suitor bent on his "dightcap," I counted them as I had from force of habit a thousand times. Ten, spreading like an estuary into my wide beautiful gulf of a porch encircling nearly the whole front of the house. I walked across that slowly, the way we enter a scene about which we're both curious and apprehensive, because instinct senses something new we may or may not like, while the brain sends through its computer all the lousy probabilities. Through the curtained oval glass in my wide door I could see part of one end of the living room. There were two kind of antic shadows there on the wall, one much shorter than the other and distinctly female, and as I pushed open the door I heard a cut-off young woman's lilting laugh and her voice saying something about whether somebody would "have a cow." I walked with the same deliberateness through the vestibule and on into the parlor, to see Randy standing against the mantel in his red silk dressing gown, like husbands caught with cookies in many, many cartoons, gesturing to this one and saying, "I believe you know Virginia Quilty."

I had not recognized the girl in the mattress-ticking pants — now dressed in an orange miniskirt and with her hair swept up and bound at the back in a dark ribbon. I decided to take a hard line, but that had to wait on other formalities, such as the introduction of Will, who knew Randy from way back and had seen him since his return, but who came forward to meet Miss Quilty as though he was going to say, "Where have you been all my life?" She gave him her hand to shake, with a smile that I'm sure made men come unglued. And as for having a difficulty for every solution, she was president of that club. Didn't she live in Evanston? Yes but now that she had graduated she was at loose ends and thought she'd visit her friend with whom she'd roomed here, the Renault, whose parents were still ruin-hopping. Should she desert her hostess in this way? It was her hostess who had gone out on a date, leaving her at even looser ends. Alone in the empty house, she was seized with the irrepressible urge to meet Mr. Rivers. Then for the sixty-four-thousand-dollar question, which I asked with all of us still standing and my hat and coat still on.

"How did you know where he was?"

"Well," she says, the winning smile something for which you shell out additional gullibility along with and over above what you cough up in believing the story itself that the smile sells you on, like the cost of the advertising that is added onto the price of the merchandise — *you* pay for the commercials that make you buy the product, "well, um, I had a hunch Mr. Rivers was here. I'd telephoned you once or twice, Mrs. Wallop, but you apparently didn't recognize my voice. Anyway, I got the usual official denial. I thought I'd just keep trying till Mr. Rivers himself answered, and tonight was my lucky night, though he didn't answer the first time. I let it ring about twenty times and hung up. But this hunch I had made me try again a few minutes later. I let the phone ring, and had this sort of absolute certainty he was doing the same thing, here alone in *this* empty house. It rang and it rang and it rang . . ."

"And it rang and it rang," Randy put in. "Maybe fifty times. I don't know. It got on my nerves. I just had to pick it up." He plowed the parlor floor, prowling among tables and chairs no less insensate than the heedless anonymous hordes through which he cut a swathe as he drove, proud and destinationless, down the myriad-footed and unkindred streets, the eyes blazing with the old coagulated fury and the leonine head giving him more than ever the look of a woolly bear. What fingers in those tortured locks would turn the mountain grizzly into a fondled toy? The ones gesturing like pale pink seafronds in the service of this tale being unfolded? How she attended the lecture he never gave, due to the unfortunate circumstance of his walking off the stage through no fault of his own, but missed the broadcast he did, as well as the paper in which the speech was printed. The home in which she was a guest did not take the Appleton *Messenger*, then, the Renault's people? No, alas.

"I'll go get you a copy."

86

Mrs. Lusk, it stands in *Medusa* for all to know, lifted her hat off her head like someone lifting a cake from a table. All right, all right! Her hats even look like cakes, round and burdened with rosettes. All right, all *right!* She removes the pin from this one and sets it down like a cake too, might as well make it complete, upon the vestibule table, finding to her irritation that Will Gerstenslager has followed her out there and is hanging up his duds on a peg.

"Randy — Mr. Rivers was kind enough to give me a copy already, Mrs. Wallop. But thank you anyway."

"So then you've got what you came for."

"Well now!" This from Will, who stands in the doorway rubbing his palms together in anticipation of an hour of delight. We may yet "oped a keg of dails." "What will everybody have?"

Mrs. Wallop, no doubt as oblong as Mrs. Lusk, moves up beside him and stays him with a hand on his arm. "How did you finally get him to talk then?" quoths she. "On the telephone. Tonight."

They exchange guilty looks, she with a little laugh delightful as the tinkle of wind chimes, he with the flustered endearing old bear growl behind one of the chairs among which he still truculently moves. "First he just took it off the hook and let it lie there, maybe two or three minutes. Then, well, um, he had to pick it up and see if anybody was still there, at the other end. And it was the funniest thing. I could hear him breathing. The exact same sound you get with one of those nuisance calls, you probably get them too. The creep at the other end just *breathes*? That's all I heard here too, only it was weird getting it after *you've* done the calling. I kept talking, anything to keep his attention, like a senator filibustering, because I knew it had to be he. I don't remember all I said. Oh, silly fan-club stuff. You know the sort of thing."

"Of course. I use to telephone Ronald Colman every night. Collect. He loved it. But the sixty-four-thousand-dollar question is still, how did you get *him* to respond. What did he finally say? How did he break down?"

"I told her to go to hell," Randy said, swinging his back to us with a laugh, blushing scarlet, and collapsed into a naughty boy.

We would never know, of course, and I paid little mind to the official account from Miss Quilty, to which nobody could give credence but which everyone could enjoy for the charming succession of well-ums to which all alike were treated, as well as the languorously waving seafronds, scarcely interrupted when she turned to sit down in answer to my invitation, save for the tinkled "Thank you" dropped like another bell note into this pile of absolutely irresistible humbug, and the way she crossed her legs, the miniskirt showing off the darling little haunches. I — what's the word I want? Improvised. I improvised my own version of what happened: how she got him to respond. Women are always wanting to sleep with writers, so they say, and I imagined this hero-worshiping cutie pausing over the wire, then in a suddenly different voice breaking down herself and saying, "Look, you're alone, I'm alone.

My name is so-and-so, my number is such-and-such," and hanging up. Then waiting to see whether he would call back. Which he did.

"But don't be angry with him, Mrs. Wallop, and don't worry. The secret of his whereabouts is safe with me."

"I have no doubt of that," I said.

"Well! This calls for a drink." Will asked us all to name our poison, which we did, and which he fetched, with a familiarity with the premises and a daring-do meant to suggest that there might be something between us too. "Cheers!"

By now everyone felt at home but me. I was disgusted with all three of them, Will most of all. There the foolish, but I must admit terribly pleasant old poop sat, pruning himself on his worldliness, his being with it, as Now as the best of them. "I'm all for the sexual revolution," I remember him saying at one point (even though his mother would kill him if she found out). "I think it's great. I think it's clearing out a lot of moral underbrush, a lot of dead wood in our thinking. The Puritan ethic has got to go."

He had to go himself, owing to the vast amounts of fluids he had taken aboard by this time, but he got back so fast and resumed so quickly with a flourish of his brandy that we hardly knew he was gone. All this New Thought of Will's being an old story to me, I concentrated on Miss Quilty's responses to it, which were the work of an artist at flattering men. A few engrossed nods and a compliment or two gave the impression of hanging on his every word, even though in a twinkling and before he knew it she had shifted the limelight to Randy. "I think it's a tribute to his genius that he caught, or I mean anticipated all this in the young even before it was in the wind," she said, batting the baby blues at him as though she could eat him with a spoon. She was a good flatterer, but she needed an editor. "Not so much butter," I wanted to say, "he's got to watch his cholesterol." She went on from his writing to his looks, which were *like* his writing — intense and lyrical, with a certain smoldering poetry to it. "Where did you get that tan, this late in October?" she asked him. He said he had spent the spring in Nassau, and most of the summer up on the Cape, soaking in the elements. "A tan becomes you," she said, evaluating him with serious little nods, a habit some people have who seem to be mentally corroborating what they hear themselves physically saying. "You've got the skin that turns that beautiful café au lait. Mine just nyah. It burns and sizzles out, like a firecracker."

At this point I lit a cigarette from somebody's pack, even though I don't smoke. Will Gerstenslager, the fifth column, kept refilling people's glasses. Miss Quilty showed no sign of running out of variations on her chosen theme, the smoldering intensity bit, or the smoke-and-flame sindrome. How unfortunate it was that Randy Rivers had elected to remain in hiding all these years *Medusa* was having such a vogue. He should give the public the benefit of his appearance too. Compliments are harder for most of us to keep our composure under than criticism, as you well know, and I must say I admired the way he managed not to look like a horse's bustle at all this, smiling or shrugging as he brushed cigarette ash off his knee, existent or non-existent, or reached for his glass to take a drink or rattle the ice cubes disclaimingly. I remembered the remark of the Boston lady: "Gross flattery is good enough for me." It was good for Paul and Silas, and it was good enough for him. La Quilty charmingly knew no shame. At one stage of the game, so help me and as God is my judge, I heard her say, "He's got charisma."

"Well, he certainly doesn't look well, does he?" I said. "And we suspected it from the tests. Rest, that's what he needs. Plenty of rest!" And rose, clapping my palms together to indicate that the evening was over.

This got nobody out of the house but Will Gerstenslager, after whose departure, maybe fifteen minutes later, I went up to bed myself. The female eyelids were still fluttering in the parlor like two moths a-mating. Straightening a rug in the vestibule with a heel, I said to the floor, "You can lock up and turn out the lights when Miss Quilty goes. Good night." I left them there, with Miss Quilty still praising the merits of deep tans for certain types of men, urging Randy to keep his as long as possible, and declaring that her mother, another sun worshiper, remained brown till well into November by using one of those reflectors under her chin.

Sleeping with my bedroom door slightly ajar, as is my want, I could hear their low murmurs floating up the stairs, punctuated with occasional soft laughter. So that "sleeping" was in this case a misnomer. After a while, just as I was managing to drop off, there was silence — which woke me up again. I laid there it must of been an hour, straining to catch even a scrap of sound, hearing only the loud hush of the house.

I finally got up and went to the bathroom for a glass of water and a non-prescription sedative called Slumbereez. I walked softly, in my bare feet, how's that for being made to feel an interloper in your own house, pausing once in the hallway to listen. There was no sound whatever. Had they perhaps gone out while I dozed off without knowing it? On the way back from the bathroom, I stole in a round-about route toward the head of the stairs, with those exaggerated steps we use on tiptoe, and paused there. I leaned my head over the bannister, cupping an ear. I fully expected to hear some more heavy breathing, only this time mutual and not over the wire, but couldn't catch a trace even of that. Maybe they were down in the furnace room, like Greta Garbo and John Gilbert in *Flesh and the Devil* in what? 1927. The light I had left on in the vestibule made it impossible to tell whether there was any in the parlor or whether that was dark. I shook my head and, with a sigh loud enough for any other ears within reasonable distance, turned and went back to bed, my heels thudding normally on the floor and making no bones about shutting the door behind me with a smart clap, as much as to ask whether a person could ever expect to get some sleep around here. Before climbing in, I glanced out the window to see whether a blue convertible I remembered noticing in front of the house as we drew up was still there. It was.

I awoke about nine o'clock, late for me. Randy was still asleep. I had breakfast and set out for my morning's marketing. The convertible was gone.

When I got back to the house he was nowhere to be seen. He wasn't in his bedroom, I could tell by looking through the open door. I went downstairs again and back through the parlor and dining room to the kitchen, where I had left my sack of groceries, without finding a trace of him. Nor was he in the television room. I was emptying my bag of groceries when a sound outside caught my ear. I went out to the back porch and there I found him, down in the yard.

He was lounging in an Adirondack chair, his elbows on the arms, holding two skillets against the sides of his face at an angle calculated to trap the rays of the sun and deflect them to his cheeks, to supplement the little he could get head-on at that time of year. His eyes were closed of course. He probably heard me, because he opened them.

"Hey, no kitchen privileges, remember?" I called down with a laugh.

He scrambled to his feet in a flustered way, dropping one of the frying pans. "Probably doesn't really do any . . ." he mumbled in his confusion.

"No, wait," I said. "Stay there."

I went back in the kitchen. I tore off a length of aluminum-paper cooking foil from my roll of Reynolds Wrap, shaped it into a kind of scoop, and tied it under my chin with a piece of string looped around my head and down again, knotting it into a bow at my throat, like a maiden putting on a bonnet, or rather like a pioneer woman fastening on, upside down, one of those pokes that were intended to shield you from the rays of the sun rather than intensify them by reflection. "If this paleface turns a little pink," I said, pulling up another Adirondack chair to join him, "why, you can still get a little. If not, it's no use." And there we sat, eyes closed, chatting away, for all the world as though the Lord God was really a tinsmith and we were his children.

"Tell me about Miss Quilty."

"Oh, there's nothing to tell, really. She's quite a little — number, is that what we said? A cute trick."

"Does she want to be a writer?"

"Oh, vaguely. They all do at that age. I told her what Faulkner once said about all that. Do you really want to write, or do you just want to be a writer?"

"And she took it in good part?"

"Oh, sure. She laughed. She's one of those who just want to be a writer. It's what weeds them out. They fall by the wayside after a year or two, once they realize the backbreaking, bone-breaking, heart-breaking —"

"My son, Osgood, you remember him. He wants to be a writer *and* he writes. He battles away at it. He'll make it all right. I'll have him show you or send some of his stuff, if you don't mind."

"Of course not. But getting back to Virginia Quilty, she's one of those women — and she now is a woman — who'll settle for nothing but the best of what they want — in this case talent, but when she finds she hasn't got it

94

herself she'll be perfectly content attaching herself to a man who does. A woman really does respect creativity, and can rejoice in a man's achievements the way a man won't in his woman's. Difference of the male and female egos here. For the rest, it's this identity-crisis business of today, finding out who you are. Virginia just wants to be herself."

"That seems little enough to ask. One individualist is very much like another, of course." I shifted into a more comfortable position on the chair, with a wriggle of contentment. "I got pork chops for tonight. That sound all right?"

He suddenly became very spirited, with one of them bursts of elation that I remembered would alternate with his glowering spells, from the old days.

"No, by God, I'm going to cook dinner tonight," he said. "I've become quite good, you know, living alone."

He would not be discouraged, not that I tried. Batching had no doubt developed his gourmet side, or made a gourmet out of the healthy eater he always was. He had a number of specialties, among which for tonight he picked his short ribs and vegetable casserole, with horseradish sauce. Before I knew it I was on my way out on another shopping expedition, with a list that included also a bottle of white wine called Montrachet, which he insisted on giving me the money to buy at a liquor store he telephoned first to make sure they had it. By now a mood of gaiety had quite enveloped us. I began to get the giggles again, like in church that time I said that contemporary literature has no need of villains, the heroes are deplorable enough? I was commencing to enjoy Will Gerstenslager now that he wasn't here. Laughing like a couple of fools, I told Randy he might as well forget picking up any more tan out there in the yard, where the house shadow now eliminated all question, but that I remembered a sunlamp bulb left behind by a law student I once had. I dug it readily out of a storage cabinet in the basement, and screwed it into a bridge lamp standing next to the sofa in the living room, first removing the shade. I left Randy stretched out there, but with the warning not to take more than eight or ten minutes on either side, the first time. If that.

This marketing trip had suddenly become a lark. I would be tickled to death to tell future biographers and historians he was a man of great good will, once you got below his frostline. As I was getting the last item on my list, the wine in Mr. Spangenberg's very fine liquor store, I suddenly began to worry about the sunlamp. What if he had fallen asleep under it, as people often do? I once had a case of it, as a matter of fact, a young woman who damn near didn't pull through. Wasn't there a famous Broadway actor who had all but scorched himself to a cinder getting an artificial tan for a role? It didn't take much to get you a first or second-degree burn, or even a third (these burns always sound like stages in the Masonic orders). My anxiety turned to panic, so sharp that I hailed a passing cab and hurried home in that. I ran up the stairs and into the house — heaving a sigh of relief at the empty sofa.

His Nibs was in the kitchen, peeling potatoes and scraping carrots for our dinner.

It was a superb dinner, and so was the wine. He took his table drinking as seriously as he did his food, and I was glad to see the grape somehow mean more to him than the grain. He worked his lips after each swallow of this beautiful Montrachet — evidently the Shakespeare of white Burgundies to hear him tell it — and finally asked me my opinion of it. The stuff was certainly boss, there was no doubt of that. I took a swallow. "This wine has bouquet, character, body, breeding and finesse, and it tastes good," I said, adding the detail usually omitted by epicures enumerating the merits of what they're drinking, to my observation. He nodded thoughtfully after a gulp of his own, as though this last item had escaped his notice also.

It was soon after that I began to observe something was wrong. He kept blinking his eyes and stopping to rub them. "Hurt." He turned away from the table, pressing into them with his fingertips. "I thought at first it was a touch of my hayfever coming back, but it's too late for that, and this is worse. Worse than just burning or itching. I can't stand to keep them open — or closed." His feet danced in his misery.

"You didn't expose them to the sunlamp?"

"Not directly. How could you? Who could look into one?"

"But you kept them open."

"Some of the time. I don't remember. I didn't think

97

that . . ." He became very nervous, fidgeting and swiveling about on his chair. "You'd better call a doctor. Hurry. I can't stand this." It come on that suddenly.

Eyes aren't my line of country, but I had my ophthalmologist, Doc Hamilton, on the phone in thirty seconds. Luckily he was home, and said he could be in his office in ten minutes, about the time it would take us to get there in my old Buick. Which I backed out of the driveway while Randy sat on the front steps with his hands in front of his face, still dancing. I had to help him down the walk and into the car, in which he sat writhing beside me on the front seat. "Christ, I can't stand this," he said. "It's like a hot cinder in each eye. I've never felt anything like this before. I can't open or close them. For Christ's sake can't we go any faster?"

We were doing fifty in a residential zone. "In five minutes the discomfort'll be all over," I said. "Four, three . . ." I kept on, recalling how I'd once had what seemed like a clinker in my eye, and the bliss when Doc Hamilton had put into it one of those anesthetic drops whose effect is literally instantaneous. "Two, one . . ." I helped him, stumbling, up the steps into the office where Doc Hamilton was already waiting, thank God. We dropped big Randy into the chair and the doctor tilted his head back and squeezed the drops in straightaway. Randy blinked a few times, and laughed like a relieved child the way we all do after great pain or distress. "Whew!" he said gratefully as he wiped his streaming cheeks with the tissues the doctor handed him. "I wouldn't like to go through that again."

His joy was short-lived however. After a few minutes of

letting him pull himself together Doc Hamilton said, "Now come over here and let me have a look."

He sat Randy down in the chair behind a slit-lamp microscope of the kind used for this type of examination, got Randy's chin rested on the stirrup and his beaded brow against a band attached to the apparatus for steadying the patient's head, and settled in the chair opposite him, flicked off the office lights, and peered first at one eyeball then at the other under varying illuminations and magnifications.

"Mmm," he murmured at last. "Yes, you've burned the surfaces of both corneas some. A condition we call a photo-phthalmia."

Randy gulped, very loudly due to his throat being stretched away out forward to accommodate his propped chin. I could hear it across the room where I stood quietly watching with folded arms. "Does that mean my vision . . . Maybe even . . ."

"Now, now, don't holler till you're hurt. It doesn't mean that at all, necessarily."

"But possibly. We don't know for sure. Bleeding Christ . . ."

"Who's the doctor here?"

"You are, Doctor," said Randy, like a rebuked school-child. But he gave another loud swallow and asked, "The damage won't show up right away, is that it? Just like with any other sunburn?"

"Yes, you've put it exactly right. You've sunburned your eyeballs, to put it in plain English. I've seen this a number of times, and you can bank on the extreme dis-comfort being gone in twenty-four hours, or forty-eight at the absolute most, during which I'll give you some of these drops to put in yourself, so you won't feel anything. And I've never had a patient end up with anything but very limited impairment, if any."

"But it could be extensive — or complete? Oh, my God."

"Come over here and read the chart for me."

Doc led him back to the original chair, switched on the illuminated chart, and asked him to read the letters and numbers, beginning with the familiar big E at the top. Randy started eagerly, rattling off the larger characters at high speed, but as he got to the lower and smaller lines he began to stumble, and his voice took on a more and more frightened pitch. His throat went dry, and his face finally became so pathetic that I laughed to put him at his ease.

"That's what vanity gets us," I said. "Doc, he needs glasses *anyway*, but it's the old refusal to admit we're getting over the hill. He's one of those people who when they read a book look like a trombone player. You know — 'There's nothing wrong with my eyes, it's just that my arms aren't long enough'? So this shouldn't be a total loss, why don't we go on and examine him for his first pair of specs."

"Fine, but I'd rather wait till tomorrow afternoon. Or better yet the next day. That'll give me time to check this other matter. Let's see what my appointment book looks like for Friday . . . Well, Emma, so you're still in there pitching. An example to all of us . . . Friday at two looks O.K. . . . Well, Emma, so that's where he's hiding. I won't tell anybody, young fellow. Your secret's safe with me."

I had a terrible time with Randy from the minute we got back in the car. He sat beside me with his head in his hands again, only not in discomfort now but lamentation. "There's damage. I could tell by the way he acted. We'll have to wait. Don't holler till you're hurt. It's just like a regular sunburn — doesn't show up till later." "No, *you* said that, not him," I reminded him, trying to negotiate both him and the potholes in the disgraceful streets around which I had to steer my old Buick, like a boat among treacherous shoals. We did hit one or two, making Randy give out with fresh groans as his head bumped the ceiling. He was a poor patient, one of the worst I've ever had, I'll say that. Not that I wasn't happy to be doing for him. Not that I wasn't tickled to death for the chance to be of service, now. I was careful not to show my own concern. The No Sympathy rule had never been more important than now. A single word, the merest cluck of compassion, and I'd have a really collapsed character on my hands. Not that it wasn't bad enough as it was.

"I'll be blind," he said as he sat drinking in his favorite parlor chair.

"And damn soon if you keep sucking the jug at this rate."

"A blind novelist."

"A regular Joyce." I rose. "We haven't finished dinner. How about that lemon soufflé you were going to whip up for dessert?"

That got his mind off himself at least partly, and for a while. The concoction, new to me, was superb. The lemon pudding, done French style, the way they like it there apparently, remains runny under the rising bonnet, to form a sauce over what you scoop out first onto your plate. He seemed to relax a little over this culinary triumph, and the good black coffee we sipped with it. But I began to notice him sneaking looks at any reading matter lying about — magazines, the labels on bottles, anything to test himself on, with a casual pretense at not doing that at all. This was a very foolish game to be playing with himself, and I rose from the table and said, "Now the thing for you to do is go to bed and forget all about it. Get a good night's sleep. Go on now." He insisted equally strongly on washing the dishes, or at least helping with them. We did them together, by which time the anesthetic had worn off and he began blinking and carrying on again. He did such a poor job of putting fresh drops in, blinking just as he squeezed the little rubber bulb of the dispenser so that the fluid ran down his cheeks and chin, that I made him lie down on the sofa while I did it myself. Relief was again of course instant, and again accompanied by such happy laughter that I was able to seize his mood to pack him off to bed for some much-needed rest. He took the suggestion willingly enough, though carrying a bottle upstairs with him as a fortification against night thoughts. I locked the house up and slipped gratefully between the sheets myself.

I awoke in the middle of the night with a figure standing beside my bed, wild-eyed and disheveled in his pajamas. His hair was like the thicket Abraham's ram got caught in. I detected the familiar fragrance of Old Crow.

"I can't see."

I climbed out of bed and into my bathrobe.

"What do you mean?"

"Can't read."

"Can't read what?"

"Clock."

"Which clock? Show me."

He jabbered away as I led him out of my bedroom and down the passageway lit by a lamp burning in his own. It was over. He was through. He could write no longer, and that being the case, could not earn a living. He would become a ward of the state, a burden to all. He gabbled so convincingly as we tripped and stumbled about among the rugs encountered by our bare feet on the polished floor that, in my own befuddled state, I began to panic myself, half beginning to believe him. "I'll be a beggar," he went on. "Now, now," I murmured, but I vividly saw him begging alms in the marketplace, my imagination for some reason wildly placing this in an Oriental bazaar in which he groped along with his arms out before him or picked his way with a stick or simply sat in the dust of the street crying, "Alms! Alms for the love of Allah," like Otis Skinner in what? *Kismet*, while he held out a tin cup to passersby, not Otis Skinner, Randy, held aloft a tin cup beseechingly to passersby, his arms thin as twigs, his face emaciated and his body covered with sores. Christ, what a night! So befuddled and confused was I in my half-

103

conscious state that it hadn't occurred to me that I had a clock on my own dresser to settle all this with, but let him make us go consult the one on his. Just before we reached his room we slid on an especially treacherous little oval rug, a new one for which I'd long intended to buy a pad. It shot out from under us, almost bringing us down in a heap of tangled arms and legs, but I caught us both just in time, miraculously getting a firmer grip on him as I steadied myself. We wobbled and slithered along like a couple of amateur ice-skaters. We got to his doorway and I said, "Now. What is this all about?" He pointed at the electric clock on his dresser. "There. I can't tell time. I can make the hands out, yes. *But I can't see the numerals.* Oh, my God."

"It hasn't *got* any numerals," I said. "Just dots-like. It's one of them chic clocks Osgood gave me for my birthday once. My God, it's been here since you moved back in. Haven't you noticed it just has those black dots instead of numbers, and them only every quarter hour, with little grains of caviar every five? That that's the way you've been telling time all along without realizing it? It says three A.M., but the real time is, it's time you stopped drinking. Give me that bottle." And up I snatched another empty.

"Who's Osgood?" he said, sinking gratefully down on the bed. "Oh, that's right. Your son." In this fresh spell of ecstatic relief he seized my free hand and put it to his cheek. "What would I do without you?" he said. I had never seen anybody quite this maudlin before — for any reason or under whatever influence. He pressed my hand in both of his. I set the bottle down on a table and laid the other on his head, feeling the thick luxuriant tangles of hair, moist and matted now. I was by now certainly quite awake, though hardly realizing any more than I had what I was doing. Any unscrupulous woman could of taken this man in his present state. What flashed into my mind was the scene in the movie of *Philadelphia Story*, where Jimmy Stewart tells how he carried Katherine Hepburn drunk to her room, and refrained from taking his will of her as he certainly could without any trouble. He didn't because — and here we had the essence of the decent wholesome all-American boy — because, he says quietly, "There are rules about those things."

I got him stretched out on the bed and soothed back to sleep again in a few minutes. Then I returned to mine, where needless to say I watched the dawn seep slowly in through the gray window-panes.

From *that* sleep I awoke around ten, and staggered down the steps to find him reading the paper at breakfast, the only trouble being again that our arm was a good six inches too short. "Good morning. Nice day." I again let him save face by not saying anything myself. I would not be rotten in that area. I was only too glad for him. The only jolt, then, would be his first pair of specs, nothing compared to what he had feared. We were over the hump. Everything was O.K.

But hold it. Just a minute. Not so fast. There's the

105

telephone, and wouldn't it be Miss Quilty, offering to take him for a ride all through the golden afternoon. Bringing our real problem, finally, into clear focus.

The question to me was plain.

Was the woman who'd caused the recent narrow squeak by a foolish appeal to a man's vanity, foolishly taken up, the right woman for that man? A few dates would not make it a worrisome matter, but the frequency with which he now saw her suggested things were warming up and might be getting serious. The question nagged me in a dozen different ways, but basically put it always boiled down to this: For a male so obviously in need of a tower of strength in his personal life, whatever his merits as an artist, would Miss Quilty make an even remotely conceivable helpmeet, if it came to that? That was the nitty gritty. I longed to put her to some kind of token test, something that would make her show her true colors before it was too late, and there would be regrets, regrets, regrets. I had a pretty good idea how I might, but when it came right down to it, I just hadn't the heart. It was none of my business.

Then something happened that made it my business —if Randy's future happiness could be so classified. I'd never of gotten my notion out of the drawing-board stage had it not been for this incident, which gave me a fresh glimpse into his particular frailties, and his absolute need for a woman he could lean on, not one interested only in spending her life basking in his reflected glory.

Randy had been having his mail forwarded from New

York. One day he got what I knew he'd been anxiously watching for — his royalty statement. He got two a year, and the check last spring had shown a sharp drop in sales over the previous six-month period. I knew the instant he opened the letter that this was more bad news.

"My God," he said, walking the floor with the crumpled statement in his hand. "Only twenty-eight hundred dollars. That's even worse than last time. Hardcover, paperback, foreign sales — everything's slipping."

"You'll have to write another book," I said. "Better than *Medusa.*"

He'd been hammering away at one in New York, but it was going poorly. It wasn't flowing. Out tumbled all that on top of this. He was in a terrible state, he was crushed, something more for a woman to handle with all the tact and affection in her being. I thought with a smile of Miss Virginia Quilty. Imagine her standing up under all this, after everything else we'd just been through! Quite a mighty fortress she'd be — I didn't think!

One last resistance to my own plan remained — to be toppled by what happened now. Miss Quilty called, and when he heard from my end of the conversation who it was, he waved both hands and shook his head no. He didn't want to talk to her, much less see her, just now. That did it. I knew then my course was clear. I need have no qualms or scruples about my little plot. When she telephoned again later that day, Randy was out for a walk, but I told her I'd like to see her. I thought we should have a little chat. We arranged to meet at a tearoom in the center of town at four that afternoon. *Some* cocktail hours could be spent in sipping oolong.

I was having mine when she finally arrived, at twenty after, carrying a box with a new dress or coat in it as well as some smaller parcels. She set them on a chair and sat down breathlessly, apologizing for her tardiness. She ordered coffee, the arrival of which found her gossiping about Randy's hypochondria in a humorous way that gave me a perfect transition into what was on my mind. It all sounded completely natural and unpremeditated.

"The thing about that," I said, "is that some of it has a basis in fact, though not always what he complains about. He has some legitimate problems that almost certainly mean trouble ahead, in the years to come, and that's why I'm glad to seem to see you two hitting it off. Because — if an old woman may butt in where she probably has no business — I think you'd be great for him. Just great."

"What do you mean?"

"You've got stick-to-it-iveness," I said, avoiding my reflection in a mirror.

"I've got what?" She had probably never heard of that virtue, and her puzzled frown made it sound like some kind of ailment itself.

"Stick-to-it-iveness. It's what built this country, and may still save it. Coping. That's another old-fashioned thing people don't want to be bothered doing any more. Just plain cope. We're all too spoiled, too soft. But you're not. You'll cope when the time comes — as come it will. You'll show you've got grit. True grit."

She turned and looked over her shoulder, as though I must be talking to a third party not visible to her. All she wanted was the waitress to fetch her some saccharine. Having emptied a small sack of that into her coffee, she stirred it and said, "What's the matter with Randy?"

"You must be kidding. What isn't? He hasn't told you about his bum stomach, for openers? Probably slight from a medical standpoint, but always there. What the statesmen use to say about the problems of the Balkan countries. Hopeless but not serious. What we call a perpetually pre-ulcerous condition. He may never pop one, but it's bad enough having to worry about a bland diet without the other, more major problem."

"What's that?"

"Decency probably prevented him saying. A man like that shouldn't drink. But when drink on the other hand means as much to him as it does to Randy, as a cushion against reality . . ." I shook my head gravely as I contemplated the possibilities. "It's bound to be hell on everybody. Hell and high water."

I took a cookie from the plate between us and nibbled on it, drinking off my cooling tea.

"You may or may not know, Miss Quilty, that he had hepatitis the year before last. You do know that's a virus that colonizes the liver, so that it's essential the patient doesn't drink for from six months to a year. He had a bad case, as far as I can make out from all accounts, but he was drinking again inside of less than three months. Whether he made a laboratory recovery as well as a clinical one — this is jargon we use for the liver chemistries — I don't know. We do know from all that how important booze is to him. What we don't know is how badly he's damaged his liver going off the wagon prematurely. But he's certainly going heavy on the grape and the grain these days, and I frankly see a cirrhosis up ahead there, too. It's only a question of time. His teeth . . . ?" I sighed philosophically and looked away.

"What about his teeth?"

"They're perfect. But you know the old saying among dentists. 'Your teeth are perfect, but those gums will have to come out.' The old villain, periodontal trouble. Responsible for more sets of dentures than decay. It's only a question of time there also when whomever his helpmeet is will have to see him through that. They put you into the hospital when they pull them, provided you've got enough left to cut that much ice, and I've had one or two such patients in my time, and I can tell you I'd rather have anything. Name it, and I'd rather have it. Having your mouth fitted for a row of tombstones is bad enough without knowing you're going to have to come right back for a colostomy. That's when they take out your colon, you know."

"He's going to lose *that?*"

"No, no," I laughed. "I meant one of the patients I had. No, Randy'll be spared that, let's hope. I trust he won't be that ulcerated, for a while. All as I'm trying to do is review with you his general medical picture. And to say that, knowing what he's probably got in store for him, I thank God he'll have somebody by his side who's loving and devoted. Who'll *stick*. Who loves him for himself alone, not just his money. Oh. That brings us to another thing."

Miss Quilty again screwed around in her chair, apparently to see if there was a bar. But no strong drink was available here. "What's that?"

"He's told you I'm sure. How the sales of *Medusa* have been slipping steadily? In a way that suggests what a lot of people have been saying, that he's been one of a number of the vogues that come and go among the young people these days. One of you said that very thing the first day you called on me. Or speculated as much. Well, I've seen the latest royalty statement and" — I shook my head — "to put that in medical terms, the prognosis is not good."

Miss Quilty now nodded her head, slowly, in a way that indicated she was really a thoughtful girl at heart, or could be, given the right circumstances, not jumping to rash conclusions or into a rash move, but taking all the factors into consideration. I noticed in the silence what an exquisite complexion she had. It possessed a creamy pallor, a smooth richness that reminded you of the paper the better magazines are printed on — coated stock I believe they call it. I pressed on.

"So give it a year or two, and he may have had his day. I don't notice any pilgrims coming through any more. Yours was the last really big batch. The furor here has been a local one, a quite natural head of steam built up over the years when he was our local star, but spent now. The rocket's gone off. Not that the picture is all dark — far

111

from it — and I don't mean to imply that the rewards of living with him aren't great, though naturally with a writer there's always the hell for a woman of nursing him through the next book, if any. I had that with *Medusa*, I'll let somebody younger and stronger do the honors on this one, thank you."

"He's at work on another?"

"Oh, sure. For years. But he tears everything up. Undoubtedly guilt over what he did to his mother the first time out has given him a block — probably permanent. But," I sighed, "he'll survive it. After all, he's peasant stock."

"Peasant?"

I poured myself a fresh cup of tea, steadying the knob of the pot-lid with a finger. I put in sugar and a new lemon slice and took a sip. I met her gaze levelly across the table-top.

"He's a Slobkin."

"A what?"

"Slobkin."

"What on earth are those?"

"Slobkins? You don't know that fine primitive strain running all through our Appleton population? Randy's mother was a Slobkin, and a solider, sturdier stock you wouldn't want. Though in the end her own version of the sensitivity that in him resulted in the artist — But never mind all that now. The thing is, we couldn't survive a week without them, the Slobkins. *They* fix our cars when they break down and our tires when they're flat. *They* see to it that our driveways get plowed and our ditches dug and our gardens weeded. Any girl would be reassured to see that clan descending on her wedding reception. *They* haul the garbage away, *they* — Where are you going?"

"I thought I'd like another cup of coffee, but on second thought, never mind. I must be running along soon. You were saying?"

"Oh. Well, I'm only trying to point out that Randy is by no means a weak reed, shaken by any wind. Not with that stock. So what if he doesn't write another line? He can always teach, or something like that. True, it doesn't pay much, and the life is far from glamorous. But with a wife who'll stand by him, see that he's fed, his clothes washed and his socks darned, who'll raise his children right. . . . Such a woman is, in my estimation, the crown of God's creation."

Miss Quilty nodded again, more reflectively than ever, gazing past my shoulder as if off into a distant vista, whose factors she had the sober good sense to evaluate at a glance, as though in her own aristocratic veins ran the blood of forebears guaranteed to steady her course and keep her from decisions of a flighty nature.

We chatted a little while longer and then she looked at her wristwatch, drawing up a natty linen cuff to do so. "God, I didn't realize it was so late. This has been wonderful, Mrs. Wallop. I'm glad we had this little talk."

"So am I. I just wanted to stress again that I can recognize the real article when I see it, is all. I won't say anything to Randy about this, so don't mention it to him when he calls you, as he probably will."

"Or I'll call him. I'm going home in a few days, you

know. I'm afraid I may be wearing out my welcome with the Baldwins. But I'll be seeing you. You probably want to stay and finish those wonderful-looking cookies with your tea. Goodbye then."

I knew she wouldn't call. I was sure I'd never see her again. And I had no hard feelings about her, or felt anything but a sense of satisfaction, as of matters probably well sifted and sorted out. I admired the trim, beautifully groomed figure as it picked up the parcels and strode lithely among the tables and out the door, the dress box carried by its handle, like a suitcase, somehow making me think of the succession of domestic servants leaving in a huff that are the special problem of the rich, a full share of which I honestly and sincerely and with all my heart wished her in a long and happy life.

five

As I hurried homeward from a job well done, I could imagine the interpretation that would of been put on it by the delineator of our "Mrs. Lusk." Her motives would be impuned. Oh, sure, psychological analysis, that major industry of today. Not by their fruits shall ye know them, but by their roots. Criminals are understood, do-gooders unmasked. All that. I could read the going-over Mrs. Lusk would get as clearly as though it was before me on the printed page: "By ridding him forever of a parasite, she had beyond all cavil done him the greatest favor of his life — exceeded only by the favor she had done herself. Under cover of yet another worthy act, she had appeased an older woman's sexual jealousy of a younger, while by erotically frustrating her slanderer into the bargain, she had accomplished her revenge on him at last — to find it as sweet as proverbially rumored. What a harpy!"

The time had come, in short, to pick my bone with T. Randall Rivers.

My delay in doing so till now served a purpose. These few but eventful weeks of fresh exposure to his subject — far, far more intimate than the first time around — would give him ample opportunity to decide on second thought whether he had been right that first time around, or might, mayhap, wish to reconsider his position in re her. What are we told in the Gospel According to Saint Matthew? "If thy brother shall trespass against thee, go and tell him his fault between thee and him alone . . ." In other words, spit it out. Don't let it fester inside. Yes, the hour had struck. The time had come. The confrontation was at hand. Nothing to do but pin up my hair (snakes and all) and hop to the very urgent business at hand.

I chose an evening when we would be relaxed and needn't rush. First I softened him up with a good dinner and a good bottle of wine, which I let him cook and choose respectively. The meal was sweetbreads à la Deutsch and the wine a red Burgundy called Chambertin. It cost twelve dollars a bottle, which I thought we could ill afford what with so little money coming in, and the royalties slipping and what not, while we were spending money like a bat out of hell, but he insisted. It was the best wine to which I have ever treated my entire palate, and the same goes for the sweetbreads à la Deutsch, though I did feel I should warn him against eating internal organs as a general rule, with his uric acid count.

"Randy," I said when we had discussed that, "there's something on my mind."

We were sitting in the living room with coffee, he swirling the usual brandy around as he lounged back in the biggest chair in the place. He had one leg slung over an arm, and he was in shirtsleeves, the collar open and the black knit tie he often wore hanging with the knot slid halfway down. "Oh? What is it?"

I was darning his socks, but at my elbow was a copy of *Medusa*, with slips of paper in it marking certain passages a person might be prepared to read. When he saw me set the socks aside and glance at it, it's possible he suspected what was coming, because he planted both feet on the floor, as though to brace himself. I only picked the book up long enough to wag it in my hand.

"Mrs. Lusk," I said. "The character of Mrs. Lusk."

"Oh, God," he said, and put his face in his hands. "Not that."

"Yes, that. I feel I must speak. How could you?"

He sprang to his feet and began pacing the room, looking as though he would like to go right on out the door and into the alien manifold inhospitable streets, despite forecasts of rain. Heatedly and then more violently and at last wildly he poured out explanations, apologies, protests, in a torrent of self-justification. He raved away about the artist, his rights, prerogatives and indeed his final *obligation* to be ruthless. He ranted about the demon which consumes the artist, driving him relentlessly to consume others in turn for his purpose, which was both divine and hellish. He stripped himself to the buff in creating portraits, why

117

not others? Personal feelings must be ignored. He cited cases, gave chapter and verse. Dickens, Joyce, Wolfe, all were merciless in regarding anything in real life as grist for the mill, including friendships. Ibsen even went so far as to *avoid them,* so he would have no compunctions about pillorying anybody in his plays. "What did Faulkner say about how an artist would never hesitate for a second to crucify his grandmother to produce a poem, and why should he? The *Ode on a Grecian Urn* is worth a hundred old ladies."

The silence that followed this tirade was hardly that, the rain having suddenly started to fall. It came down in buckets, one of those downpours that make the whole house sound like a cooking pot. At the moment I had another fancy. Seeing the streaming windows made me feel we were caught together in a great big wash machine through all of whose cycles we had to go to the end like a wad of dirty clothes, churning and thrashing through hot, warm and tumble-rinse, to say nothing of something else in which we would have yet to be spin-dried, coming out at last, it was to be hoped, fluffy white.

He stopped abruptly in front of me and said, "Have you ever heard of Hubris?"

"No," I says quietly, smoothing down my dress. "Is he somebody I ought to know?"

"It's not a he, it's an it. It's a Greek word meaning pride, or rather the insolence and violence that often spring from it. Every artist worth the name has this self-ratifying arrogance. What did Hemingway care about the poor devils

118

who sat for their portraits without knowing it? What did ... ?"

Well, by now I have learned a few big words of my own. As he dilated away, I tried to recall one recently acquired. It came to me in a minute, though I wasn't sure how to pronounce it. Using it for the first time here was like breaking in a new pair of shoes.

"That is all very well," I said, "but it has no bearing whatever on the central problem, which to me is one of verisimilitude."

"What do you mean?"

"How true is the portrait, and therefore how fair to the person portrayed? The one in real life. Especially one recognizably so. Have you a right to paint the subjects blacker than they are?"

He turned away with a shrug, flapping out both arms. "All I can say is, that's the way she was. I didn't exaggerate her in the least."

" 'She'? 'Her'? Who?"

"My mother. Isn't that what we're talking about?"

I don't normally drink after dinner, or brandy ever. I poured myself a stiff one now, in the first glass I found available. The wash machine had slipped into a fast spin cycle, sending me into a giddy confusion. My whirling head was scarcely cleared by the drink, which we often belt down in moments like this because it sets up a distracting sort of bonfire in our stomach, a small favor not to be sneezed at. My eye caught a newspaper lying on a

119

nearby chair of which the headline of one story read: "Wider Research on People Urged."

"Why did you make her a landlady?"

"Purpose of disguise. Those are just surface details a writer arbitrarily shuffles around to blur the identification somewhat and spare people's feelings."

"You just said they didn't have to. The Hubris and all."

He rearranged some air in front of him, in loo of gestures more consistent with what he was going to answer, whatever that might be. "Not in the essences. Secondary matters are just that. A landlady is the last thing my mother could conceive of her being, so I thought making her one would prevent her ever recognizing the portrait. But she did, with the aid of kind friends. Also it was convenient. I was rooming here at the time I was writing the book, and hence familiar with the mechanics of a landlady's life. It offered me a *setting*. None of that is important. It was the essence I was after. I was trying to pin down a universal human type. One of those 'dragons of respectability,' as I described her, who are usually trying to live something down or cover something up, as she was. The do-gooding I simply transposed to another key. Simply transferred from a moral to a physical plane. Club and churchwoman to professional nurse."

"Like me."

"Yes. But my mother was always descending on the sick in the way I said, you know, and for the rest, I again borrowed from my immediate observable environment because it was easy to . . . I suppose I drew on you more than I realized at the . . ." He stopped and stared at me, open-mouthed. "My God! You thought Mrs. Lusk was *you?*"

"What else was I to think?" I said, quite firmly and in clear tones, determined not to be switched from plaintive to defendant now that I had at last brought this case to trial.

"But — but . . . But you, of all people. Why, Mrs. Wallop, you're one of the nicest, kindest, sweetest, and most considerate of God's creatures it has ever been my pleasure and good fortune to know."

Moving right along, I gave a vague grunt of grateful acknowledgment the way we do at a compliment, and then after a moment of murmuring something in return about being glad to have my faith in his grasp of human nature restored — it was important to him as a writer — lit another of his cigarettes. My second that month. I also made a mental note to read the damned book *all the way through,* and not to be put off, misguided or misled by loose and irresponsible blabbermouth small-town gossips going off half-cocked. So *that* was his mother. Not that all of this excused him. Far from it. He was still guilty as sin in my book.

Now as I turned back to look at him, it was to see him watching me with a slowly broadening, cunning, slightly wicked grin on his face. There was even a glint of malice in his eye as he studied me speculatively. "Why?" he said.

"Why what?" But he had more or less put the question to himself, as he did his further observations.

"Why would you think the shoe fit?" he went on,

slowly. "Interesting. Very fascinating subject for a psychological study. Why would a woman recognize herself in a portrait of which she had never been intended as the target? Fairly insist that it was she who had been tarred with the stick, and, thereby, tar herself with it?"

Here I drew myself up quite straight. "Mr. Randy Rivers, just what in heaven's name are you jabbering about now?"

"Nothing. Just thinking out loud. Idea for a book that suddenly just hit me like a ton of bricks . . ." He poured himself some more brandy. "A kind of parable of universal human guilt as well as a study in feminine psychology. Ordinary sort of woman, in an ordinary small city, who sees herself in a fictional character not meant to be her at all, and in her resentment becomes the bitch she thinks she's been called. By over-reacting, she comes to *deserve* the lampoon she's undertaken to disclaim. The us-chickens thing. Giving her guilt away by the very protestation of innocence. *Us Chickens* might even be the title. No. But anyway, my *God*—"

"Randy, there is something I feel I should tell you," I said, only too happy to hear about his new book, but not now. I experienced just then the keenest, most overpowering desire to deserve the compliment he had just paid me. To all the virtues he had reeled off as mine, I would certainly insist on adding that of honesty. I would never flub in that area. "Randy, I told Miss Quilty a few things about you, oh, nothing much, nothing very damaging, but that may be, well, just enough to be responsible for her having made herself so scarce. I know you're concerned about not having heard from her for three or four days, and not being able to reach her yourself and all, either. I may of scared her off. It's all my doing." I noticed my voice had become shrill with fear. The belief I had been called a vixen had turned me into one. How's that for modern irony!

"You *what?* . . . Oh, hell, she's probably no good for me, and I don't want to talk about that now. I must think this through while I feel it boiling inside me at white heat. Let's see, her very defense cancels itself out. Denying the charge proves it . . ." Before I knew it he was out of the room and going up the stairs two at a time to his notebooks, emitting little squeals of ecstatic joy. Oh, our chuckling wanderer ran upstairs. "She becomes the meddling old bat she saw in the portrait. Give a dog a bad name and all that . . . Oh, my God! . . ."

Like Auden says, "And the writer runs, howling, to his art."

So the whole unfortunate misunderstanding is cleared up. The confusion is resolved and we are once more squared away. Blue skies above, bright days ahead. We live again.

But oops, hold it. Not so fast. Just a minute. Who is this coming up Crown Street as I descend it, swinging my shopping basket? Hold everything. Isn't it Cora Frawley, the news behind the news? None other. And wearing the expression of unmistakable relish a woman wears who has something she is sorry to have to tell you? Another woman's radar can pick that up a mile off.

"Hello, Emma. Well! You must be the proud parent. I just read Osgood's novel. Novella, really, I guess you'd call it," she said. "The one he has in the *New Voices* anthology. You've seen it I'm sure."

"Yes," I said, though this was the first I'd heard of it. Osgood's reason for silence was instantly obvious in the very next blip I picked up, if instinct hadn't already told me. "That's something he's been working on for some time. I told you he was writing a modern novel."

"The portrait of the mother! I mean it's certainly, well, astringent, to say the least. And the description of your house and the early years together is especially vivid." Be charitable, I said to myself. Consider the source. How would you like to have tweed skin and a husband who spills? "What did you think of it?"

"I agree with you. Very good of its kind. But you know mothers these days. They're very much in — as punching bags."

"Yes, I know," she laughed with me. Then she looked off and said, "Of course some of this stuff today goes pretty far. I mean it seems a bit — would thankless be the word?"

I laughed again. "The way of the world. What can you expect of a boy with a mother? Or a girl?"

I think clairvoyant is the word I want. I was quite clairvoyant about what I would find when I finally got to curl up with this one, which I had hardly expected when I left the house would be the first thing to fall into my hand-basket, namely a copy of the paperback anthology containing *The Duchess of Obloquy*. I had little doubt as I skimmed through *this* little valentine at Freitag's that the title character would be another ball breaker I believe they call them, in the charming parlance of the day, or that what she had done *to* her family was far, far more than what she had ever done *for* them. I knew the plot backwards, having heard it before. It would deal with some sensitive youth unable to make a dime with the girls because of you-know-who. It's open season on mothers. They pin everything on us — except a rose. Why don't they try that sometime, and knock us over dead with surprise? Knowing this all in advance, I figured I might as well be hanged for a sheep as a lamb and reimburse on the spot the friendly neighborhood currier who had brought the good news from Aix to Ghent.

"Cora," I says, "I simply must compliment you on that hat."

"Oh?"

"Yes, it's been on my mind for years. I've admired it for longer than I can remember, and have always felt guilty about not saying so. Now I have, and it's off my chest."

So no more than the wind had cleared in one quarter than it sprung up in another, blowing an even stronger odor. Because this really was a family matter where the other strictly speaking wasn't — not my family at any rate. Of course there was a certain poetic justice in it. What I thought Randy Rivers had done to me but had actually done to his mother, I now discovered my son had done to

125

me, in any case. So it all evened off in a sense. So the beef I have been airing all the time turns out to be legitimate after all — which is a relief to me for your sake, dear reader, as it means I haven't been wasting your time. At least you can make up your mind whether it's legitimate after reading *The Duchess of Obloquy* for yourself, which follows in full. After that I will be back for more equal time, if I may. In the anthology of new writing in which it appears, it follows a short story with a somewhat more sympathetic portrayal of a modern young wife and mother, who after a typical day of cleaning, sewing, and cooking for a family of six, is seized with labor pains in the middle of the night and rushed to the hospital, where she gives birth to an eight-pound pot roast.

I certainly believe in self-expression, and know it's bad to hinder or hamstring the artist in any way. But I sometimes wonder if we don't carry this realism a little too far.

II

THE DUCHESS OF OBLOQUY

by Osgood Wallop

1

My mother imbued me so strongly and so early with the puritanical view of sex prevailing in the pious and Godforsaken corner of the Middle West whence I come that even now, more than twenty years later and from nearly a thousand miles away, she casts her shadow over every bed in which I try to lark it up with another woman. Have I really said "another woman," as though those formative pruderies have indeed shackled us together in some incestuous bond? Yes! You know those husbands who can't take a mistress because it would be cheating on their wives. I can't take a wife because it would somehow be two-timing Mom.

Here and now, trying to lark it up with little Mary Hackney, down even in this scrupleless barnyard, the Village, I am afraid that if I reach out and cup one of her darling breasts Mom will learn about it, and take down my britches and give me a dozen. She will discover it as she discovered me at the age of six, playing doctor with Evelyn Lee in my "office," a neighborhood barnloft into which I urged little girls to come for regular checkups. Why can't I *feel* the lazy, post-ecstatic prowling masculine expertise I affect as my palm grazes downward along Mary Hackney's cooling flanks? My mother will get wind of it. Someone will snitch. Someone already has, she knows I am here, wallowing among the abominable sheets. I can hear her now. "So, playing thorough checkup again, are we? Maybe this will teach you, and this, and this. And an extra dose of castor oil tonight." The umbilical cord stretches like a nine-hundred-and-some-mile leash that in the end smartly snaps me back, like a tethered figure in a Looney Tune. It is that tether that has fetched me up short here in New York, only partway to the Paris for which I was originally bound. I can hear her on the telephone yet. "That's one good thing about being born and raised a Hoosier, you know. You don't have to leave the country to become one of them expatriates. All you have to do is move East. That's the same equivalent as leaving New York for the Left Bank, just as there would be exile enough right here in Tiverton, Indiana, if you hailed from Oklahoma City or Bozeman, Montana. So let's not hear any more crazy talk. You stay right where you are, and write home every week without fail, hear?"

For Mother was wise, and from her mouth did issue words of counsel. For she sought out and set in order many proverbs, wise words as goads, as nails fastened by the masters of assembly, which are given from one shepherd. But she has ruined my life, wrecked my summer, and now threatens to spoil my evening.

130

Her explanation of the mystery of life had nothing in it of bees and flowers, and was a far cry from the Maeterlinckian view of infants as mystic cherubs waiting in a kind of blue heaven to be born, the position espoused by a next-door slattern who, asked why she had all those eleven children, answered, "Because they needed me." My mother did not even use my own birth to satisfy my curiosity, but seized on a neighbor girl's illegitimate pregnancy to make her point. "Lars Hanson put his front thing into Marjorie Pemberton's front thing and kind of 'went' into her." My father left the room with a shudder of despair while my mother dilated on this theme. "That's what happens. Something comes out of a man then, that makes babies. A sort of pus."

A sort of "number three."

With a groan I roll away from little Mary Hackney, twisting the squalid sheets and folding the pillow into a sandwich around my face. If I married her I would be upon her nightly with my gasping loins and a mind as vile as sauerkraut. Memories of boyhood intruding unremittingly into it, then as now. Memories of my mother saving string, saving newspapers, magazines, even old bills, tying everything into bundles from the ball of cord swelling steadily under lengths and snippets salvaged from a lifetime of packages received. Memories of myself in high-school years at last warning her that these were quirks of behavior for which psychological explanations now existed. "Hoarding refuse like that is supposed to show an anal fixation, Mom," I said. "Anal my ass," said my mother, waddling up the stairs with yet another load of things to store in the attic.

Is my own life scientifically definable as a quest for the feminine ideal as typified by Mom? Little Mary Hackney hardly fills that bill! Daintily boned and slimly proportioned, she is the creamy pink of those china cherubs encircling mantel clocks, fadeless nymphs forever afloat about eternally fading hieroglyphs of time. She is also a tough little cookie. She sits up and clears her throat in a manner that makes me suspect the worst. The piper wants his fee. She wants to talk about "us."

I feign sleep, even affecting a light snore, no harm in suggesting right off that one would be no bargain, one would not be all that good a catch, that felicitous a mate. After a few minutes the springs creak beneath me, and out of one eye I see her sprint into the bathroom, with a laugh I find utterly charming as a giggle provoked by my seed running down her leg. "Why are you so long in the tub?" my mother would say. "Let me tell you that it will do you no good. If kept up it softens the brain and makes an idiot out of you. Use the bathroom for what it's supposed to be used for. Anything the good Lord intended to come out of that thing don't have to be pumped out." Now Mary Hackney and I have been enjoying a novel on the subject. "That's what it's about, and that's *all* it's about," she said in first recommending it to me, with the rippling breathless giggle I find so entrancing, so hopelessly envy as a kind of animal naturalness forever beyond my reach. "And you may not believe this, but he pulls it off." "Oh, I believe it, Mary, I believe anything I hear."

My mother met my father when he was working as a bouncer on the dance floor of an Indiana lake resort, where one of his jobs was to patrol the crowded pavilion with a ruler to make sure couples were dancing at least eight inches apart. In the classic manual *What a Young Man Ought to Know*, which most of us children there and then were given to read as preparation for life, the evils of the waltz are graphically depicted by an account of a young woman who reports the giddy lust she experienced when whirled about in the arms of her partner, or rather the hands of a partner holding her at arm's length, to the strains of a tune in three-quarter time. At least such is my recollection of the guidebook, of which I wish I had a copy now to check also my impression that it confirms what my mother warned about the madhouse and the cemetery as the rewards of flogging our own meat. My father, at any rate, performed the task of seeing to it that defiling contact was kept to a minimum at Lake Takoe. He would sidle among the couples in a straw boater and shirt with sleeve garters, as I can readily imagine from fading period snapshots, the ruler at the ready, challenging any pair orbiting cheek-to-cheek and in otherwise censorable proximity to the strains of *Yes, Sir, That's My Baby* and *Toot, Toot, Tootsie!* "All right, all right you two, back a ways," he would bark at some blazered Romeo cuddling his piece too closely. Any offenders would be allowed one warning, and at the second misdemeanor — off! "You! Belly to belly again are we? That's two I think. Out! Skidoo!" The blade might mutter an "I got your eight inches," or something of the sort as he slunk off with his tootsie, flapping bell bottoms

133

then in their first, and straight, vogue, the sign of sporty types known then as "sheiks" or sometimes "cake eaters." I must defend my father against the charge of sincerity, here. I doubt that his heart was really in any of this except for a slight and ephemeral enough sense of power it gave him at a job undertaken, in any case, because it provided him an opportunity to hang around a place where he might get a chance to play his trombone. He was at best an indifferent performer on a musical instrument an unmusical wife soon discouraged his blowing around the house. Once he found himself going steady with marriage necessarily in view, he learned a skilled trade — floor work — that stood him in good stead the rest of his life. How remote now seems a point of view that I, nevertheless, took in through my pores. Tiverton town had even more repressive elements in its Dutch Reformed folk, who considered dancing all right as long as girls danced with girls and boys with boys — arrangements I was later to rediscover in updated New York. Mixed up in all this was the quaint principle of chivalry embodied in clichés about being unworthy to "kiss the hem of a woman's dress." The term conveyed respectful distance well enough when dresses swept the floor, but at today's miniskirt level such a tableau would seem a little forward, if not downright salacious.

The bathwater runs away and a fresh nymph returns.

"Hey, you."

My father snored when he was awake, a light stertorous sort of snuffling buzz that continued all evening over his paper, filtered through a verdant mustache probably not unlike that of old Jolyon Forsyte, in which the bit of thistledown caught as he sat dying in the summer garden. I mustn't overdo this pretense at being asleep, just sustain enough of a honk to drive thoughts of matrimony out of her head. "You," she repeats. "Mmlaah?" I mumble, heaving about, and, once again winding myself in these disreputable cerements, play dead. With a resigned murmur she goes to a chair and sits brushing her hair. It is a short-cropped brown mop whose natural curls she cultivates by brisk upward strokes, which crackle pleasantly in the otherwise silent room. The steady rhythmic noise makes my spine begin to tingle, as though intangible fingers are massaging it. After five minutes or so, she drops the brush and comes over to the bed.

I had thought it only fair we level with one another before becoming lovers, and so we had talked freely one night before doing so.

In a day when we have resolved that individual fetishes are nothing to be ashamed of, that anything that gives pleasure, or is necessary to it, is to be openly owned and unabashedly indulged in — morality alone being taboo — I had admitted a rather outré specialty of my own to Mary Hackney, who had then racked her brains over what it might be. "What do you have to do?" she asked, somewhat apprehensively, despite having herself spiritedly put the case for latitude. "You mean before you can experience gratification? Is that what you mean?" I nodded, looking away. "What?"

"Guess."

She ran through the gamut of known specialties and perversions as encountered either in personal experience or through hearsay, to no avail. She was not even warm. As an educated and enlightened woman she thought she knew every sub-variant of anthropoid conjunction, everything that might have to be touched, tasted, plied, entered, bitten, fondled, flailed or flogged, before orgasm could be attained. But no. This was an associative so exquisite, a requirement so far out and unheard of, as to be surely one of a kind. It was unmentioned in Freud, Kinsey and Havelock Ellis. She would comb Krafft-Ebing in vain for it. By now she was genuinely alarmed.

"My God, what is it?" she said. "What on earth do you have to *do?*"

"I have to" — I blushed to speak of it — "I have to hold hands."

She now glided softly back into the bed, slipping a palm into mine as with the other she undertook a tactile journey aimed at reviving excitements in abeyance.

"Why are you so uptight?"

"Why must you give *them* candy, if they're coming there to you for regular checkups?" I can hear my mother again now. She has a terrible memory (total recall) and is not asking questions at all, but putting accusations. "If you're the doctor, why is it you have to pay the fee when you examine them? An Oh Henry or a package of Walnettos for each visit."

With the mind that inevitably resulted from all this, I was naturally interested to hear from an intellectual

friend in adolescence that there is an orgasm in the over-
ture to *Der Rosenkavalier*. Fact. Playing a recording of it,
I was readily able to identify the brass-depicted emissions,
for the orchestra actually comes three times in the *Voor-
stuk*, as distinguished from the single tumescence and re-
cession said to underlie the pattern of the "Liebestod" in
Tristan. My mother was believed to have fed my father
oysters because she'd heard they were good for virility —
thinking that was something that had to be cured.

"Christ, if my love were in my arms, and I in my bed
again!"

I get up and run into the bathroom, but when I turn up
the tap water to drown myself out, there is Mary in the
doorway, leaning against the jamb with her arms folded
and laughing. She wants us to become as little children —
completely wholesome and natural. I must decline. It has
taken Nature several billion years to entangle my urinary
and reproductive organs in so baroque a fashion, and it
will take me at least that long to adjust my dim view of
the result, even without a nereid looking on. I try to push
the door shut but she slips prettily in and sits on the edge
of the tub to watch me, smiling prankishly, her arms still
folded over her little Cranach breasts. Minutes pass —
nothing else. I stand there like an urchin in a European
town fountain with the water shut off. It is a form of uro-
logical impotence. I remember those psychological test
questionnaires aimed at evaluating cretinous applicants for
stockroom work. "Do you find it difficult to micturate
with somebody else in the room?" Yes, except for the

reading room of the public library. There I am O.K. Oh, how I wish I were like this uninhibited pink sprite skipping lightly back to bed. But — Mama don't allow no spontaneity here . . . Oh, Mama don't allow no untrammeled self-expression here . . .

When I return myself, however, I see that her expression is serious. She sits propped against the headboard, the polluted sheet drawn to her chin. I can see that we are in session. We are going to talk about "us." Oh, God, how I hate all this self-analysis to which we are all nevertheless prone and by which we are all in any case inescapably trapped. We sort through the emotional rubble of our lives in search of some primal reality called Love, like excavators gingerly picking through the debris of Cnidos in search of the statue of Aphrodite, or rather the fragment of it they fear they will probably have to settle for . . . But this is serious. Mary has undoubtedly been trying my name on for size. It's a fancy name, any woman would like it: St. Cloud. Clearly she is aspiring to it: "I'm Mrs. St. Cloud." She frowns thoughtfully at her hands a moment and speaks.

"Bunk, you're essentially a moral person. I know you think people should level with each other. Not take and enjoy each other under false pretenses. You're basically decent. You want to do the right thing."

"Oh, I don't know." I snuffle repellently — *snnk* — like those chaps forever correcting sinal seepage. Warshawski is one. Where is he now? Isn't he overdue? I may borrow the mannerism.

"A kind sort of guy at bottom. Sentimental, in your way. You should have a family."

"Thanks, I've got one. *Snnk.*"

Sheer fear of getting any more deeply involved makes me try to kill the discussion aborning by turning the radio on. It is a rude thing to do, and I find it hard to forgive my mother, well as she meant, proper though she thought the training that has rendered me unfit for a permanent relationship. Issuing from the radio are the strains of Ravel's *La Valse*, whose sardonic eccentric rhythms always suggest to me a roomful of waltzing cripples.

Mary Hackney gets up and shuts it off.

"Bunk, we've got to square with one another. I've got to be honest." As she returns to the bed, heels thudding on the frayed carpet, I note again that a woman's backside is cruciform, the horizontal crease just below the sweet cheeks being transverse to the long downward cleft — which by itself, when she is lying down, is, however, like a kind of smile. O moonflower! O pulps of Paradise! "Honest and say I don't want to encourage any false expectations on your part. There comes a time when both parties have to lay their cards on the table. I owe it to you to say I — Well, I just don't want to get married."

So. I am to be given the air. Discarded like an old shoe. Mother was right. Modern girls don't want to cope. They don't want to pitch in. They don't want a home any more, responsibilities. I would find New York especially teeming with these pleasure-loving swingers. Is nothing sacred to

139

them — not even this mucking about? No, nothing — except possibly their careers.

"You know I want to sing more than anything, Bunk," Mary took up, echoing my very thoughts. "That's got to come first, and no marriage ever works that comes second."

A rather interesting exercise in casuistry followed. I used the unexpected development to embezzle, as I suppose you might put it, a great deal of moral credit to myself by pretending, at least taking no pains to deny, that I was indeed the earnest-hearted chap she cracked me up to be, willing to do the right thing by a putative "steady" by marrying her; even hinting that secret hopes were being dashed by *her* not secretly hoping to become Mrs. St. Cloud, the name in fact not like a bright parasol already opened in fancy, twirled in anticipation. "Good afternoon, I'm Mrs. St. Cloud . . ." All of which again proves how much life is a game, not to imply that it's any less worthwhile for all that, or "meaningful." "Lamb," she said, turning to me and fondling my head. I take a breast to my mouth, a long, leeching kiss. "I'm sorry but . . ." Her comforts take an inevitably amorous turn, and we are soon again appeasing one another, and, of course, ourselves. "At least I have to see whether I've got any talent," she continues later. "You've got talent." I reassure her. "You have a lovely voice." "All right, then at least till I see whether my talent is going to get me anywhere. I'm going to make the big pitch. I've got a press agent now as well as an agent. Warshawski's being a real busy beaver. He's gotten squibs in several columns lately."

The evening takes a fresh turn with the arrival of Warshawski himself. He is expected, so we are dressed when he arrives about a quarter to ten. He is a black friend of Mary's and, as a consequence, lately, of mine. I have no idea what his Georgia family's name is. I assume the Warshawski is assumed, like the succession of dialects with which he apparently enjoys spreading further confusion. My allergy to put-ons makes me especially resist the thick Irish brogue with which he greets us at the door. "Sure and it's sorry I am that it's so late that I am, but me job keeps me jumping at all hours, at all, at all, and devil a penny I make the best of days. Hello, Mary. It's good to see you, Bunk me by." Christ, I think, even your wop and your Swede are better than this — even your darky. Warshawski himself I like, with his octave of white keys for a grin — who could not? I leave soon, knowing they have business to transact, or at least discuss. The conversation is not hard to reconstruct from the squib I read a week later in one of the metropolitan gossip columns:

"Rising chanteuse Mary Hackney belts them out with special fervor at the Grape and Grain these nights. Rumor has it that she is singing her heart out for a swell guy who's eating his out for her."

There was presently this in another tabloid:

"What part-time waiter in a Village chophouse goes home nightly to work on That Play — with a fish-hook in his heart? He's carrying the torch for torch singer Mary Hackney, currently wowing them at the Deep Philip."

I complained to Mary about all this foolishness, but she

had troubles of her own. She had yet to get her first real job, the bars mentioned by these scrounging journalists being nothing but showcases for entertainers willing to perform free for the experience or the chance to be seen by producers themselves dropping in at such joints to get a look at any aspiring new talent, deluded or otherwise. The "turns" were little more than auditions; the collective result often little better than Amateur Night.

Suffering for her as I did, I gave off, and took my grievance straight to Warshawski himself. But before I ran into him again, I had become a legend. I was known in nightclub circles as the Heartbreak Kid.

2

I didn't go straight to him, actually, or hunt him down directly my dander was up. Nursing a beef I knew warranted a good stiff punch in the nose, I naturally avoided him. I shouldn't have wanted to answer for the results. Once I spotted him coming down Houston Street and turned and ran in the other direction, around a corner. The dread of such a confrontation was no doubt partly sympathy for the underdog (as domestic colonialism the Negro is certainly

America's unique creation), partly the white man's instinctive fear of the black man's bruited sexual superiority. "Where *is* it?" my mother would joke, drying me off after a tub. "Oh, there it is. What a cute little button." Those were the days when I tied weights to it, hoping to elongate it. Small and then heavier metal objects, like the lead sinkers on a fishline. Worn there inside my trousers, they produced as I walked down the street or into the schoolroom at least a convincing facsimile of the end desired. My mother liked nothing better than a good fight, I mused as I sprinted up the street away from Warshawski, and for her own counterparts of the bone I had to pick with him would lustily quote something from, I believe, Matthew: "If thou have ought against thy brother, go and lay it on the line" — or whatever the Gospel author's no doubt finer choice of words happens to be.

Trotting round the next corner, I run smack into Warshawski. He has been hustling in the other direction. We knock the wind out of one another — the little we have left.

"Oh, there you are, you son of a bitch," I pant.

"Bunk! I'm a look all over for you. Look a da high, look a da low. No find a Bunk — till now. *Snnk*."

"Oh?" I lean against a building with the flat of my palm, crossing one foot over the other. We're both breathing like race horses. "Go on."

"Well." He swallowed and looked off, as though to collect his thoughts. "I'm a get three, four one-liners in the papers about you and Mary. Sometimes two lines. Special a mention the lovely roman*tic* a feeling that's a prevail. Mean nothathing to you," he goes on with a shrug, the hands upflung in endearing wop spontaneity, the black lips curled in a smile of wop persuasion, "but good a for her, whaaat? Make a da legend maybe?" He poked me in the stomach with an arch suggestion I'm a gay dog, prepared to go to any lengths to put his woman on the map. Bit of a cynical bastard maybe. "De end justify a da means, hah?" Another knife in the gut with a long thumb. Then with a pantomime of bowing a fiddle tucked under his chin, "We feed 'em a da pap, a what?"

I decide to accept this apology. Which is what the guilt behind all the hanky-panky implies. And for Mary's sake I decide not to resent the role of Heartbreak Kid, sometimes Bittersweet Boy, the unnamed object of the sentimental songs she is struggling to make her specialty in the neighborhood joints, struggling like herself, in which she nightly sings for nothing, or at best the price of supper and a few drinks. She now began to preface selections with a few words about the "very, very dear friend" to whom she was dedicating them. Since I often went to hear her, I was frequently pointed out as the guy who was carrying the torch for her, and I must say that, slumped across the bar with a glass in my hand, and past my first resentment, I began to enjoy the role. I even began to believe it, such are the attractions of self-pity. *Snnk.*

Mary was on the point of getting somewhere when something happened. She telephoned me late one afternoon and said, "Come right over."

144

"Is it important?"

"No, just urgent."

I had several things to do, including pop apprehensively into a bar on the spur of the moment for a few quick ones, and so it wasn't till nearly an hour later that I arrived, quite out of breath, if not snoring when awake. "Sorry I'm late."

"You're not the only one."

"I . . . don't . . ."

"Three or four days."

"Oh, my God." I sank into a chair with my head in my hands. "How long have you known?"

"That I'm three or four days late? Oh, I'd say three or four days."

"Oh, my God." I rocked my head, still holding it in my hands, covering my face for shame. Oh, the regrets, to no avail. I flew in fancy to my years as a lad. I had promised my mother that I would save number three for my wife. I wished now it had been a deathbed promise. I wouldn't be in this jam now, with a vow that binding. What a bitter pill to swallow.

"It's that damn pill," Mary said, uncannily contrapuntal. "After taking it for a while you suspend it, or you forget it, but keep the false confidence. That's the insidious part. Did you read about that report by some Swedish royal commission? There's been a rise in unwed mothers in Sweden because of the pill, and in pregnant brides."

"Oh, Mary, what'll we do?"

145

"Maybe you can think of something, or know of something."

My mind at high speed ran off a scenario of girls jumping from chairs and tables, bowling and bouncing on trampolines, to say nothing of the story about the horseback ride taken by a topless one with bazooms so large she wound up with two black eyes — a fate hardly likely to befall our Mary, what? I found it harder to forgive Mom for these churlish thoughts than for most provoked by the spectacle, or news, of a fallen woman — no doubt because I was up to my neck in this thing myself.

"I'll see what I can do," I said, at the door. "Let me do the worrying for the time being. I can't promise anything, but I'll try."

I naturally wondered what Warshawski would think or say when he found out. He did when Mary's condition made it impossible for her to sing in public, by which time he had doubtless already formed his suspicions. He was then in his redskin period, whose genocidal echoes might be thought of as supplying an apt mirror-symbol for his own sorrows — to say nothing of its convenience in easing the strains of communication. He spoke in Indian lore when he came to pay a ceremonial call on me.

"Me hear. Me heap surprised. Could knock me over with eagle feather."

"Yes, I know. How about some beer?" He continued as I poured us glasses from a half-gallon bottle of Ruppert's I had in the icebox.

"After many moons, have manchild or womanchild, one

146

or other. Heap many precedents, all through centuries, make that dead certainty. Meanwhile She who Sings will wax like the moon herself, slowly, surely, quarter-moon to half-moon to full, as she swell with child. We change her name to that — Waxing Moon. Spirits of many ancestors tell me this, come to me in dream last night with much good medicine, and say call her Waxing Moon. So from now on she Waxing Moon, while you waxing floors. Must pitch in and help, so not have undue strain. Also want to keep mother-to-be in good spirits, so that when her hour come, she give you manchild which you hold up to rising sun and cry 'Aiyeee! Aiyeee!' with much joy and triumph, in strength and glory of your manhood." Warshawski had paused before something tacked to my wall at eye level, a strip of three pictures taken in one of those automatic photographic booths. "Who is this?"

A tale hung by the souvenir, which I related.

Several years before, I entered such a booth in an amusement arcade in Chicago, where I was stopping overnight on a visit back home. I inserted a quarter, disposed myself in a variety of agreeable poses, waited the interval required for developing the film, and was at length rewarded by a digestive rumble from the mechanism which then extruded a band of three snapshots showing a maiden in the first blush of her Maytime, with fair hair and wide eyes, smiling prettily under a straw bonnet secured at the chin with a large bow.

Feeling faint, I stumbled out of the booth clutching this product, and stood leaning against the side of it, breathing heavily as I waited for the next customer to come along in hopes of seeing how he, or she, made out. A machine in ill health can be a monster, even one merely off a notch in its sequence, and one can only speculate what the girl with the flaxen hair had got before me, or who, coming after, might have been dealt representations of himself in triplicate as a Midwestern blade-about-town with patent-leather hair. I slipped another quarter into the slot but nothing came out at all that time, and I left, murmuring something to an attendant about putting an Out of Order sign on the booth.

Some errant sentimental fancy for the girl, such as often seizes us for the anonymous, made me take her back with me and tack her to my living room wall, where Warshawski was now studying her and listening to my story. He shook his head dubiously.

"Bad medicine to let anybody catch your spirit in the box, anywhere. May be enemy wanting to work evil magic. That why I never let anybody click box at me, especially stranger on street, if I can help it. This not good mixup. Somebody else got your spirit out of box and you got hers. Or maybe yours still in box. Not good. Ugh!"

Little Waxing Moon was rarely in an agreeable mood as the weeks rolled by. She groaned especially resentfully at the loss of her figure, loathing in particular the defaming maternity slacks bought in the cheap Village shops among which we disconsolately scrounged. She made no secret of feeling herself entitled to at least one uptown shopping binge at Lord and Taylor's or Bonwit's.

148

"We need more money," she declared flatly one night, at her place. She snapped off the phonograph we'd had going. "Lots. And right away. We've got to get it. Period."

She fixed herself an Old Fashioned, using artificial sweetener. I had given her a Medici ring, in the "poison cup" of which she kept saccharine tablets. Twice a week she allowed herself one piece of candy, making her selection from a box of assorted chocolates we kept around for this ritual, in a manner that was something to behold. She would sit for minutes pondering the contents like a chess player his board. Even now, with her figure temporarily compromised, she continued to preserve her posture by walking around with a book on her head — on which *War and Peace* was now precariously balanced as she stood in the doorway assailing my improvidence. One of the squibs, perhaps more, that Warshawski had got in the columns about her before he was let go had to do with her superior cultural level. "Mary Hackney, the model turned singer presently slaying them at the Twelve Cats, is one of your more literate entertainers. She would never think of doing her posture exercises with a book on her head that she hasn't first read."

"How did you like *War and Peace?*"

"What?"

"That book."

"All right. Look, we've got to talk about money."

"I don't know where we're going to get any more, Mary, unless you got a temporary job of some sort yourself." I was still working part-time at the steakhouse, only dinners,

149

which left me a good part of the day for the play I was writing, or trying to. "You wouldn't want me to work at the restaurant full-time, would you?"

She darted me a look as she circled the room, her arms extended in an informally elegant attitude. She did have a pretty carriage. She threw the book down at last and sat on the couch beside me. "How about your mother? Couldn't you touch her for a loan? You tell me about the jolly wad she must have socked away with that growth stock that's been zooming. That you say she hoards like she hoards old newspapers. What's the matter with you? You're white as a sheet."

"You are never, never . . . under any . . ." My voice is foggy with fear, my knees turn to rubber in my mouth. "My mother must never hear a word of this. She would —" I was about to blurt out she would kill me, but caught and reversed myself. "It would kill her. No, that's out, absolutely. Just give it another three or four weeks and by that time I'll have my play ready to show Jakes, and he may give me a contract."

"One day you offer to take a full-time job and the next day you take it back. You told me you had integrity."

"Where did you ever get any such idea? I never told you that. *Snnk.*"

"You did so. You laid right there and boasted about how honor went first with you, decency —"

"Ooh, you liar. *You* said I did. You said I was an innately moral person, whatever that means. How about your father? Wouldn't he help you over a stile?"

150

She shook her head as at a proposal with no foundation in reality whatever. Her mother has been dead for years, and her father has just recently married a woman with a headache. They now live in Jersey. I've met him once, a tall man with thin lips and a smile like a snarled bootlace. He's made it clear that his current marriage takes all his time and money.

I get up from the couch, fidgeting at a pair of trousers that seem to have become extremely uncomfortable around the waist. A ballooning middle is oddly unaccounted for by any increase in weight.

"Look, let's forget our troubles and make a night of it."

"Where, Voisin? We've got enough for a pastrami sandwich apiece and some more of those loathsome pickles you seem to crave as much as me. What are you undressing for? If you think I'm in any mood for —"

"No, it's not that. Look, I'm going to make a request that may seem peculiar. I'd like to borrow a pair of your maternity slacks. My middle seems to keep blowing up right along with yours. In fact I can hardly button these pants. The button snapped off another pair the other day. It must be this thing called sympathetic pregnancy they say husbands can get, apparently."

"Jesus Christ, you mean we'll have to buy you a whole new wardrobe too?"

The phenomenon seemed to surprise as well as annoy her, though it does occur with great frequency according to an article in *The Ladies' Home Journal* that I read while waiting for Mary in our gynecologist's office. The distention is often quite marked, in some cases making it necessary to let out the expectant father's clothes, or even buy larger sizes, as he hysterically keeps pace with his wife's swelling progress through the months. It all sounded excruciatingly cozy, in a kind of family-solidarity, America First way that I linked incompetently with certain speeches by the Vice President, especially during my bouts of morning sickness. "Who's effete now?" I would seem to be saying as I retched over a bowl of ice cream at breakfast, holding my fecund middle in a sort of nauseous rhapsody. An extremely slipshod equation typical of my confinement, that made me understand Korzybski's concept of "colloidal jazz," for the sheer dance of cerebral and glandular electrons we call thinking, and that gave me an insight into women's seasonal instability while making me doubt their right to the vote.

In rapidly deteriorating spirits Mary dug from her closet a pair of trousers the color of those she had on, which fit me to a T. Together we took the evening air, a look-alike couple as ever was, identical even to our moderate sizes, except for my being perhaps an inch or two taller, with matching tummies. We strolled arm-in-arm, allowing for the constant readjustment of Mary's grip on my biceps as necessary to stabilize herself on some new high heels, and greeting neighbors we encountered. "Evening, Miz Wishengrad . . . Hello, Snedecker . . ." Short of the delicatessen for which we had been originally bound was an Italian restaurant we had always wanted to try, and which looked seedily within our means. We went in. It smelled disagreeably of cooked food, in a way that reminded me of a spaghetti house to which my father would often take us on Saturday nights, when I was a boy. Filaments of memory again played about in my mind, momentarily caught, then again lost, in the thalassic depths of recollection, like phosphorescent broken gleams of light in plashing night water. Mother had two wardrobes herself, being one of those women who (another phenomenon) alternate bloat and recede, independently of parturition, for reasons apparently having to do with water-retention. She was always more polemic when the larger was required. I can see her yet in her tweed skirts, eating an ice cream cone as she pedaled down the street on a bicycle with a sticker on it reading "Stamp Out Smut." My recollection is that she grew each year more contentious with my father, who himself lapsed into a state of resignation broken only by protests at having his own words twisted.

"That does it. I'll never open my mouth again."

"*Will* you be still."

"Never, never again will I utter another word. I shall take a vow of silence."

"Oh, shut up."

After a heavy dinner of ravioli and beer I rose from the table to go to the men's room, and as I did so remembered that the maternity slacks I was wearing had no fly. That was the least of my problems. I have always found slightly tedious the "Kings and Queens" and even cuter designations on public lavatory doors, such as silhouettes of top hats and frilled bonnets. Worse are those in a foreign language, except for French, and possibly Italian, though even here the non-linguist must pause a moment over his choice of suffix to "Signor." Most galling of all are a pair of cryptic symbols such as confronted me here. They were designs unfamiliar to me, and completely beyond my powers of exegesis as distinctions in gender, even on a guesswork basis. Vaguely heraldic in feeling, they could also be construed as derived from the Greek alphabet, or Egyptian hieroglyphics, not that any of that would help the layman wishing to take a leak. I hung about waiting for someone to go in or come out either door, as a clue, and when no one did, picked the one that seemed the more masculine to me as a sort of Rorschach selection, and plowed ahead.

It was a swinging door which, halfway, met an outcoming occupant of superior strength, or at least determination, who slowly but surely forced it back in my direction. I fell back, to recognize the sturdy figure of Adelaide Bagshaw emerging, a slight acquaintance.

"Well, Bunk. So it's come to this."

"Hello, Adelaide. It's these damned symbols. I suppose I want the other, then?"

"I earnestly trust!"

"I've been out of touch. We must have lunch sometime."

By now I was thoroughly out of sorts, and resolved that if I ever got myself knocked up again it would not only be when I was making more than a teacher's salary, which was all you earned waiting on tables part-time in a chophouse, but in another and simpler part of the country, where

154

there were real people, the old ways were good enough, and the sun rose and set on townfolk pursuing humble tasks according to plain old-fashioned values. How I longed suddenly to be a lad again, going to the Christcapades with Mom and Dad, walking hand-in-hand between them, our ice skates slung by their knotted laces over our shoulders, as we made our way to the frozen pond in the park where the Tiverton Chamber of Commerce every Christmas time set up the giant illuminated Nativity crèche, or Christo-rama. There with the other good folk of the town we swirled about on the ice like microbes on a slide, uniting, dividing, spinning gaily apart and together again as we caught one another's mittened hands, round and round to the music of carols pouring from loud speakers set up near the triumphantly blazing stable, laughing as we cracked the whip, the casualties almost spinning off into the Wise Men and the Holy Family, laughing as I grasped Mom's hand or missed it to snatch it next time around, Pop the melancholy skater orbiting the rink by himself, bent over with his hands behind his back like the Dutchmen from the old-country canals, negotiating the circles with sure, steady strokes, an icicle gathering on his nose like a festive scrap of holiday tinsel, joining in the laughter only when I fa down and go boom, or Mom lands on her fat hiney, sitting there with shrieks of mirth and for intervals of a frequency that gives new meaning to these scheduled periods as "sessions." We always made the one-to-three session on Sunday afternoons as long as there was skating, walking the half-mile homeward hand-in-hand again, our cheeks winter apples, tired but happy, contentedly spent, ready for the mug of hot cocoa in the kitchen, none of us talking much but Dad completely silent, in fact morose in a way that becomes infectious, Mom at last, though in a good mood and not inclined to be really captious, giving him a glance as much as to ask, then at last actually asking, "Matter? Cat got your tongue?"

"Remember? I've taken a vow of silence."

"Hush."

Will I be as good a parent when the time comes? Let that wait — the gynecological problems are enough for the moment. When I feel the child kicking inside me I figure it's time to go see Dr. Wilmot myself, alone. Yes, he's familiar with the phenomenon, waves away the frazzled *Ladies' Home Journal* with the article entitled "When Father Is Pregnant" that I carry in from his own waiting room to show him. "Take these for gas is about all I can suggest," he says, shaking from a bottle some pills the size of mothballs. "And eat what you have a craving for, though all those pickles have enough salt in them to swell that potbelly faster than anything I can give you will take it down. Quite an alderman you're getting," and he laughs. Then he must be from the Middle West too, where we always called a paunch an alderman, for the caricature of a ward boss it suggests. Before I leave I have him prescribe a specific for migraine, something stronger than aspirin, because this crisis isn't just a bellyful — it's a grade-A headache.

Often, when first making love with Mary Hackney, I

156

had vividly imagined the child we might conceive in our careless raptures. I woolgather constantly. My erotic fantasies are interrupted by almost nothing, not even lovemaking itself. Often I would *think* about possessing Mary while in the act of doing so, chimerically flavoring my lust with mental images of our essaying other and more unusual anthropoid positions than those in which we happened to be conventionally thrashing. Amorous delight would also, finally, be spiced by fancying that the next paroxysm would land us "in trouble" — bringing down upon our heads the shame against which my provincial mother warned me, and that I secretly wanted to bring down on hers for having spoiled sex for me by polluting it with morality. I could feel my hot seed spurting to meet hers, Mary's that is, lying in wait for it there, for mine that is, in the dark mammalian grottoes of her flesh, the blind primordial still unfecundated but plenipotentiary mother muck. This became embodied in the form of an actual nipper out there, somewhere mystically lurking in the wings, as it were, ready to "fix us," to do us in. I mean that the peril itself flavored our revels with an extra zest. Often, while holding back with the "after you" kind of courtesy a man extends to a mate taking a longer time to her crisis, in Mary's case often involving delays of up to a half and three-quarters of an hour, like the Long Island Railroad and the New Haven, now Penn Central of course, that vehicular ghetto — where were we? Oh, yes, the periods on the copulative siding when I would pass the time by imagining the nipper, in most vivid detail, impatient for me to get on with it. "Fow Chwist's sake, let's get dis show on de woad, shall we?" he would say, beating his spoon on the high-chair, figuratively speaking, clamoring to be born. "I haven't got all day, you know. Let's get de lead out, shall we, Pop? Don't go blaming her now, maybe you ain't de exciting ball of fire you pween yourself on being. Chwist, I could be two, thwee months old by dis time."

Now that the nipper was actually on the way, the situation sometimes became ironically reversed. Freed of the fear of pregnancy, now that she was pregnant, Little Waxing Moon had seizures of desire I was put to it to accommodate in terms of responsive energy, quite apart from the sheer physical problems of getting our two "aldermans" together in anything like the sheer number and variety of animal conjunctions with which she now lusted to experiment. Oh, of course one wants to try everything, and does; but "different positions" turn out to be like the elk steak or the bear steak one keeps seeing on restaurant menus and at last orders out of curiosity — not all that good. To say nothing of the fact that the particular member ultimately responsible for achieving all these hyphenations may not always have been all that expandable. The problem posed by two ballooning midriffs can be pictured in terms of a dumbbell the progressively swelling ends of which relatively shrink the interconnecting stem. Waxing Moon thirsted also for a full complementary repertory of oral and labial delights, till your correspondent's back, neck, legs and shoulders ached, not to mention a half-torn ligature under his tongue. Held to her ripening breast, in moments of exhausted repose, he could turn his mind to the financial problems. Why couldn't we give up one of the two flats we now separately occupied, and move into the larger — hers? No, that was out. We would both hate it, in each other's hair, in each other's pockets, finally hating each other. We were not going to marry anyway, she reminded me. The new emerging American woman had plenty of glamorous confirmation for this independent point of view just then, there being several actresses in the news as unwed mothers — not that anybody even bothered to use the term any more. All that had gone by the board. It was a new era.

Mary certainly emerged a new woman. After the birth of the boy, she immediately recovered her figure, and came back stronger than ever as a singer. Her voice seemed to have deepened, her tone to have become steadier. Her agent even got her work! It didn't pay lavishly, but it paid, and it gave her a chance to see the country. He booked her with a traveling industrial show, sponsored by motorboat manufacturers for sportsmen's exhibitions in various cities. Her expenses were also of course paid. She bought some new clothes and set off on a six-months' tour, leaving the baby with me.

3

It is an evening in late April. I am trying to bat out an article, "I Was an Unwed Father," for the *True Confessions* type of magazine. Another, "I Am an Abandoned Man," is making the rounds. Could I make a bastardy case out of it, the first one of its kind? "There, Your Honor," pointing an accusing finger across the crowded courtroom. "She is the mother of my child!" A smattering of Women's Lib among the spectators laugh. The doorbell rings, and I know who it is from the shave-and-a-haircut-six-bits rhythm with which the caller has identified himself.

"Warshawski!"

"Ach, ja."

He is depressed. He has just been to see the latest Broadway comedy hit, and is in need of cheering up. The plot concerns a brilliant academic scholar who prides himself on being known in his circles as a walking encyclopedia, and who learns that he must have both legs amputated. Subplots include a son expelled from veterinary college for bestiality, while romantic interest is supplied by a daughter who is in love with the boy next door, who is in love with the boy next door to *him* . . . No wonder Warshawski is dejected. How can he hope to write a comedy as fine, humor as compellingly contemporary, as that?

"Maybe we can collaborate," he says. "Got any ideas?"

"That reminds me. Come on over here."

I beckoned him to the bassinette, where we stood smiling down at the sight of Ed, just awakening among the blue bedclothes. "Doesn't he strike you as kind of dark?"

"What do you mean, dark?"

"Dark-complected. Dusky." The penetrating glance I attempt to fire into his eyeballs lands on the back of his neck as he turns away with a philosophical shrug.

"*C'est la vie*. In my cawntry, fathers often thought their kids looked light. Mine did, and Mother would often say, 'Don't you pay your father no mind, chilo. He's no kin o' yourn.' Haven't you got ancestors with a swarthy streak? Some Spanish great-grandfather you said was more than half Moorish? What's that in the Bible about the sons of the fathers being visited upon the children to the third and fourth generation or something?"

"It's the sins of the fathers."

"Yeah. So that's where it's at."

All this while the kid was gurgling and swinging his head impatiently from side to side as much as to say, "Teach me to talk, wiw you, because I've got a few things to get off my chest. If we have to inhewit dis fwiggin' world at least get us in shape to deal wif it. Was it Talleywand who said, 'Man was given the power of speech in order dat he might conceal his thoughts.'? Well, not dis baby! So leave us give me no infant-cwying-in-de-night-and-wif-no-language-but-a-cwy cwap. Dat's a baby's pwayeh at twilight."

161

"So play it loose. And let's not be in a rush to write this play until we're sure we've got a good comic idea. They're everywhere, if we only open our eyes to them. But humor has to have substance today. Audiences won't settle for filigree anymore. Not these times. Laughter must have an honest root in reality, and that means a necessarily melancholy undercurrent. Anything else is false. Any notions?"

"Two garbage cans are buried to their necks in people."

"Don't be frivolous. Quit the jiving." He paced slowly, in sober concentration. His gaze swept the floor, which was more than the cleaning woman had. She prettied up by making paper napkins double as antimacassars on a couple of second-hand overstuffed pieces, which aided them in feigning a resemblance to chairs. "What about this mother of yours you always talk about. She must be something, to hear you tell it. I've often thought there's something in her as a character. Why don't you pour us each a beer while we kick her around some more?"

I nod and get two cold cans of Schlitz, which we drink through the flip-top openings.

"I remember once," I relate, walking the floor now as Warshawski settles down on the couch, "a period when she briefly took in roomers. 'Selected Lodgers' the sign in the parlor window said. She wouldn't take anybody unless they applied. I remember once as a boy I went upstairs and as I was about to turn down the hall I saw my mother peeping through the keyhole of one of the rooms. It was rented by a girl student at the local college and it was directly across from a room occupied by a young interne. Or maybe orderly. I think she suspected — that is, secretly hoped — there was some shenanigans going on between them, from the low moans audible through the closed door. I now sometimes wonder whether she didn't misconstrue them as calls for help, since her own life must have contained no precedents of amorous outcries of sexual fulfillment from the woman's side. The wails of a woman being attacked, you see. But no matter. She saw something going on between a man and a woman, and there she squatted watching it through the keyhole, and there was me in the passage watching her watch it. That was Mom for you — making a voyeur watcher out of me. And how much lower can you sink in the scale of libidinous specialties? Then let's see. My father. What she did to him was nobody's business, so let me tell you about that. 'Wipe your feet when you come in — and the dog's too.' I mean when he came back from taking his dachshund for a walk, especially if it was wet, how he'd get down on all fours and, taking one of the dog's paws at a time, wipe it on the doormat. That terrible, Warshawski? That tear the heart out of you? Is it any wonder my father would turn the doormat around so that he read the word 'Welcome' on it *as he left the house?* Glad to leave it, to sally forth into an outside world ready to greet him more warmly than anything ever did as he entered it? My mother always — we all have something in our craw —"

"Yeah, I know. Go on."

"My mother always wanted to be born in Boston. And

there being now little likelihood of that, being this wide
of that mark she took correspondingly extra pleasure in
looking down morally on people she couldn't, of course,
upstage socially. Hardly even, if it came to that, the
hunkies swarming into the neighborhood with better cars
and more money than my old man could bring in with
his floor sander. She referred to them as the 'element' we
were getting in. She still warns me about the 'element' I
get mixed up with here in New York. It's — Here — Let
me just throw out to you the image of Edna May Oliver's
sniff? You've seen her on the Late Late Show, as though
those beneath her are discernible on an olfactory level? Of
course we know such vulgarians fill their brandy snifters
to the top, and of *course* they supply us with our chief
vindicatory satisfaction in the form of fallen daughters,
they used to call them. I can hear Mom yet: 'Always
thought so much of that one, always bragging about her
marks in school, and her so choosy, so stuck-up, and pure
as the newfallen snow. Yeah — but she drifted!' That
type humor. Way we talked then, Warshawski. Oh, I wish
I had her tongue! Have this play — one long screed,
you know, like Beckett or something — have it batted out
in three weeks flat, and by myself too. But — Where were
we? Yes. Sex. There is no doubt Mother's chastity is one
of the seminal values in my life. Basically, sex is dirty. As
it plain has been to millions before her and will be to
millions coming after. Naughty, mustn't, *ich!* Is it any
wonder that we next see me, a boy of twelve, with his new
bow and arrow, shooting flaming Tampax through an old

barn window? Where is the lad that only yesterday was out there in his — Get this, Warshawski, the picture, we must try to ignite one another with this quintessential image or that — the lad out there in his Yankee baseball uniform, to which is affixed a sheriff's badge, ambushing the Wells Fargo stagecoach with a toy rifle? That an engaging composite, Warshawski? That beguilingly mixed up? But where is that lad now? Like I say, shooting flaming Tampax through an old barn window. Through which it still in memory chimerically streaks, meteoric trajectory of some burning dream of pudendal shame, guilt-stoked lust and lust-combusted guilt, in whose phantasmagorical wake our mother-made miscreant still deliriously streams, the tail of the eternally exploding comet of himself!"

The sudden rifle-crack sharpness of my voice brings my listener's head up off his chest, onto which it has slowly begun to drop. He springs to renewed attention, as far as one can do so in a seated position, and reaches for the can of beer he has set on a table. I continue my odyssey.

"Fade in to a few years later still, an adolescent getting pimples from impure thoughts. His first date in the family car, he does number three all over his girl and the front seat, which is worse, as Mother identifies the stains on the upholstery quite readily without catching him try to get them out with spot remover, and even *then* tries to take down his britches and give him a dozen, administering the birching about the legs at any rate with a stout switch, and making him get down on his knees with her and pray for an hour for forgiveness and guidance, then requiring him to write a hundred times the Bible text, 'Wherewith shall a young man cleanse his way? By taking heed thereto according to thy word.' I doubt whether my mother renewed my father's franchise of her flesh after I was born, and in any case now doubt that, with the limits her own erotic life must have had, she understood the low moans issuing from the bedroom into which she peered. What else? My mother taking things to the poor, or even the fairly well-off when they were going through a rough period, coming up the steps with an armload of clothes, in this way working off her hostilities. One set of neighbors had such ups and downs that I once saw the Salvation Army truck in their driveway and told my mother, and she said, 'Picking up or delivering?' . . . And let's see. The man next door had six fingers on one hand."

"None of us is perfect," says Warshawski, taking another gulp of suds.

"A rudimentary extra finger growing out of the thumb. He was born with it."

"Then that explains it."

Another of the lad's early recollections is of his father leading his dachshund about with a rag around its throat, when it had a cold or infection of some sort. The dog was a hypochondriac who kept running back to the vet for every little thing, once he had been taken there and knew where it was. One time the vet sent us a bill, which my mother refused to pay, on the ground that we had not taken the dog to him. "But he turned *up* here," the vet protested, "with a cut on his foot, and I treated him for it because I knew you'd want it that way. You're that kind of people." Mother finally did pay it.

"Well, now then. Our collective miseries being what they were, everyone driving everyone else crazy under one roof, my mother, recognizing this state of affairs, offered a solution: 'We must do something as a family.' And now it will be seen whether, walking up the stairs to the bowling alleys, we conformed to those billboard scenes advertising, whether for churches or chain restaurants or the bowling industry itself, a family group happily bent on joint recreations. Perhaps we did as we trudged to the park to ice-skate in the Christcapades. Maybe we did going up the steps to the bowling alley. But as we came down, it was to find that the dog had committed suicide. Where are you going?"

"Is there anything to eat?" Warshawski's face shows the strains of literary composition as he rises from the couch. Scrounging in the kitchenette, I find a couple of small pies for us, those individual cellophane-wrapped commercial pastries of the kind I like because they come accompanied by little slips of paper telling you what flavor they are. He assumes a more reclining position on the couch, using one hand as a saucer as he eats with the other, and looking, in a single earring, anything but piratical.

"Bruno," I resume, pacing the floor with my own tidbit devoured, "has been taken along, but left in the car. He often was. It's a sedan, with one of the windows partly lowered so he can breathe. His leash grip is secured to the inside handle of the door in such a way that he can't jump out. But he can jump, or climb, or scramble halfway out, and at some point has. Was it to follow us, so that if his plan succeeded we would find him as we came out the door, waiting for us, wagging his tail as in an old *Saturday Evening Post* cover? Or is he sick of the sight of us, the thought of us, of everything, the whole everlasting irremediable botch? I think the latter. He is Fed Up, full of some dog *Weltschmerz*. That is what the spectacle tells me that greets us as we hurry toward the car: the hound dangling from his leash outside the front door. He has ended it all . . . . Christ, Warshawski, you're a hard man to please. Don't ask too much of a comedy. There's only so much futility to go around, you know."

"I know. I think it's great," he says, munching the last of the pie as he nods with the gravity of all technicians when struck by true perfection. "I'll dine out on that, if we don't use it." Warshawski is noted for the emetic tales with which he keeps the conversational ball rolling at table. This seems to meet his standards, as does my anecdote of the mouse the cat caught and jumped up on the stove with, to drop it into a pan of gravy there, prior to partaking of it. Or the post-obstetrical case my mother attended, whose baby drowned in the enema traditionally given expectant mothers.

"Now then. I went through a religious period when I cursed God and all his works, as represented by this mudball earth, as Thomas Hardy put it. Then cooled down into stoical atheism. A very persuasive Catholic priest once converted me to agnosticism — that is, hauled me that

168

distance back toward the fold — but I again settled back into plain unbelief. But this hot period I'm talking about followed a funeral I went to. It was my last ride on a train, I mean aside from these rolling slums like the Long Island and the Penn Central. After that I flew. I slipped away from the bedroom I was sharing with my parents and went to the club car, where a bunch of Uncle Franks were yacking it up with cigars and booze. They were on their way back from a convention in Akron, which was where I had just been to my Uncle Harry's funeral. The vignette I want to give you now concerns his last hour, as we heard it described. My aunt, the widow-elect, sits at his bedside, not sad, oh no, because they have Faith? They know they'll meet again in that great beyond. They know what the tinted placard on the mortician's office wall assures us, that our mortal ship in each case leaves one shore lined with loved ones waving farewell, to sail out of their sight and into that of others who have gone before, awaiting us on that bank to greet us in welcome. So that as my uncle breathes his last, it is my story that Aunt Margaret is sitting beside his bed *waving*, as God is my judge, a handkerchief, fluttering it as in a dockside farewell as she says, 'So long, Harry. I'll be seeing you.' Is it not monstrous? What people have to go through, and what they will therefore believe? How does that grab you?"

I walk to the window, and in the silence broken only by Warshawski's light snore from the couch where he has curled up, I lean with my forearms spread along the midledge, my chin on my hands, and gaze out into the night.

The broken line of roofs studded with chimney-pots is intermittently silvered by the light of a full moon, across the face of which drifts, just then, the smoke from a passing jet, like the trail of slime left on a flower by a wandering snail.

I suddenly break down and sob, "Mom said a dog howled when I was born." As abruptly I pull myself together and, honking into a handkerchief, pocket my tears and resume the interrupted soliloquy.

"Oh, those handkerchiefs fluttered at this and what now seem a hundred funerals blended into one," I apostrophize softly at the window, "all plucked from the bosoms of black dresses and all soaked with cologne, a suffocating scent at the very remembrance of which I seem to reel, the collective reek of aunts swooping down on me, smothering me in their voluptuous grief, raining tears of orgiastic sorrow, the whole shrieking sisterhood of graveside Bacchantes. Oh, Nature can turn us out, but, Christ, she needs an editor! Then the insolence of nymphs like this brat's mother, marinating their dulcet limbs in bath oils for the sad delectation of clods slumped before their television sets, nereids so fragrant in fact, as we know who have lain with them, these singer-model-actresses, that we bleed for the fat aunts who watch them as they come dripping from their baths and spray their floral crevices with some commercial unguent or dust their poised flanks with — did you know there's a Directoire dusting powder? Directoire for God's sake! Were tufts of French meadowgrass then thus floured? Was Gallic pussy fed this catnip? Was

170

it with this confectioner's sugar that whilom gash was —?"
I turn from the window with a savage lunge and snarl:
"When and where did you two lark it up together?"

Warshawski comes to with a start, kicking his legs out
as he springs to his feet, instantly wide-awake and re-
freshed. I lie down while he now prowls the floor, a
smoothly cogitating panther.

"Man, you said something just before I dropped off that
I like. It grabs me. It hooks me here. Your mother always
wanted to be born in Boston, and takes out her social
gripes with moral vindictiveness. That frustration thing
can work in so many ways. I mind once moan mother saying to moan pappy . . ."

We kicked mothers around some more, and by midnight
had evolved a rough outline for a play springing from our
joint sense of being pariahs in a community itself already
really bad enough: his racial, mine cultural. A drama of
underdogs it was to be, which we would move forward into
the area of the contemporary struggle for the Negro's sub-
urbanization, to be entitled *Uncle Tom's Cabin Cruiser.*

Warshawski hurried home to bat out the opening scene
while it was still fresh in his mind.

"Hey," I said as he went out the door, jerking my head
toward the bassinette. "What about him? The kid?"

"If this collaboration works out, he'll have a father he
can't help being proud of. Right?"

4

4

The sound of a baby prattling to itself is one of the joys of parenthood, but now again my pleasure in the stream of Ed's cradle babbling became snagged on a phrase or two I fancied I caught, possibly quoted from something his mother had said, in the line of current truck about role-playing in modern life. "De oblitewation of wole-boun-dawies," he might be gurling in especial.

"Don't you pay your mother no mind," I told him, fixing his formula. "She's no kin o' yourn."

I had dreamt that night that I was President, and had rushed back to the White House on my way to a reception to see whether I had turned the stove off. Now I couldn't remember whether the name of the song running through my head was *Foolish Love* or *Careless Love,* but I sang lustily as I went about my chores, "Now I wear my apron high . . . Now I wear my apron high . . ."

I was warming a pan of leftover soup for myself on one of the kitchen burners, and, stooping to shade the flame, I expressed a willingness to renew the discussion I had a moment before choked off. A talk with Ed.

"All right. We'll talk about it," I said. "I suppose she also implied, or tried to insinuate, that we inflate our griev-ances to make our point — indeed hoard them. That the very office we are made by our mothers to resent — the old and ineluctable mammal office — we must seize from our wives to show them we can excel them in it. More. Show that in welshing on it they are not acceding to anything superior in the economic role they are trying in turn to wrest from us, but are walking, head high, into broader disenchantments than any they could have had in their children and that their mothers — antiphonally hostile — have already had in them. Meanwhile, among these contested shores lie many unforeseen rewards, coves and bays and commingled tidelines none can finally either obliterate or differentiate. So let her sing for her supper while I cook mine, ours, to sing by. Even if only the blues."

"Wight. And then you hit your bottle while I get mine."

"That has no bearing on any problem, being a universal anodyne. So nemine that. Where were we? Yes. For out of all this proclaimed and bruited usufruct — whether of torch singer ditching the child given birth to or the crisp and tweeded midtown secretary getting to be thirty and thirty-five and then at last regretting the child never had and now too late to have — out of all this bruited usufruct rises remorseless still and never to be circumvented world without end, whether whelped in fee simple through flesh upon parturated flesh in mortal perpetuity or locked in barren flesh, that truth to which flesh itself is immutably heir: thou shalt not go hence till thou has paid the last farthing. For what is usufruct?"

"Yeah, man, what dat? Splain dat to me, Kingfish. What dat usufruct stuff you always talkin' 'bout, mixed

173

up wit' de mammalian bit and de mother-muck kick you on. Ah know you a mother-mucker in de Freudian sense of de primordial mammy symbolizin' de evolutionary intertidal slime, and what dat Thomas Mann keep callin' in de Joseph book de mother stuff. *Mutter Stoff.* But what dis usufruct deal?"

"In Roman and Anglo-Saxon civil law, the right of enjoying all the advantages derivable from the use of something which belongs to another, as far as is compatible with the substance of the thing not being destroyed or injured. But neither the secretary nor the traveling entertainer is destroying anything of the man's by usurping the gainful office traditionally his. That is limitless. She is destroying a piece of herself, irrevocable moon by permutating moon, sun by annual sun, then at last irreclaimable as it sinks behind the last and absolute biographical horizon, her own sun's setting. From this there is no appeal: that she shall have dominion where she is also serf, slave and suzerain both of the principality of flesh, her fate sealed in the dews and juices of colliding lusts, the beads and drops and dripping exudations of two blindly slobbering loins, the blindly pumping gasping anthropoid collaboration of agglutinated meat, bathed in, bogged in, laved in, shame-locked and then shame-cloven, the wallowed in dived in writhed in very sex sty, the ten-millenial animal colloidally colliding distillates of skin and rut and crotch and burrow, the oozing delta the blind gravitation to which may be an atavistic nostalgia for the very pristine slime itself, and musk of scalp and mouth and tufted skin down to her own

174

precarious spice, the writhing gut-stuffed hides of creatures blindly begetting in this binary swoon their own disparaged and even flagellated selves, lives whose long ordeal is briefly relieved by the ecstasy that perpetuates it, the one true and at last serenely inscrutable cycle, creature sorrows centrifugally dispersed by the hot heedless deed that will but re-assemble them in another, a fresh cellular recapitulation of trials themselves ephemerally recessed to their own self-perpetuating binary swoon, mare-stallion shriek of the vatted guts —"

"Chwist."

"— seed blindly committed to seed, together committed to the dark ineluctable lurking phallo-philoprogenitive mother-muck, the self-realized self-canceling, nay self-mocking He-and-She-spindled blindly gasping — gah — gah —"

"You better watch it, man. You gonna blow a gasket, you don't let up. I hate to see you hanging over de stove like dat, clutchin' yo' chest. Better knock it off, 'fo' you get a heart attack."

"— blindly gasping ecstatically slobbering loins. But in that white-hot fusion may not their separate genders have been so indissolubly welded for once and all that any exchange of functions thereafter must seem child's play itself?"

"And that's what you're twying to pwove, eh, Pop? That anything they can do you can do better. And without becoming a bitch, biddy or battleaxe."

But what of slut or slattern? Could I arrest my now

175

seemingly precipitate decline into these? Because I now found myself doing the last thing a person should, even though worn down by child-bearing and housework. I was letting myself go. As a Cockney slattern at that, often as not, pictorially and aurally the worst. Dressed in one of Mary's castoff Mother Hubbards and a pair of soiled felt slippers, I slopped about doing the dishes, sweeping the floors or bathing and feeding the brat I had been abandoned with. "They're all alike, and she as alike as they come. 'As 'er will of 'im and then discards 'im like an old shoe, and 'im a mere virgin when they met. Off with 'er fancy friends somewhere this minute, a hentertainer she is, leavin' 'im to wheel 'is shame down the street for all to see. Come back long enough to get another stirrin' inside of 'im, like as not, and then off again to her frivolous ways. And never sendin' 'ome so much as a bleedin' quid."

This was not quite true. She sent a check every week, from wherever she happened to be — at the moment some city in the Middle West. It arrived on Monday morning, almost without fail. I would be waiting downstairs for the mailman to deliver it, for fear of the vandals and dope addicts who constantly foraged for lucrative letters in mailboxes forever, as a consequence, sprung open. Though regular, however, the check was too little. I must get back at least to my old part-time job at the steakhouse. But how? I had no place to drop Ed for that half-day, and no one to leave him with at home. The two available sitters in my apartment building were a teen-age girl who was also a prime suspect in the mailslot thefts, and a middle-aged widow who was a more disreputable-looking slut than myself.

One evening I was hammering away at the typewriter, trying to get a scene to move in *Uncle Tom's Cabin Cruiser*, when the doorbell rang.

"That'll be Soames Forsyte, I'll be bound, come about the codicil. Knows 'is fancy son's got me knocked up higher'n a kite and wants to buy me off. What's me price?" I mumbled, shuffling off in my bathrobe to the hall speaking-tube. "Hah. Well, guvner, seein' as you're a lot as fancies money, I'll try to meet your high standards. 'Ow does a straight settlement o' ten thousand pounds for me sound, wi' a thousand a year in trust for the tike till 'e comes of age? No? Then I'm afraid I'll 'ave to mike a scandal, draggin' us through mud as for me won't mike no difference, but for you and your grand lidies . . . Ow, seein' daylight, are we? I gots me own foresight saga, you know. All right!" I called down through the speaker. "Yes?"

"I'm collecting for the day center down the street—"

"Don't need any today—" I mechanically began, and caught myself. "Day center? What kind?"

"You know — the day-care center. Where working mothers can leave their children."

"Just a moment."

I pressed the buzzer to admit a plump, pleasant middle-aged woman for whom I was waiting on the landing as she puffed her way up the last of the four flights of stairs. In return for a three-dollar contribution and over a cup of tea, she told me all about the social-service agency run

177

in the basement of a nearby Lutheran church, and supported by it with funds supplemented by private neighborhood gifts. I asked, after learning these essentials, the sixty-four-thousand-dollar question. "Can fathers leave their children there too?"

The woman shook her head with a sweet smile. "No, only mothers. For no reason except that we have to draw the line somewhere. We have more applicants than we can take. We just draw it arbitrarily. Well, you've been kind, and I thank you for your contribution, as well as the tea."

That was when I knew I must take the final step into the *Charley's Aunt* situation toward which I had been irresistibly drawn. I would have to go out in drag.

My feelings about carrying matters to that extreme were mixed. Ample indoor preparation should ease a transition for which I admitted a certain appetite, of a nervously hilarious nature. Yet qualms underlay that of a graver sort, since what I was about to embark on was illegal. But embark I must, if I was to settle the kid in good hands long enough to work a few hours a day, and to see producers later, if it came to that.

I stole a pair of hose and some cosmetics from Altman's, where I then next bought a pair of brown loafers epicenely indistinguishable from a woman's low-heeled saddle shoes, the store's profit from which I saw as canceling out what it had lost on the thieveries. I debated a blonde wig, but the counter was overseen by a hawk-eyed woman who never left the corner where I stood pondering one. Also in that exposed quarter I began to have uneasy intimations of store dicks' eyes peering at me from concealed wall louvers. Snatching a peruke and running for an exit would have given the whole thing a transvestite stink I particularly wanted to avoid. Anyway, this was the heyday of the era when people couldn't tell the girls from the boys etc., a vogue which, together with necessary barber economies, had my locks hanging in Messianic strings.

These I put up with a brand of setting gel called Dippity-do and gathered into a bun behind, tied with a strand of blue ribbon. Since I had a key to Mary's apartment, I had been able to help myself to a dress or two from those she had left behind. A makeup job completed a result that convinced me, at least. Swinging one of Mary's handbags I was able not only to stroll the streets unsuspected, but to shop for groceries in an unchallenged falsetto. The time had come to put this *Charley's Aunt* to the acid test. Tucking the kid into a cheap second-hand perambulator I had bought, I wheeled him down the block and around the corner to the Lutheran Day Center.

It was at the back of the basement, and I had to wait in line with two other housewives and mothers, both seedier-looking specimens of their sex than I. A fourth who joined us at the end of the queue looked like Arlo Guthrie. Pants suits in any case gave a man whatever more in protective coloring that he might have needed. The nurse in charge at the desk smiled and gave me a form for new mothers to fill out. She did a take on the customer in the rig.

"His father is black," I squeaked in an upper contralto.

179

"We have no prejudices about that here. We're all God's children."

"Yes, ma'am."

I had after each such deposit, of course, to dash back home and get into normal civvies, preparatory to hightailing it over to the chophouse. I developed such quick-change ease, with, finally, so little fear of detection in ever-prolonged tests such as stopovers for cigarettes or newspapers and even more substantial shopping encounters, that I wondered if I mightn't turn a better buck as a female impersonator — not in the traditional nightclub sense, but as one of the transvestite cops with which Mayor Lindsay was augmenting the New York police force, as an aid to nabbing sex offenders real or potential, and creeps and crooks in general. Of course it was only an idle fancy. Still, I could imagine myself swinging Mary Hackney's alligator bag, horseshoe-stuffed, at some degenerate nudging me in the sardine swarm of the subway.

One day Mary came back, for a brief stay before setting out on another tour with another industrial show, and I wouldn't let her in.

"Go away," I said through the double-locked door. "We don't need you."

"But I *told* you I was coming back. And after this next tour I'm going to stay home. I've got a promise of work here. Nat's got it practically sewed up."

"Yeah, well, consider yourself sewed out — Mother! We don't need your element here. We can get along without you."

"Bunk? Bunk, have you flipped? Because I can get you help."

"I don't need any help. A cleaning woman once a week . . . Wolves are high on Nature's list of species in which the males play a major part in the rearing of the young," I threw out as a matter of general interest.

"You don't *want* me to do my part," she called back, thumping the closed door. "It would spoil the case you're trying to pile up against me, my sex, as woman, as wife, as mother. So that in that way you can indict your mother — as mother, wife and woman. Something like that. The eternal 'the woman thou gavest me' cry of the male, ringing down since the Garden of Eden. Oh, I know your type!"

"And I know yours. Fasting as a protest against our Southeast Asia policy, timed to coincide with a diet you were going on anyway. Oh, I read all about it in the papers, you and those other showgirls. Were they weight-watching too, I shouldn't wonder, squeezing a little publicity out of it. I don't need a hypocrite like that to raise my child."

"Oh, my God. *You're* the hypocrite."

"Oh, yeah? Well, there are so many virtues on which hypocrisy is an improvement that I wouldn't dismiss it out of hand."

"Will you kindly tell me what that statement means?"

"I'm busy. I've got my potatoes on, and after that I have to bathe the baby."

"I'll sue you!" she exclaimed, giving the door a last bang.

"Not if I sue you first!"

There came a time when I had to go out in drag after dark. It was to attend a fund-raising coffee at the church, at which it would have been churlish not to show up at least long enough to demonstrate my gratitude to the center and my moral support of its cause. I got through the evening well enough, gassing and clucking with the other dillies and bragging about how our children were coming along. "Where is your husband? Couldn't he make it?" the director asked, a pallid man in a blue pinstripe suit. "No, he's tied up," I said, outthrusting my little finger as I lifted my cup. One of our star battleaxes whispered to me out of the side of her mouth, "That's what you'll find me after this next kid, believe me — *tied up*." This was heady stuff, and I left when I could decently break away. There were only two fathers there.

This was one of the times when I had rung Warshawski in as a sitter, and muttering to myself, "Let the bastard sit a while longer," I slipped into a bar for a few belts. I had by now begun to feel I had paid off my share of "reparations," as far as that element in my tangled problems was concerned, and was getting people in my own debt. Warshawski was working on the script anyway, at my typewriter, as well as probably foraging in my notebooks for ideas to steal and use later on projects of his own. I enjoyed the sensation of moral creditor.

And along with it, my mug of draft Michelob. Added to all the coffee I had taken aboard, this had me jiggling my legs on the bar stool and casing the place for the Ladies'. It was here I became aware of a pair of luminous green eyes watching me from under a cascade of gold curls. Their owner was sitting around a corner of the bar on my left. I swung my head and returned the smile. A brush with a Lesbian was the last variation I had dreamt of in this series on a stated theme, but in this part of the country it was probably most to be expected. One of the heavily mascaraed eyes winked lasciviously, and again I reciprocated — a flash of lust for a woman in fact kindling me under my wraps.

"Nice evening, dear," she fluted.

"Very."

"Doing anything later?"

"No."

"Maybe we can do it together."

"Don't mind if I do."

By now I had both located the women's washroom and been able to determine by a reasonable time-interval that it was momentarily empty. I took advantage of the lull by excusing myself and hurrying into it. The door had no more than flapped shut behind me than it flapped open again, to reveal the dike smiling at me in the mirror over the washbasin.

"I've noticed you here before, haven't I? My name's Pam Cutler. What's yours?"

"Same thing," I cheerily sang in response.

Finding it now necessary to stall for time, I stepped to the mirror and pretended to be inspecting my makeup. The apparition floated closer in, beaming behind and beside me.

"If I may say so, I don't think you're using the right rouge to offset that mole on your cheek."

"No?"

"No. All right, bud, that does it." The mop of yellow ringlets were pulled off to reveal the crew cut and square jaw of one of New York's finest. "That mole makes me double sure you served me that steak for lunch this noon, when we were both ourself, so to speak. We *have* had our eye on you in this neighborhood for quite a while, like I say. So what's the real name?"

"Rick."

"Rick what?"

"O'Shea."

"Rick O'Shea. A wise guy. Not bad though, I'll say that for you. Also that anything else you say may be held in evidence against you, and so on."

"I can explain everything."

"I sure envy those who can do that," he said with a large, philosophical sigh that was not without its compassion. "Shall we go before the ladies join us? To the Magistrate's Court, if you don't mind."

"The *Night* Court? Where they take prostitutes and pimps? Then what?"

"If the presiding judge feels the evidence warrants it, you'll be committed for trial to Special Sessions of the Criminal Court."

"This will kill my mother," I grinned placatively as he hustled me out.

184

5

The following story appeared in a New York newspaper several weeks later:

A bizarre tale of a "new freedom" *ménage à trois* involving transvestitism, marital role-switching, both sexual and parental, and miscegenation unfolded in Special Sessions yesterday with the trial of Waldo St. Cloud on the original charge.

The twisting sequence of events began, or rather ended, some weeks ago when St. Cloud, a 26-year-old youth living in the Village, was arrested for appearing in public dressed as a female by a police officer himself wearing women's clothes, as many on the force now do as an aid in trapping offenders. His story was that he had been masquerading as a mother for some time in order to leave his baby and that of his common-law wife, Mary Hackney, 23, an entertainer who had "abandoned" them, with a church-sponsored day center while he worked as a waiter in a nearby restaurant.

According to St. Cloud's version of events on the night of the original arrest — authenticated in every detail and called by one observer as "too grotesque to doubt" — he had slipped out briefly to a Ladies Aid benefit dessert-sociable at the church, wearing a dress and accessories belonging to his wife, who was appearing in a nude revue at another church farther downtown, one with a basement serving as an Off-Off-Broadway theatre. He had left the six-months-old baby in the care of a sitter who is the child's real father, according to admissions by Miss Hackney, who claimed that she has been trying to "snatch" the baby from the man who had been concurrently her lover, namely St. Cloud, who had been persistently locking her out of their apartment, or his apartment, as unfit for the role of mother, while terming the father "the real bas-

185

tard" in the case. The sitting, and putative, father is a 22-year-old unproduced black playwright named William Warshawski. At least he has been going by that name for some time, though he now says it is an assumed one — his real name being von Weygand.

Unable to raise bail money on the night of his arrest, St. Cloud was held in overnight custody, necessitating Warshawski's — or von Weygand's — staying the night with his own child, and enabling him to let Miss Hackney into the apartment the next morning when she called. She has moved with him and the child into her own apartment, and is now locking St. Cloud out.

The trial has proliferated from one involving a simple misdemeanor to a tangle of charges and counter-charges the like of which the presiding judge, Edward R. Coffee, says he has never encountered in thirty years of jurisprudence. "This is nothing less than a cross-section of the whole current mess," he said, throwing up his hands and thus inadvertently flinging away his gavel. St. Cloud accused Miss Hackney of being unsuited to the role of motherhood, being, in fact, "not even an adult." Miss Hackney jumped to her feet and retorted, "He couldn't even make it as a child!" Concluding testimony originally to have been intended for the defense, she went on, "This whole masquerade he's been conducting has been a way of taking out his hostilities and maladjustments. He's determined to make his life a satire on women, this whole thing is a put-on in which he takes a secret glee in spreading as much chaos as possible!" St. Cloud then leaped to his own feet and shouted, "Who was it said chaos is order unperceived? Maybe we're shedding light here on many aspects of man in transition. Maybe we're breaking fresh ground."

"Enough to bury you all in, I hope!" shouted the judge, leaping to *his* feet.

A climax now ensued more rococo than any of the events that had led to it. Judge Coffee (nicknamed "Instant" by intimates familiar with his impulsive decisions) purposely hurled away the gavel he had just been on all fours retrieving from the floor and said: "I can't make head or tail out of any of this, and I don't *want* to! I'd be ashamed if I understood it! Free, we have never been so bound. Relaxed, we have never been so uptight. Doing our

186

own thing, we muck up everybody else's. My decision is
— to retire from the bench. I'm retiring from the bench as
of this day, this minute. Case dismissed on a change of
venue — to HELL!" And, rending his robe, he strode
from the courtroom through the public door rather than
into his chambers, stepping around the prostrate form of
a woman who had just fallen, dead, out of her seat into the
aisle, and who was later identified as St. Cloud's mother,
visiting New York from Tiverton, Indiana, to "see a show
or two."

6

Such was now my sense of persecution, indeed state of
paranoia, that everywhere I went I saw authorities. A
sprinkling of policemen in the course of a city hour, the
rest plainclothesmen. Eight million of them. I was hurrying
home one cold afternoon that autumn when I became aware
of three of the latter, all buttoned up in dark overcoats and
hats, hustling in my wake. A second glance darted over my
shoulder made it clear they were trying to overtake me. I
quickened my pace from a walk to a run. My pursuers
gained on me, not surprisingly — there were after all three
of them to my one. I scuttled into the hall of my apartment and, finding the outer door opened just then by a
super hauling out trash, bounded up the stairs two at a
time, the trio close at my heels, so close that I had barely

closed and bolted my apartment door behind me than they were banging on it with their fists and calling out.

"St. Cloud! Open up."

I leaned with my back against the door, a brief abortive attempt to become an actor also accounting for my inclining my head to it in a dream of terminal distress, another of those histrionic techniques having no counterpart in real life whatsoever. The only sound was my heavy panting — and, of course, that of my tormentors in the passage outside.

"We know you're in there, St. Cloud."

"I've got to get my beans on."

"Open, please. We want to talk to you."

"What about?"

"We want to give you an award."

"Don't want any today."

"The Hilda Rosenthal Award for Humanitarian Service to that person who in the estimation of the judges — that's us — has most alerted us to the problems of our common human existence in an age of bewildering transitions, and who has at the same time set an example most calculated to recall us to a sense of our traditional obligations. There's a plaque and a citation."

"Can you shove them under the door?"

"No, we don't have them with us. They're to be presented at a ceremony at Princeton at the end of the year. Please? You gave us an anthropological 'package' most relevant to our times."

"Well . . . all right. Just this once. But don't let it happen again."

That was how the whole episode ended. The award was made at a black tie dinner, in the midst of a week of panel discussions on various aspects of the central theme: America at the Crossroads. Participants included sociologists, anthropologists, psychologists, economists, religious leaders, writers, artists, historians and a smattering of disc jockeys. I was expected to look in on all of the sessions, which kept me panting heavily still, and though I was not officially billed for any of the symposia I made what contribution to each that I could, if only in terms of my moral support, "a symbol of sanity," as one chairman, or moderator, put it, "in a world gone mad."

Strain though it was, it did get my mind temporarily off the personal problem chiefly vexing me just then — the blowup of the collaboration on the play. I regret it had to be put by. Because I've always wanted to write a farce.

III

III

six

I had been trying for the last couple of hours to reach Osgood in New York (this is me again, back for more equal time) but had so far been unsuccessful. First, a completely half-baked operator had wasted I don't know how much time trying to locate him in Greenwich, Connecticut, instead of Greenwich Village where I had distinctly told her he lived. He keeps changing his phone number or his address or both, which makes it hard for a parent to keep up with him, however devoted. When I finally got his number from New York Information he was out, so I left the call in, telling the operator to keep trying. Which gave me more time to think, sort out my feelings about the story, and what I was going to say.

My feelings themselves can be imagined. I had read

the novella uttering cries that were of real dismay, emitting snorts that were of real disgust. This muck-raking of mothers has got to stop, now I want to submit. Hanging all the blame for everything on us. Why do we stand for it? Why don't we form a union, get a lobby together to put an end to this libel? Remember "mother" is also what they call the stringy guck that forms on the surface of fermenting liquid, like wine turning to vinegar? They call that the mother, that's named after us. Another charming little tribute. And all the sexual mysticism that gets mixed in with the comic valentine. If there's anything I can't stand it's dirty mysticism. To say nothing of the language. People don't seem to realize what's happening to the English language — or care. All they want is their three squares. These writers who make an issue of the freedom to use four-letter words talk about expanding their vocabulary. All right. But many of these vocabularies turn out to consist mainly of the words they've been expanded *by*. It would be interesting to see how their word-banks compare with that of, say, Jane Austen, who never had her vocabulary expanded. Not that I've read her, it's just a wild-guess example. Well, the artist is expected to set an example as one who reflects the times, and this vocabulary is no surprise in an era when letters received by the New York Police Department Hack Bureau from taxi passengers complaining of foul language on the part of the cab drivers totaled 7,643 for the current calender year, up 1300 from the year before, or an advance of over 16%, a figure which the Hack Bureau itself regards as still no measure of the problem as most riders *do not bother to file or do not know who to complain to.* To which I add that as a woman I take little solace from the fact that most of the complainants are my sex, since most young girls today, even or in fact especially educated ones, are garbage-mouths. The per diem filth issuing from rosy lips gives us more than the usually discussed environmental pollution to worry about. (Perhaps the Cassandra legend is the one for which I am all the while groping and must finally settle for?) I must in all fairness add that Osgood is a very minor offender in this area, and that he can also sling the fancier words around. All that about the ancient mammalian office and the philoprogenitive loins and one thing and another. And, ah yes, the mystical mother-muck. Mustn't forget that. The primordial life-slime I represent. Pardon *me*. I'm *sorry*. Excuse me for living. What else about me gravels you? My habit of inhaling and exhaling, perhaps, the combination known as respiration? Please feel free to say. It's a habit you'll soon have cured me of, it won't be long, I can't help reflecting as I lie here in the bed to which you've brought me, waiting for my bedside extension to ring with the completed call.

For I am indeed in bed. I have taken to it, ashen, never to rise again, probably. This thing has finished me. I shall follow Stella Slobkin Rivers to the grave pre-ordained for *her* from the moment she whelped her boyo (who is downstairs doing for me now, I can hear him in the kitchen, rustling up some nutritive goodies to coax me back to life with). I prefer to lie here till my mortal hour has struck, pray God it be soon. I prefer to lie here licking my wounds, wounds that will never become scars:

195

there won't be time. It is evening, mine as well as the day's. Soon I shall follow Stella Rivers into legend (with any luck on the part of *The Duchess of Obloquy* turning out a minor classic like *Medusa*). So it's not altogether accurate to say I'm back for equal time, in the sense of a negative rebuttal, a summing-up for the defense. I want only to let Osgood know that the shaft has gone home, the poisoned barb, and to be prepared for one last other call informing him that the millstone so long around his neck is no more, he is free — save for the one last trip home. He can then load my remains, or what's left of them, into my old Buick and drive me down to Bingham's parlors, as I'm sure undertakers won't be making house calls by then any more either, any more than anybody else. It's a world I'll be glad to leave, having gone to pot as far as any standards or principles of a professional kind are concerned. They can cremate me in the old Buick for my part. It's somehow stood up for eight years in spite of built-in obsolescence. Detroit must of slipped up somewhere.

Footfalls and a discreet rap on the door. I tell Randy to come in. The recumbent sight toward which he bears the tray of dainties is one hardly calculated to boy him up, presenting, as I know it does, repeated history. What he sees is the mother he did in, of which he was spared the sight, or which he spared himself the sight of, being conveniently out of the country when the crunch was on, returning not till she was laid away. So perhaps there is some poetic justice in his having to do for me, the surrogate mother they call them, a kind of atonement in which he can take a certain measure of suffering satisfaction. His spirits have been none too good anyway, these days. Not only are there no more pilgrims coming through; they're not writing any fan mail to speak of either. Week before last he got one postcard. Last week his mail fell off a little.

"Eat these. Come on. For me."

This time he's trying to tempt me with a few watercrest sandwiches, very appetizingly prepared and rolled up into little cylindrical delicacies, as well as a glass of nourishing eggnog. I shake my head, rolling it away on the pillow to gaze at the sycamore thrashing outside my window. I sense that he would like to get away, not just from here but from Appleton itself. He would like to bolt for New York. I don't hold him, but guilt does, with bands of invisible steel. He takes a highball he has also brought up on the tray, as well as a couple of the watercrest sandwiches, and sinks into a chair. He clears his throat. He will say something to comfort me, anything, I know the ritual. He may tell me I am being foolish, that fiction is fiction, and I am taking it all too much to heart. Or he may agree with me, saying what he thinks I want to hear. Anything to open a line of communication.

"People in the town are with you, Emma, is the general feeling I get," he remarks. "I ran into Mrs. Frawley on the street, have I told you, and she says Osgood exaggerates. Not a soul here doubts it. It's all laid on for effect."

"Cora Frawley is a blabbermouth. I'll say it to her face, and you can tell her that for me."

"She hasn't exactly been made to leap for joy by her

197

own son, I imagine. What's his name, Ralph? I met him once in New York, and brother! I think it's kind of sad, all the lost connections between the generations. She talks a blue streak about how she and Frawley see him every time they go East and he takes them out and what not, but I don't know. I have a suspicion it's all made up. All a mare's nest. He's not interested in them."

"Yes," I sigh, looking at my folded hands. "Yes, the young people talk about 'relating' today. It's one of their words. The big thing today is to relate to everybody. Except, of course, those you're related to."

Randy heaves a sigh of agreement, I guess it's agreement, looking soberly into his glass. It's at that moment the telephone shrills, making us both jump. I pick it up. It's the operator, saying she has my party. Randy gets out of his chair to vamoose, but I stay him with a gesture, and he walks the floor instead, popping another sandwich into his mouth so it shouldn't be a total loss. He knows what the call is, and he "watches with me one hour."

"Hello, Osgood. Well. I just wanted to compliment you on your novella."

Silence, in which a cagey apprehension is all too obvious. Then a queasy, "Oh, you read it? Did you like it?"

"Does a rabbit like hassenpfeffer?"

"Aw, now, Mom."

"I don't want to talk about it."

"Is that what you called me long distance to say? That you don't want to talk about it?"

"It's a brilliant job of matricide. With emphasis on the

198

mattress. Because I've taken to my bed, Osgood, I'm taking this lying down. There are things that flatten people for good, and I don't see how I'll ever have the strength or the will to stand up on my own two feet again, until this flesh is raised incorruptible. *Snnk.*"

"Oh, come on. It's a work of *fiction.*"

"To which the artist has a divine right to sacrifice anybody. I've heard that before," I say, darting an eye at Randy, who is plowing the floor as he rakes his hair and pops yet another watercrest fingerling into his mouth, from which little wretched cries concurrently issue. "Well, the pen is mightier than the sword, when it comes to inflicting wounds. This is one of the things What a Young Man Ought to Know. At least you can't expect me to leave the house again and face this town, so I might as well waste away in bed. Now, I've left certain instructions with Will Gerstenslager, my lawyer. You're to get in touch with him — though of course that won't be necessary since he'll call you. But don't feel too badly about it. And above all don't pity me. I don't want anybody's pity. I'll die decently if it's the last thing I do."

"Oh, Mother, for God's sake! We must have a talk."

"Well . . . All right, Osgood. I'll go out there and visit you. I'll come to New York."

"No!" A cry of horror, quickly checked. "I mean you don't sound well enough to travel. Tell you what. I'll come out there."

"That's my boy. Always thinking fast. 'If I go home, I can leave anytime I want, but if she comes out here, God

199

knows when I'll get rid of her.' *Snnk.* That does it, Osgood. That tears it, as you say today. That was all I needed. I can die in peace now. You've revitalized my death wish."

"What the devil does all that mean?"

"Just what it says. I'll be glad to go — after one last trip to see you. Randy Rivers is still here, as I told you if you've been reading my letters, or if they ever get forwarded to you. Do you?"

"Of course, Mother. I read every word you write."

"Then it's mutual. So here's what we'll do. Randy's anxious to get back East too, so maybe we'll go together. Let's see now, today is Friday. I'll arrive, say, the first of the week, or the middle at the latest. I'll wire the exact time. O.K.? Fine. Goodbye till then, Ozzie. It'll be good to see you again. We've loads to talk about."

We were the only ones on the train to New York except for three men about whom there was an air of mystery. Though together they never exchanged a mumbling word, between gulps of their highballs and gazing glumly out the window of the club car where we first noticed them. A brakeman with whom I fell into conversation there told me in whispers who he guessed they were. A committee from the Interstate Commerce Commission taking a check ride on a train the railroad had filed for permission to discontinue, on the oft-repeated ground that there wasn't enough business to warrant it. "When the management learns the ICC is sending representatives on a run they want to bump," he told me behind his hand, "they'll give orders to ticket agents not to sell any space. You probably got your accommodations before the tipoff."

"Tipoff?"

"Yes. The ticket agents are instructed to tell anybody wanting to buy space on that run that it's all sold out. So when the boys from the ICC ride it, it's empty. And the owners can say, 'You see? Nobody rides the railroads,' and *chk*." He slit his throat with a forefinger to signify another run lopped from the schedule.

Well, one of the first things I did in New York was to get ahold of the ICC and investigate this brakeman's story. It was wrong in every detail except the basic truth. The ICC don't send representatives to case specific runs up for the axe, much less committees, they don't have to. All they have to do is ask to see the records on them. And all the railroads have to do to make them look bad enough to scratch is not to sell space on them, just like my brakeman said. That they resort to this practice the ICC knows from its investigation of complaints from people who wanted to buy space on a certain train but were told it was sold out, when a back-check of the records showed it was anything but. So the brakeman may of been crazy and the Downcast Three a group of bell ringers who didn't have their option picked up in Hollywood, without invalidating what the brakeman told me and the very nice man in the Railroad Department of the ICC who took time out to see me verified, tipping back in his swivel chair and lacing his hands behind his head while we chatted. That the railroads as a public service will haul freight and cattle, but people? Yech! And this is the system them wild-eyed young radicals want to overthrow. If they don't like it here why don't they go to Russia. Maybe such cynics will have their faith in human nature restored by learning how generous the White House can be in flying free of charge, on Air Force planes often similarly empty, vacationing Congressmen and their families who vote with the President on key issues, while those who don't are much harder put to it to get such handsome side-boodle on jets costing us taxpayers $325 an hour to fly. Your government does try to draw the line on wasteful expenditures wherever humanly possible.

Getting back to the railroads, a more direct method they have of putting an end to an era is to kill off all remaining passengers by letting tracks and rolling stock together go to hell. The road bed made my own bed in Upper 12 anything but a place for peaceful dreams, though a few more lumps on the old coco as we rocked along would of put me over the line into oblivion land for good. There were times as we shot through parts of Ohio that your correspondent thought we had lost our wheels and were belly-guttering over straight cinders, if not scudding in the wrong direction along the floor of the Grand Canyon. When lateral motion equaled forward and backward and up and down, it was a tumble-dry your local Laundromat couldn't hold a candle to. "Thank God I'm *not* asleep," I thought finally as I clang to the edges of the bunk with both hands, "or I'd be a goner. Maybe I should of taken a plane at that. I'd be safe in Havana by now." From cursing insomnia you were glad you had it; you had to stay awake to stay alive. What would a phrenologist make of me now? I had every bump but the bump of direction — that I lost along about Toledo. As I gripped the steel side-flanges of my crib I wondered how the big shots from the Interstate Commerce Commission were making out. Like jumping beans in their own snug abodes no doubt, as they groped for pad and pencil to jot down vivid phrases that occurred to them to include in their reports and that they didn't want to forget — always provided that total amnesia from skull fracture hadn't drove out even the memory of who they were, let alone why they were on this particular vehicle.

My night thoughts got increasingly graphic. I tried to frame a suitable prayer, something along the line of Humperdinck's fourteen angels guarding the bed of the tikes in the opera, but all I could think of was the words of a song the band played at the lakeside pavilion where my intended was busy keeping the jazz-dancers eight inches apart:

> Railroad, take me back,
> Got the Thirty-first Street blues;
> Don't you hop that track,
> Got the Thirty-first Street blues.

Perhaps I should ring for the porter to hold my hand and read to me portions of the Bible I see him nodding happily over in his seat as I went by on the way back from the diner (where I had cowchips Aquitaine, whatever claims were put forward for it on the menu). Memories passed through my mind like objects going down a Disposall on this Walpurgisnacht, probably for the last time. Of the morning Osgood come into the kitchen where I was eating breakfast, bobbing on his toes and swinging his short arms as he followed his custom of closing his eyes as he went by me, on the way to the refrigerator. With his head in that, he said, "I'm writing a book." I must even then of had premonitions of what was to be, because I remember thinking of pushing him into the icebox and clapping the door shut, like the wicked witch was shoved into the oven by the children in the fairytale, only the other way around, a modern switch bringing things full circle.

"Anybody in it we know?" Keeping munching my toast and spooning up my eggs.

"Call this bacon?"

"Not I. There's some link sausages in there with an oxygen interceptor for great stability. If you don't believe it read the label. Is it going to be about real people, your book?"

"Christ, I hope so."

"No, I mean based on actual ones. Like, well, family members."

"Everything good is based on reality somehow," Osgood said, and yawned, his eyes tearing as he went by me again on his way around to the stove. He kind of smiled to himself, but it was the way he shut his eyes as he walked past that struck me, the way a bird I once had, a parrakeet, would shut his eyes as *I* went by his cage, on some occasions falling off his perch and laying there among his own refuse and birdseed hulls, as though it was all too much, he wanted out. I remember that at the time of this breakfast we had a hamster ceaselessly treading an unoiled wheel, squeaking away day after day as though he was being paid so much an hour by the intellectual establishment to illustrate the principle of futility. Osgood was having trouble facing the world those days. Many's the time I would say to him, "Lots of young people have been known to drag themselves out of bed and come down to breakfast. It can be done." Now he was down all right, but evading the issue. Which way the wind blew I could tell well enough by the questions he began putting with utter innocence.

"Is it true that when Dad proposed to you, you asked him to supply three character references?"

"It's done as a matter of course in hiring an employee. Why not for the most important relationship in life? Your father swept me off my feet. I knew him exactly four days when he popped the question. He was from another town, I knew absolutely nothing about the man — except the best foot we all put forward, and what's that? For the whole thing about matrimony is this: We fall in love with a personality, but we must live with a character. Behind the pretty wallpaper and the brightly painted plaster lurk the yards of tangled wire and twisted pipes, ready to run a short or spring a leak on us without a word of warning. I was perfectly willing to give him three references of my own. In the end we skipped it, we were that in love."

"Do I recall Dad saying the coldest room in the house

was the sun room because you always kept it sixty there for your plants? Never mind us?"

From fourteen to twenty-one they're impossible. Then at twenty-one, presto it suddenly changes overnight. They're possible. But win with them you never will. No matter what you're doing — pinching back begonias or throwing out leftover soup — they'll equate it with castration. This one and I are on a collision course, headed for that obligatory scene the playwrights call them, that confrontation when he will say to me, "Mother, you're suffering from penis envy," and I to him, "Maybe that's your trouble too, Son." And that'll be it. And it's back to the Greek tragedies to see if there's any parallel covering *that* little situation, or any symbolical guide to where do we go from there.

"And a far, far better temperature for humans also than the eighty your father kept the parlor at. Well, memories. How they come flooding back. When your father took sick, I would wheel him around, leaving him on the glazed porch when I went out to do my marketing, among the plants, where they all got the afternoon sun."

"Did he really want you to plant vegetables on his grave instead of flowers? He'd had enough of them? Was that his last request?"

"Certainly not! His last request was could he offer a lady his seat. He died in his favorite chair, you remember. He was recalling how we met. It was a crowded streetcar and he saw I had my arms full of bundles. 'Chivalry isn't dead,' he said, tipping his hat as he yielded his place, and

I said, 'No, but it's breathing pretty hard.' We were destined to have many another such joke, along the course of our married life. Did you ever hear his one about where does the money go, what do the womenfolks do with it? George Washington could throw a dollar across the Delaware because money went a lot farther in those days. That was one of his cracks at the church banquets, where he was always called on. Would you like to hear some more, for material?"

"Later. Just now I was trying to remember the months here with Randy Rivers. He accused you of spying on the guests through the keyholes. What made you a Peeping Tom?"

"I had standards to maintain. I had a right to know if there was anything out of the way going on under my own roof. No immorality, please. Not over my dead body."

"The expression is *over* my dead body."

"I suppose you have loads of personality. Anyway, as far as my lodgers were concerned, there was to my knowledge only one woman he was ever promiscuous with."

"Which is something in itself. Now just a second. Hold it." Osgood is standing over the range frying the bacon. He pauses to turn the strips in the skillet. "I seem to remember one night Rivers was down here in the parlor holding forth on the theme of women. The hard time they have biologically, which accounts for the hard time they give others. Do you remember how that went again? There was a lot of evolution mixed up in it."

Pounding through the black American night, in this year

of our Lord, on a railroad throwing in a chiropractic treatment to its last few remaining buffs, I try to recapitulate
the argument. This is how it went to the best of my ability.

Once in the dear dead days beyond recall, after I
wouldn't know how many million years of asexual reproduction, splitting down the middle and one thing and another,
Nature took a whack at another experiment, or a fresh turn
in the old one. Sexual specialization. There would be a
part of the organism (hereinafter called male) whose
function it would be to impregnate the female and then
forage for food for his mate and her young, so the female
could be left to reproduction and rearing. O.K. But the
unexpected happened — or the expected. The male took
advantage of the free time he had on his hands, after
scrounging up the food, to do a number of other things
besides. He took it upon himself to organize the life the
female produced, to say nothing of foraging for a little
food for females other than his mate — to wit, giving
lunch to some cookie in town and maybe even dinner,
whilst the Mrs. is locked up in the kitchen back home
where he left her that morning. The result is predictable.
The battleaxe, the nag, the bitch, choose your own term,
seeing the life she produced passing from her control to
that of the intended biological mere supplement, or serf
or flunkey. Until by the time she is middle-aged, that is,
finds even her role in the *production* of life gone by, she
can become a real dragon. There are gynecologists who
think women should be liquidated at forty-five, as the only
animal that outlives its reproductive usefulness. The dur-

208

able unendurable woman, as *Time* called her in a particularly charming story. Terrorizing her children, backbiting her sisters under the skin, and clobbering her husband into an early grave. Nature's supreme product: the widow. Swimming alone up Park and Madison Avenues, Michigan Boulevard, or just plain Main Street.

Now, the way your Women's Liberation Movement feminists of today probably fit into the picture, you might call them pre-marital battleaxes. Battleaxes without husbands. Most of us need a good ten years of marriage under our belt to get to be as feisty as they are from scratch. They're to the manner born, as we say. And a word of advice, they'll never hook a hubby with that attitude. No siree, Bob. They'll just have to change their tone.

Those were a few of the night thoughts with which to while away the wee hours as we pounded across mid-America on one of the male's more notable triumphs: the railroads in menopause.

But at breakfast the next morning the stewed prunes were good, my favorite eye-opener as you may recall I told the young scholars who called on me that day in Appleton, and I recommended train travel? Now I pressed the prunes upon my two companions. I speak in the plural for Will Gerstenslager had joined Randy Rivers and me at the last minute, insisting that a fling in the Big City was what he needed just then. Nor did the Babylonian high life wait till we got to Babylon. Will had bad me good night on a note of devilment 2nd to none's. He chucked goodies such as candy bars and bags of peanuts into my berth and then laughed like a fool as he took off down the corridor to his own. Even Walnettos, which I thought were out of print. Talk about decadence. We're through, washed up, kaput if revelry like this is any example. The barbarians are at the gates. A hand would reach through the curtain as I sat propped in bed reading my magazine, toss the tidbit onto the blanket and retreat, the prankster's slippered feet scurrying on the floor of the speeding pie wagon, as I keep thinking of Pullmans with their narrow aisles. A night in the cement mixer had taken all the mirth out of him. He and Randy both looked like death warmed over, and as for the Three Wise Men from the ICC, they were sitting at separate tables, apparently unable to face each other.

"We're stalled," Will said when the train ground to a halt in the middle of nowhere.

"Thank God," said Randy. "Give us a chance to recover our chemical balance. My blood is homogenized. Whose idea was this?"

"Eat your prunes," I said. "While they're ice-cold. It's the chilled edge that perks you up. Don't take a person out of context."

From a newspaper in his lap Randy observed that a man in Oklahoma had poisoned his wife, dismembered her, and stuffed the separate portions into culverts, public lockers and the like. "If you examine behavior like that closely," he said, yawning, "you can detect a certain undercurrent of hostility." Will was staring glumly out the window at a Holstein standing beside the track where we stood, staring glumly back. "That cow got up awful early, especially for the East," he said.

Farther up in the field a man with a pick and shovel was digging a hole for a dead cat, or trying to. It took me back to the days when we Wallops had so many aging pets that I would often dig a hole in the late fall, before the ground had frozen too solid, so we would have a grave in readiness for one or another of the animals that a hard winter would generally carry off. The trouble this man had getting his pick into the crust of his backyard justify a policy some, back then, deemed worthy of more than passing note. One day in early November, having just got my bulbs in, I went into our woodlot to dig a last resting place for an old tabby I knew would never see another spring. Osgood, then perhaps ten or twelve, came back to watch.

"You like to bury things, don't you, Mom?"

"If they're dead. Otherwise I can't say as I ever give the matter much thought, one way or another. Well, we've got quite a cemetery here by now, haven't we?"

I gazed around at this clump of maples under whose rustling boughs reposed the remains of more once-cherished dogs, cats, rabbits, birds and sheep than I could easily enumerate, though a moment's respectful pause between us called them individually back to mind before I turned back to Osgood and asked, "Have you put the drops in Tinker's ears yet?"

"No, I thought you did that."

The old man on the hill finally shouldered his own pick

and shovel, tucked his furry problem under his free arm, and shambled off to try elsewhere.

I returned to my table companions. They both looked as though they had just been exhumed. Randy's face had a mangled appearance, as though he had lain with it mashed into his pillow all night. The knot of Will's tie, surely worn to keep an election bet he had lost, was half hidden under the collar of his shirt, and there were red flecks on his jaw like razor nicks, although he hadn't shaved yet. Possibly my eyesight had declined since the last time I'd broken bread with him. They both possessed the three nostrils that are the product of astigmatism, as well as some other interesting features that made me decide to get out my specs and put them on so as to get them into focus — hardly a net gain. They looked like drawings of them that had been done by skitsophrenic children. Randy twisted around in his chair to flag the steward. "I wonder if we could get some wine."

"Nothing goes with prunes," I said as serenely as possible.

"No, I was thinking of champagne. Seriously, there's nothing better with sausages than champagne. It's wonderful. Few people know about it."

The steward, when finally summoned, dashed that hope, and I felt so sorry for Randy that I started to agree with him that railroads were finished, but when he started in on the glories of air travel I hardened my heart and swerved back in my thinking.

"In the future, even jet transportation as we know it

will be a thing of the past," he said. "We'll go in rockets, fired up, then down, in a sort of angular trajectory. It'll take us twenty minutes to get to New Delhi."

"If it only takes twenty minutes to get to New Delhi, why not stay home?"

"Check!" chimed in Will. Just then the Holstein and the old man with his cat slid slowly into our past.

"Old ark's a-moverin,'" said Randy listlessly.

That's the way it went all morning. A half hour later we really stalled, because, the conductor told us, "something is hanging down." That was as specific as they would be, despite pleas, cajolery, and finally outright threats of reprisal. Still, woefully inadequate as this intelligence was, it also seemed uncalled for, because of its crude overtones. And so on and so on. But at last we rolled into the train terminal and there was Osgood smiling in a lot of steam though engines are all Diesel and electric now, and coming toward us with his bobbing gait, each springing step giving him momentarily an extra inch of height. A loop of red wool scarf was flung across his throat, high against his chin, so that he hitched it down in order to kiss me. You could see that his real excitement was in meeting Randy Rivers again, at whom he gazed in awe as he pumped his hand. "It must be seven years since I've seen you," he said. Randy nodded, without any interest in checking those figures. It was clear my companions were eager to get to their respective destinations, Randy to his uptown apartment, Will to the Biltmore, where he had a reservation. Osgood and I were presently in a cab, creeping

213

through dense traffic to his Village digs. He sat looking out his window, the muffler held around his mouth. After some minutes of silence I dug out of my bag a copy of the *Reader's Digest* I'd been reading on the train.

"There's a nice piece in here," I said. "A young man's affectionate memoir of his mother. It's full of interesting passages, but just let me read this sentence at random, if I can— Oh, here it is. 'She was a gentle soul, and her winds were from the south.' Why don't you write things like that about your mother, Osgood?"

"I don't know, Mother. I guess I'm just not that kind of writer."

I tucked the magazine back into my bag without further comment. We were inching our way down Fifth Avenue, and I rubbered out my side with a woman's natural instinct for shops. High on the list of dry goods stores to be visited was certainly the one we were just passing— Lord and Taylor's. There were some mighty smart-looking outfits in those windows.

"Randy's changed. He looks like hell," Osgood said, getting us onto more pleasant matters.

"He's been through a lot. So have I, so do we all from time to time. Not that such things are necessarily all bad. We all need plowing over from time to time, to keep from stagnating. Provided we don't get plowed under. We ought to stop short of doing that to each other."

"Oh, Mother, you take everything so personally."

"Said the spider to the fly."

"It's a *story*. It's not to be taken literally in every respect.

You said in your letter you didn't remember a lot of the things described in the book. Of course not. They were made up, or exaggerations of what did happen, distortions if you will. Picasso said, 'Art is a lie that tells the truth.'"

"Pablo Picasso?"

"That's the one."

All this while Osgood continued to hold the muffler around his mouth, so I couldn't swear to the dialogue, even though I owned a half-interest in it, but such was roughly its gist. Watching him give the scarf another tuck around his bearded lips and chin, I said, "Have you got a toothache, or are we going to hold up the Brinks Express?"

"I have got a sensitive tooth, actually, and a sort of sore throat beginning."

"I'll take a look at it when we get home, see if it looks angry."

"No, no, no. The cold gets me. Tell me more about Randy, Mom. You had an episode with him, eh?"

When I was a little girl living in Edgartown, Indiana, my grandparents came all the way from Idaho, where they worked a potato farm, to spend Thanksgiving with us. It was the same time of year, and the railroads, then in their infancy, were working their way upward from a stage ours, in their deterioration, have about dilapidated themselves back down to. No, I shouldn't say infancy, it was more like their prime, but that's no matter. The main thing is that our dining table was pulled out as far as it would go,

and my grandfather sat at the head of it carving the tur-
key. The term "groaning board" could be taken literally,
because of the decrepit condition of that piece of furniture. As he bore down with knife and fork, the dowels
came out of the dropleaf at his end, or the slotted bolt
holding the sections underneath, or whatever, and the
dropleaf descended into a kind of chute down which the
entire bird, platter, fixings, gravy and all, slid into his lap.
"That does it," he said, while many willing hands wiped
him down. "I'll never come East again."

Now I had come what was for me East, to visit my own
son, with the year entering likewise its holiday creshendo.
Osgood was determined to hear about Randy, apparently
quite impressed with his mother's hobnobbing with the
bigwigs, so I spent the nearly half-hour it took us to get
to his apartment relating the recent adventure. I was still
at it when he rose from his chair to rustle us up a little
lunch, expressing as he did so the wide-eyed hope that
he might get to see something of Randy here in town. "I'll
give him a ring tomorrow or the next day," I said. "We'll
tie one on." And for the first time really took this pad in.
It was exactly as described in *The Duchess of Obloquy*.
No attempt to graduate or transform there. All I missed
was the paper napkins for antimacassars on the ruptured
chairs, the fictional cleaning woman's touch, proof there
wasn't a real-life one here. I gave the place a drubbing it
will never forget. I was still at that when Osgood got back
from his marketing for dinner, and after that meal I knew
it was time for another confrontation. The hour had struck,

as it had with Randy Rivers. The occasion chosen was the same as in that former instance, when both parties were eased and mellowed by good food and drink. Osgood poured us glasses of some Greek liqueur whose name I forget, which works minutes faster than the four other leading nasal decongestants.

"So. Medusa," I said, summing up the account given of the misunderstanding straightened out between Randy and me. "It was all a mistake, cleared up when we put our cards on the table. But hold it, what's this? Another literary work? Yes, and it turns out the rejoicing was premature, she is Medusa after all, and her own son is — Perseus!"

"What the *devil* are you talking about? Perseus wasn't her son."

"He is in this little drama. I've looked the whole thing up. Mythology is big these days, we can go back to the Greeks because our own gods are dead. Well, if you'll recall, she was such a fright her look turned men to stone? But that didn't stop Perseus. Our old Percy had it upstairs, he had it here. He cut her head off by — how? Remember?" I says, picking up my glass for a leisurely sip.

"Look, Mom, if you're going to conduct a quiz —"

"By watching her reflection in his shield. That way he avoided looking at the hag in question. But wait. Here's the switch of all time, the sequel to your little valentine, enough mythology to win you a Pulitzer. The bag can hardly look at her own reflection without turning *herself*

217

to stone, but she sees it — ready? — in her son's shield. My own Perseus."

Osgood leans his arms along the mid-ledge of the window, his chin on the backs of his hands, but I know the musing pose is false, or think I do. Maybe, pondering his image in the dark pane, he is flushing beneath the black beard.

"No, wait. Something better. A topper for even that. It's not in his shield she at last sees her reflection. It's in — *his sword.*"

Whirl is king, having driven out Zeus. He spins toward me with such vehemence that he goes right on past and out of sight, unless I twist to keep him there over my shoulder. "Oh, Mother, for God's sake! Why do you make a federal case out of it?" He raises his voice not in volume, but register, the way a man will in a domestic quarrel — which in a sense this is. "It's a *story*, can't you get that through your —"

"Might 'thick skull' be the phrase you're groping for?"

"If you like, but at least give me the chance to grope for it. Medusa's what you want too, so Medusa it is. Why should I argue with you? You *want* the grievance, you positively revel in it. You wouldn't for the world want to be deprived of your complaints. It's your inalienable right as a woman, the right to be wronged. If I went through the damn book line for line and told you what I took from fact and what I made up, you'd fight me every inch of the way, insisting that what I made up was true too but had no right to say it. You'd collect either way, as a martyr.

I suppose now you did tell me a dog howled when I was born. That I never made up what I thought a rather neat touch."

"That's what I mean. Putting such words in your mother's mouth. What will the neighbors think? That on the outside here's this decent person they know, but in the house, oy, what a harpy."

"Oh, my God," he says through his teeth, imploring heaven with fists raised and his eyes rolling in his beard, or such is my hallucination without my glasses at the moment. This is the pass things have come to. His teeth are biting his throat. His words certainly bite into me. As a confrontation it leaves nothing to be desired, except maybe that we're back to back half the time, the way he keeps pivoting in and out of view. "Why, *why* are you so positively, so mortally determined to make me feel guilty?"

"Aha!" I spring to my feet. "Now we've got to the crux of the matter. The key word in our culture, our country itself brought to focus on a pinpoint. Leave us dwell on this a moment. Your hero's guilt is what your book is about. The guilt instilled in him by his mother that makes him unable to enjoy sex and get himself on a decent footing with another woman — on whom he has to turn the tables by a line of behavior calculated to make *her* feel guilty. Doesn't that give you a clue to all this guilt stuff we're suppose to have in the national character thanks to our Puritan heritage? You know what? I don't think we feel guilt at all, any damn one of us. If we did, why would we let people starve, rot in ghettos and disintegrate into

219

perverts and beasts in prison? The Puritans never caged people up for life for their crimes. They whipped them publicly or hanged them and got it over with. The Puritan conscience is what we've *lost*. If we had any conscience why would we discriminate, climb over each other's backs for promotion, get rich dealing cancer in the form of cigarettes and death on the highways by manufacturing cars with horsepowers nobody on God's earth needs, to say nothing of concocting a lot of lying advertisements advertising these things with the profits from which we can subscribe our share to a country club costing a million dollars five blocks from where we successfully opposed a Synanon for the rehabilitation of drug addicts in a remodeled old livery stable? Yet, responsible for these and a million other monstrosities, we go squeaking and squealing about our precious guilt, coddling ourselves with that — taking that what-do-you-call-it to our bosom. Flattering unction. What we've probably got on our conscience is that we don't feel any guilt. *That's* what we've guilty about, and little wonder. No. The American problem isn't guilt at all — it's accusation. Self-justification. Because — hold it, equal time, remember? — because I've read a dozen articles and as many novels on the subject of this famous guilt of ours, America's chief product, right? And it always come around to finding some doorstep to lay the blame on. Somebody to pin it on. First it was the Puritans, then it was the old lady, then for a while it was the wife, she was the ogre, and now it's the old lady again. We're not tearing our breast, we're pointing our finger.

We're not confessing, we're leveling charges. But I must be fair, I mustn't go too far. Or rather I must go back really far, to where we can see it's not exclusively an American trait but human. To the very beginning: 'The woman thou gavest me.' Remember? That ring a bell? Yes, the Garden of Eden, the very dawn of time, the first flicker of human shame, it's all Her fault. And I guess it'll be that way to the last syllable of recorded ditto. Her. The central all-embracing, all-smothering, however-much-life-giving philoprogenitive Her, the corridor of shame, the slimy vestibule of sin, the old mammalian muck. How are we doing? We cooking with gas now? We making with the mystical hoop-de-da? But lay it on us. We started it all. Is the national debt up? Unemployment show an increase of 2 percent? Hard-core poverty on the rise in Appalachia? Show us no mercy. Hang it all on we mothers. When are they going to stand on their own two feet, these pip-squeaks, and shoulder their own responsibilities, instead of blaming somebody else for their shortcomings, usually their parents? So wear a chiropractor's tunic because they give you false values. So get a guitar and knock the culture that developed the system that enables you to amplify the protest. So your mother was a little straight-laced. She was a little repressive. You should of got a load of mine! She made the Amish look like a Roman carnival. I wish you could of seen the freedom I never had, to say nothing of the Casper Milktoast she made of my father. You're lucky you never knew those two dreamboats!"

"No, but I knew my own father, and from that I can see

you were your mother's disciple. Maybe it's true what the psychologists say. That all women are afflicted with penis envy."

"And not a few men!"

The church was only three blocks up the street. I had noticed it coming down in the cab. There I knelt at the altar and asked forgiveness. There among the statues and fluttering candles of a religion totally alien to me, but the only place convenient or even open at the time. For deliverance from the terrible remorse over what I had done. Bowing down to sticks and stones is not my style, all sorts of distracting thoughts crept into my mind in that twilight grotto. Pagan gods I might better be running through instead for some informing myth that might give focus to my life and direction to what, God willing, remained of it. A sketch in the copy of *New Voices* that carried Osgood's novella, of a grim-lipped housewife-type with arms folded on a bosom consisting of two boxing gloves, a four-page-spread entry of an artist regarded as another Calder. It was too early to tell what he was another, as anyone still burning with memories of the last random tangle of wire hangers he's seen in his hall closet would know.

"Lord, help me do my best," I said, pulling myself together. "As a mother and as a human being. And lead us not into castration, but deliver us from that evil . . ." I'm never much satisfied with my own prayers, and usually fall back on standard ones. I wound up on an old family wall-text you still see around, and no wonder: "Give me the strength to change the things I can, the courage to accept the things I can't, and the wisdom to know the difference."

When I got back home, Osgood was in the kitchen fixing some hot cocoa, whistling at his task. He knew he had me. The tables had been turned, the burden of guilt was mine.

"The fight we had was all to the good," he said, as we drank our hot chocolate in the parlor. "It was long overdue. But the air is cleared."

In that sense we could be more relaxed. We could even laugh now about my mother. "She warned us against snappy ginks with roadsters who would shift gears with our knee," I related, "and when that was permitted, go farther up our leg, as far as they could go with their 'socialistic tendencies.'"

He nodded, removing his nose from the mug. "You got it off your chest, said what you said, and now I can speak freely about my plans. My way of life. You don't like this apartment. The fact is I'm going to move out of it. Or at least I'm thinking of doing so."

"Good idea," I said, sipping. "I hope you'll look for something a little bigger as well as a little better. Maybe I can help you with the difference."

"That's very nice of you, Mother, but thanks, no. I've got a place. I may move in with somebody else."

"Oh?" I smiled archly they call it. "Is she anyone I know?"

"Yes," he said, setting his cup down and then picking it up again. "Ralph Frawley. I'm going to live with him."

I finished my cocoa and moseyed on back to the church. It seemed colder at the altar this time. There was only one other worshiper kneeling there, one of them old ladies always seen in Catholic churches, who seem as much a part of them as the statues. I noticed that she had a glove on top of her head, in loo of a hat, and I recalled the custom of ladies covering their heads in such churches, with whatever article of apparel or even accessory was convenient, the principle of reverence being important, not its outward manifestation. With neither hat nor gloves in my own instance, there was nothing for it but to set my bag on top of my head, for the sign of respect that now seemed important to me, in view of past petitions proving so unavailing. The problem of keeping it balanced of course reduced the angle at which I could bow my head, but I figured what I had lost in the posture of contrition I had gained in its spirit.

"And now, my Lord, he's mixed up with the confusing spring warblers," I said. "Where, *where* did I go wrong?"

seven

"And just who are you not to suffer fools gladly?" That was what Bubbles Gerstenslager use to say, and I was to think of it often in connection with the people I now met and the events through which I was pressed, to a conclusion I still think must be a dream. I did not protest, make scenes, or anything of the sort. We would see what we'd see, play it by ear, and all that. People have to rub along, like everybody else. Osgood said he imagined I'd like to meet Ralph, that is see him again after all these years, and why didn't we all get together and make an evening of it. This was easily seen through as a ruse to cultivate Randy Rivers, both for himself and to impress Ralph, whose ilk, as you know, set great store by knowing famous and glamorous people, and who, truth to tell, flew in pretty high circles even by New York standards. Anyhow, I went to work on such a get-together, which must naturally include my visiting-fireman friend Will. Being the oldest and the best-heeled, he wound up as host, an interesting development in itself. It probably necessitated his wiring home for money if not dipping into principle, because we went to a fancy place in the Fifties called the Niçoise.

"By George," he said, playing the man of the world over the menu, so blasé he's eaten everything except the commonplaces, "do you know I've never had steak Tartar? Can you believe it? I think I'll try that, waiter. Medium rare."

Everyone thought this a gag and met it with a burst of laughter that baffled Will, whose expression they then thought a further part of the act, and laughed some more. It was partly courtesy toward a host who was hardly on their wavelength, but not altogether. Poor Will. He was simply beyond the pail, as we say. Still you couldn't help loving him for it. My heart went out to him, in his gray-blue suit and a tie that was surely another election bet, looking around with the roasted-apple face as though he was trying to take *them* in stride! Including the Negro called Pilsudski who turned up with Ralph. I got the general idea they were living together at the time, but I wasn't certain. In any case he was obviously the original of the Warshawski in *Duchess*. "You didn't make *him* up," I whispered to Osgood, after hearing Pilsudski talk.

"But I did make up the dog's suicide," he whispered back. "Don't tell me Bruno hanged himself on purpose."

"He had been despondent for some time."

226

All of this was later. Over cocktails we were five, awaiting Randy Rivers who had said he'd be late, and could he bring a friend. Certainly, Will had said. Randy now made an entrance as we were sipping our drinks and nibbling on a platter of assorted appetizers. All eyes were fixed upon him as he came down the short flight of carpeted stairs and made his way toward us with a young woman on his arm who was made to arrive late and who visibly relished doing so. She seemed familiar. Who was this, I wondered, until they actually reached our table and I recognized Miss Virginia Quilty. She positively shimmered in an apple-green minidress of shot silk, with no jewelry but simple pearl earrings — and those perfect teeth hardly bigger than grains of rice. The world is a madhouse in which most of us are lucky enough to be visitors rather than inmates. It's about as much as you can ask. Why should I be surprised at this development, or non-development? She'd kept in touch with Randy, or got back in touch, or whatever. My radar picked up nothing more "between" them than formerly, though to that I couldn't swear. She wound up sitting on my right, with Osgood on hers, and was instantly in deep conversation with him about his novella, which she'd read and loved. I made a concerted effort to catch all this, catching also the vague sense of their hitting it off, a forlorn hope quickly dashed by its developing that she had come to New York to try to make it as an actress. She had met a producer who saw either a play or a movie in it, and of course she'd adore to play the girl. "Actually," said Osgood, laughing gratefully into his plate, "I frankly see it more as a movie, because you can weave in and out with

227

the scenes from the boy's past more fluidly than on the stage." "And that mother. I can see her hovering over the bed in the love scenes," said Virgie. "Sort of surrealist technique would be the way to do it. They can work wonders with split-screen stuff these days." Her own laughter tinkled musically among the crystal and the cutlery. "What a marvelous battleaxe," she added in a lowered voice, and I looked modestly away. "Actually," said Osgood, exactly the same height as her, "I've been diddling with a screen treatment. Oh, it's all on spec. Still this producer is ready to go if he likes what I turn up. So he says. Tell me . . ."

I turned my attention to the Negro, who was sitting directly across this large round table from me, next to Randy who had Ralph on his other side, chattering away twenty to the dozen in an effort to impress the lion. Pilsudski was quite slick and handsome in an African tunic that at the same time made him look like an impostor, not only because he was light brown rather than black, but because his features were completely un-Negroid, with a short straight nose and lean mouth, so conventionally attractive that even his color seemed a disguise. I'm not uptight on the subject. We have a certain amount of mixing even back in Appleton. One colored girl we had there frankly aspired to cross the line and marry a white boy. She got her way, marrying one who wasn't only white, but an albino into the bargain. You can't have your dreams come truer than that. This Pilsudski could play the clown, but I noticed in a group like this he was content and even careful to let Ralph carry the ball. He had a grin rather than a smile, but at least the grin was always at the ready. Ralph was square-faced and blue-eyed, with dense waves of blond hair and even blonder beard and mustache, all clipped and well-groomed. He wore a blue velvet jacket and a Paisley necktie that really picked up the marbles. He had a mannerism that I suddenly realized was typical of this type: darting the eyes about without turning the head. Giving a coquettish air to everything they say. It was these eyes that included everybody in his attention, even the poor host who by now didn't know *what* streetcar he was on. Such brittle dialogue, I thought we'd all bleed to death from cuts and scratches before the night was out. Once a man at a nearby table was overheard remarking, "The will's been probated, and I'm coming into a million dollars." "I wish I'd said that," said Ralph. He strongly recommended to Randy that he read his own book, *Medusa*, which Randy said he hadn't looked at since the galleys. "Underlying it all, and in spite of everything," Ralph said, "is the thing no work of art is anything without — compassion." (His sets had compassion.) "You could even go so far as to call it pity. Remember what Oscar Wilde said to Gide when he picked him up after his release from prison. 'Pity is the most beautiful thing in the world.'"

"I never realized Gide had been in prison," I said.

Will Gerstenslager was simply out of it, especially when the conversation took a literary turn, but he didn't mind. He nodded along, looking at the table and smiling to himself, tickled to death to be part of the group. This was a night to remember. He would dine out on this dinner. I

229

could hear him already back home, come summer, on some patio in Big Toe.

Ralph called over to him. "Will, could we have another bottle of this Latour? I mean do you mind? Let's let the wine be on me."

"Wouldn't think of it." Will twisted in his chair to summon the wine steward. "I'll just call my broker in the morning and sell some municipals."

"I just had an ominous call from *my* brokers — Mene, Mene, Tekel and Upharsin," said Ralph, and darted his eyes wickedly around the table.

I didn't know whether Will knew he wasn't kidding on his own end of this financial banter, but he found out soon enough when the check came, or checks, there being also an invoice from the vintner. It was one of those places where credit cards simply aren't mentioned. Will looked at the bills and then over at me. He was ashen. He stole over to my chair under cover of a brisk boil in the conversation, and whispered, "Could you let me have fifty or so, Em?"

"Certainly," I said, and excused myself to go to the Ladies'.

I always carry plenty of spondulix on me when I travel, especially to New York, but I generally keep it pinned to my corset in the form of tens and twenties, and maybe a fifty. That way a malefactor will never find it unless in addition to robbery he's also intent on carnal knowledge, hardly likely in my case. I had to strip myself halfway down to the buff to get at the coin of the realm, owing to the nature of the dress I had on, the details of which are beside the point here. But it kept me in the booth so long the maid on duty there became worried and called over, "Are you all right, hon?" "Okie doke," I called back, wriggling back into this and that, and tucking into my bag, which I had set on the floor, the fifty I had unpinned from the right side of my corset. I trusted this would see Will through. I reassembled myself, took the needless wash for which the maid had already filled the basin, gave her a quarter and returned to the happy party. It was still clipping along so merrily I could slip Will the money with no more risk of detection than he'd run in asking me for it. I hoped the round of liqueurs ordered in my absence did not escalate the emergency unduly. I returned to my seat and, sipping the lubricant freshly placed there also, watched Will conclude the evening's transaction with a waiter who hovered behind him. I never asked, but my hunch was that he gave the fifty for a tip, out of insecurity, or in his eagerness to get out of this as soon as possible and with a whole hide. That done, however, there was still something lurking on his flank which we both spotted at the same time: to wit, the sommelier, a thickset, stolid figure standing with his feet planted firmly apart, the key around his neck being not merely to the cellar but to the kingdom itself, and whatsoever he bindeth on earth it shall be bound in heaven, and whatsoever he looseth on earth it shall be loosed in heaven. To say nothing of the mater dee posted like a sentinel beside the mints. Will threw me another stricken look and came back over.

"Have you got any more?"

"I'll see."

This time the maid was really baffled and alarmed by the goings-on. "Are you sure you're all right?" "Positive, dearie," I sang back, "Thank you." Another ritual wash, costing a further two-bit piece, and I was out in the passage, where this time Will was waiting, pacing between the two johns. "Here's a ten and a five," I said. "Give the mater dee the ten and the wine steward the five. It's plenty." And back we sailed to our party, in time to disband it.

So with the wealth a little more equitably distributed, we got home tired but happy. I made up my bed on the couch in Osgood's parlor, where I insisted on sleeping, refusing the bed he tried to press on me. I didn't feel the least sleepy. He looked pretty chipper himself, for reasons I hoped I guessed aright, though I carried that hope carefully, like a bucket from which one fears to spill a drop.

"You hit it off very well with that girl," I said. "Virginia Quilty. She seemed to take a shine to you."

He grunted something embarrassed and even resentful, but pleased. He continued poking about the living room. I had a hunch he didn't want the subject dropped, any more than he wanted to talk about it.

"Why don't you ask her to go out with you?"

"Good God, Mother, are you matchmaking?"

"Would I be a woman if I wasn't?"

"But isn't this the one you shooed off of Randy, or tried to? Whose clutches you thought it your duty to rescue him from because she was poison?"

"Don't split hairs. Poison for him, for you she might be your meat. Did you get her phone number?"

"Yes, but . . ." He sighed, plowing his hair some. "I think she gave it to me because she hopes for a part in the script — of which I haven't even written a treatment! And assuming Bogomil wants to produce it."

"What of it? Women generally have an axe to grind. I'm grinding one right now. Some girls' affections have to be bought and paid for, they're simply that type, and though it isn't the best thing in the world, there are a damn sight worse — ahem! — if you get my drift. So. Let's hear about the treatment. I'd love to see a movie get under way. I've had enough of literature for a while. I need a new art form."

Lying in the dark parlor waiting for sleep to carry me off, I reminisced about the time Osgood was an underachiever at Brown. Not as a college student, but as a high school pupil; and not studying so much as *being* studied. It was at Brown University, one summer, that a staff of educators conducted a survey of carefully selected underachievers, secondary-school-level scholars with good minds who were not performing up to potential, or snuff, as we use to call it. Once the term underachiever was coined it was bound to carry prestige of its own weight — a whole new intellectual category was born. The study was made on a special grant from the Carnegie Foundation, in the hope that some light might be shed on why underachievers were not hitting on all the cylinders God gave them, and that the cause might be eradicated in time for them to be working up to potential by the time they got to college — or even so they could get *into* one. Osgood certainly qualified. His marks would of been enviable as golf scores, for nine holes. The six-weeks course as a scholastic guinea pig cost me six hundred dollars, and having laid that much on the barrelhead I thought I might as well treat myself to a little trip and go to Providence with him, and as long as I had gone that far, stick around a while and close enough to him to find out what his trouble was. So there he was in his element — *belonging*. Glowing for the first time with a sense of that. There he was with close to a hundred other boys, hand-picked for their poor records from all over the country and one from Hawaii, being well fed and comfortably housed in a new dormitory and every need looked after and seen to, because they had spent the year goofing off, while those who had applied themselves and done their duty had to spend the summer working in supermarkets or in restaurant kitchens washing dishes.

I stayed for about two weeks, living at a motel not too far from the campus. Wither I would repair every day shortly after noon when the classes where the scholars were being studied were over. I would watch from a safe distance while the underachievers poured out of the building and horsed around on their way to the dining hall for lunch. They had lessons to do, their failure at which was under scrutiny, so there were study periods, after which they would again emerge and hack their way down the streets, usually to a coffee shop which became a favorite hangout. Osgood mingled very well with everybody, but I noticed when groups of three or four would pick up local girls and go for walks, he would be sort of out of it. Oh, he was definitely part of the bunch, included in the conversation and his jokes laughed at all right enough, but always the last to pair off with a girl, a fifth wheel, a schlep when it came to that. I was glad to see the girls, whoever they were or whatever group they were from, disappear from the scene and the boys once again roam the streets in larger bands. One day I saw about a dozen underachievers lifting a parked Volkswagen off the street and onto the sidewalk. The leader was a huge hulking boy from St. Louis, but the winner in the sexual area was a little Florida kid named Rennie Mays, who tried to date one of his teachers, a divorcée of thirty-five.

Whether anybody ever got to the bottom of their performance lag I don't know, but there must be a lot of profiles and opinion sheets on file at the Carnegie Foundation. On my last day there, I had a conference with the project supervisor. Waiting for him in his office, I stood at a window and looked out into a kind of courtyard. In it was a large maple tree with a typewriter ribbon entangled in its branches. My most vivid single memory of that summer — the red and black streamer wound among the rustling branches, and a robin singing above it. The project supervisor was no fool, and knew that he couldn't tell me anything I didn't already know, that Osgood had brains but lacked confidence, and as a result would fall into funks and torpors.

They were familiar enough to me, and had often been accompanied by sore throats, nosebleeds, headaches and other incapacitating things. As a younger boy he'd had a newspaper route. Then in mid-October he took sick and I went out and peddled his papers for him. So now we see me pedaling my bicycle under the falling leaves, a canvas bag slung over my shoulder, pitching the folded evening *Messengers* onto front porches. Another year he lined up some summer work mowing lawns and again took sick. Nothing the doctor could find physically, or any thermometer recorded a temperature for. He was just on dead center. I was not going to see his yard work go the way of the paper route, so once more I pitched in. "Oh, no!" he howled, rolling over in bed at the sight of me dressed in blue jeans and sweater, and drawing on canvas mittens for the chores ahead. "Oh, yes," I said, and went out there and mowed those lawns. Something seemed to cow him, some shadow to hang over him.

After Brown, he spent his last high school year in a private prep school. I hoped that the taste of an Ivy League campus would sharpen his appetite for a good college and bolster his determination to get into one, but no dice. His marks were nothing to write home about, but of course Dalton Hall had to write home about them, regularly once a month. His highest grade was Unsatisfactory Plus, whatever that means. He squeaked into a college that shall be nameless, it having hazards enough in the way of its reputation. The same story. He'd start off with a bang, then along about the second or third week it would be in effect,

236

"No more pencils, no more books, no more teachers' dirty looks." He dropped out after one semester, then thought he would shoot pool for a semester. That is, he had got attached to a snooker parlor of which the owner needed a temporary manager, having gotten laid up with something himself. The pay was irregular, but then Osgood spent most of his time there at the tables. Then he drove a truck for a semester (his college years were flying by), a delivery truck for a large dry cleaning establishment. He seemed to like that, zinging around town in a new rig and trotting in and out of houses with fresh clothes to be delivered and bundles to be picked up. His zest was obvious to me, who again trailed him at a hundred or a hundred and fifty yards in my own car, once in a while. Perhaps whatever he was writing at night was going well. For a while. Because in time he fell into dead center again; the typewriter stopped and his house-to-house spring lost its verve. I climbed to his room one night when he was lying on his bed, listening to good music, and told him that he must make an immediate effort to get back to college or he was a goner. He promised to apply to several right away, but I wasn't fooled. Trailing him with a heavy heart the next day I noticed we were tooling along a main highway well off his established route. A right turn, then a sharp left and we were off on a country lane petering down to a stream, where I knew he often went to mope. You know the contemporary type. Everything is too much and nothing is enough. He shut the motor off and sat there staring into the water. I got out of my car and came

237

around to the side of his and stood there shaking my finger at him through the cab window. "If you don't watch out you're going to wind up driving a truck," I said, "mark my words. You'd better pull yourself together and finish your education, or you'll be lucky to get even that."

"You dropped out," he said mildly, looking down from his eminence.

"That was different and you know it. That was grade school. It has absolutely no bearing on this, on you, on today. And it's altogether another matter for a man — if you intend to become one!"

I picked my way back to the car, sinking to my ankle in a puddle of spring mud, thinking as I lifted my spattered skirts, "I should of sent him to dog obedience school, along with that dachshund." I was very sensitive to his mood swings. That night, thank God, the typewriter was suddenly going again, the "thunder in the ceiling" that foreshadowed the imminent Randy Rivers days. That winter he quit his job and went to New York, with my blessing.

Now here I am in New York myself, sitting on the living room couch trying to give him searching glances from under eyelids I pretend are closed. I am trying to evaluate from his own expression how the dates with Miss Virgie Quilty are going. For he had another with her last night. It indicates something less than a resounding success? At least something less than resounding self-confidence. He is an underachiever still. He will never get a wife.

I climbed off the couch.

238

"We're going to see a marriage counselor."

"You're out of your mind."

"That's right. Or going out of it. I can't stand this — this air of defeat. *Something's* holding you down, some weight is crushing you, and we're going to find out what it is. You don't need psychiatry, any of that depth consulting. A marriage counselor can often go deep enough, and some of them are quite good. That magazine I had on the train, what did I do with it? There was an article in it by a New York marriage counselor who seemed to know what he was talking about."

"But I'm not married."

"Hair-splitting again. People who plan to get married go to them too, just to air their problems. They're sometimes even consulted to patch up affairs. You'd like to get married I know, but something makes you shy away from it like a skittery horse. So talk to somebody. Let your hair down for God's sake." I had been pacing the room while looking for the magazine, and now fetched up behind the chair in which he sat in his pajamas, staring out the window. "Does Virgie like you? As much as she seems to?"

"Oh, for God's sake, Mother."

"Women like that are expensive, but they respect achievement or even just talent, as much as they do money. Because the one leads to the other. Randy and I talked her out. He doesn't want her, they don't want each other. Anybody with talent has an inside track. So how's the screen treatment coming? Why don't you knuckle down and finish it?"

"It's *buckle* down, and *knuckle* under. Good Christ."

239

"So. Stuck on dead center again. Can't get started for fear of failure. All that. We're going to see this Louis Leland. That's his name. Here, read this piece. Then we'll call and make an appointment."

" 'We'?"

"Yes. If I'm the culprit shouldn't he get a look at me? I'm game, so why shouldn't you be."

He drew himself up to his full height, albeit he was laying down again at the time, and said, "I can take care of my own affairs, thank you." Then: "Virgie's the type you always warned me against. She won't cope, she'll never pitch in."

"It's not what I warned you against then. It's what I'm saving you from now. With my last ounce of strength and, yes, penny, if it comes to that. You're not going to move in with any Ralph and Pilsudski if it's the last thing I do. You're not going to play house with any tomboys. I may be from hunger, as you say, but I think I can see Virgie Quilty straight. She's a snob and she's out for the main chance, but she's no — sick as I am of the word, sound as it may be — castrater. That one's no mutilator, a regular Delilah creeping up on her Samson with her scissors to leave him shorn, stripped of his power. She'll want her man to *have* power, to send him out into the world so he can help *her* cut a figure in it. No. She'll supply the spark a man needs, help you put fuel in your engine, inspire you by her own example. To look to yourself. Dress better, pick out shirts and ties for you, get those bangs sliced off your forehead so you can look the world in the

240

eye for Pete's sake, not go around like a sheep dog — a Roman emperor sitting for a sculptor after sending legions into Africa though the Empire is in decay! For decay is what that little affectation now days reminds me of. So good riddance, so you won't look like some ancient decadent bah relief."

"You make her sound like a proper nag."

"So what? Better you should be nagged to death by a woman than live in peace with a — Don't make me say it. Because the one is with Nature and the other is against it. The Pair is nature's supreme concoction — *but her way.*"

"Ralph and Pilsudski are always quarreling."

"That don t reassure me none. I don't hold with all this liberalism about sex — be loose, do your own thing, whatever turns you on, sex is sex, everything goes. Because then everything *is* going. It *is* the Roman Empire rotting and the barbarians are at the gates. You're going to get yourself straightened around and fixed up with a wife, and I hope she's half the woman your mother is. And that in the end, when she's gone, you'll think of your mother that way. Oh, you don't have to write about her like the author of this memoir — the magazine just happens to fall open to that page. 'She had a heart as soft as a ball of yarn.' That's the way to write about mothers, it seems to me. Your father use to say, 'The happiest hours of my life were spent in the arms of another woman — my mother!' It was one of his cracks at the church banquets. No, Ozzie, you don't have to say your mother's heart is a ball of yarn. Just think of it as being in the right place, is all. And

consent to see this marriage counselor. What do you say?"
"Oh, God, all right. What can I lose?"
"We'll see," I said, heading for the telephone book to make the appointment.

A large painting hung in the waiting room of Leland's office. The canvas was covered from top to bottom and side to side with blobs like those in the Rolaid stomach-mint commercial, that absorb 47 times their weight in excess acidity. But at last we were shown in, and seated on two chairs facing the counselor across a desk the size of Rhode Island.

"Now then."

Always an ominous beginning. King Solomon had wavy dark hair and a smile like the juice of ½ a lemon. "Keep your mouth shut and eat," I suddenly remembered saying to Osgood when he was a little tike talking out of turn at table, and Osgood retorting, "How can I?" He was all right. A smart kid.

Leland was assessing me with a gleam in his eye that seemed frank admiration for a woman that age being found desirable by such a young man. I knew then already which way the wind was blowing, or about to.

"The age difference is no rarity," he said, "if I may assume this to be the difficulty." A shrewd analysis of the affair. "Except in the sexes. It's usually young girls wanting father figures. But young men sometimes need mother images."

Osgood started to say something but I gave him a nudge

242

in the ankle with my foot. Let me do the talking, it conveyed. I had this klutz's number from the start, this Leland.

"Even when they've already got a mother?" I said.

Yes, even then. What was needed was a mother *figure*, which the mother often was not. Someone who, neither dominating nor over-permissive, but warmly supportive, could make sex wholesome and from whose example he could go on to a mature relation with a partner of his choice. This client's mother had evidently failed in that respect, or he would not seek a substitute and possible solace in a woman twice his age. "Of course the problem can also be a weak father . . ."

"It depends on what Sunday supplement you read," I agreed. "One Sunday it's the one, the next it's the other."

My thoughts were far away. Something had been plucking the back of my mind. This Bogomil, the producer. He would let an author bang away at a treatment without taking an option, without at least some kind of *advance*? I would go see him tomorrow, and ask him what his trouble was.

243

eight

Bogomil had very few characteristics, but those he had went far. One was a spluttering delivery like that of some Shakespearean actors famous for spraying the first three rows during impassioned speeches. Well, you thought when you got too near Bogomil, the farmers need it, and stepped back or out of range in some other way. It wasn't always easy, for a prowling restlessness kept him on the move when talking, especially in conference, so he could directly confront whoever he was addressing; one trait better appreciated when not accompanied by the other.

A worse nervous case was his sidekick, Prackup, who directed their pictures. He had little or no hair, as though it had all been torn out in bygone frenzies over versions never got right, deals never consummated. He had beautiful teeth, which he ground constantly. One look at him warned you that his nerves were a can of worms today, any day. The same was true of Bogomil though to a lesser degree. Both were men of voltage, and you could sense the currents running through them the instant you stepped into their presence. If you grasped the extended hand you might be electrocuted. There was a general aurora of power about them, but physical and artistic, not yet financial power. That would come later.

They were together when I kept my two o'clock appointment to meet them in the room of Bogomil's apartment that served as their office. Prackup took a matching armchair near mine, as though we had both come to see Bogomil rather than I the two of them. Bogomil came around from behind his desk and leaned against it, smiling at me above folded arms.

"What kind of parts have you played?"

"Mother parts."

"I see . . . Well, the mother role in this is rather . . . tough. Special, quite demanding. I don't know if . . ."

As he studied me the wild thought entered my mind to seize at the misunderstanding and audition for myself, which in some wild but not incredible mixup they thought I was there for. Why not? Real people, cinema vérité, it was all the thing today, to save money and make art honest.

"Do you have an agent?"

"Not yet."

"There's no script either."

"Then that gives us a bargaining basis. I can read from

the book. I'm familiar with the part. But one condition. If I'm not right, there will be no hard feelings prejudicing the main purpose of my call. I'm Osgood's mother, as I believe you —"

Bogomil nodded, eyes closed, as though the obvious must not detain us; we would get on with the audition for which I had come here assuming my pull gave me an inside track. "Where is our copy, Steve?" he asked Prackup, who readily produced one.

They both paced the floor as I read, their heads down and pulling underlips, ear lobes, noses, everything available. When I finished they smiled courteously and let me down with a gentleness that did Bogomil, who did the talking, credit as an actor in his own right. "Very interesting, but you're not" — sweetly he broke his hands apart — "the battleaxe type."

"I was afraid of that." I handed the anthology over to Bogomil. "Now then. My boy is working like a dog on this property without having seen the color of anybody's money. Nobody seems to be putting that where their mouth is. I don't think that's a respectable way for a producer to operate — even an independent one."

"Mrs. Wallop." He rolled a yellow pencil in long pale palms as he advanced on my chair. A full explanation of the facts followed, accompanied by a three-minute car wash. Everything was absolutely openly a gamble. They saw a good movie in *Duchess*, yes, provided somebody dug a script out of the book. They had told Ozzie that and no more. Taking a crack at the treatment that must

246

even precede the script was his own idea. Had they *asked* him to do one they'd of paid him at least a modest advance, as an option on the property. The script would be authorized if they liked the treatment, then the movie produced if they could get the money — from a major studio or a bank. "Nothing could be more iffy than this business," Bogomil concluded.

"How much would you pay him for a treatment?" I asked. "If you asked him to do one."

He shrugged. "Thousand or two. Twenty-five hundred."

"I'll give you the money to give him. Without mentioning me, or even letting him know I was here. That is an absolute condition. Supposing I make you out a check for a thousand dollars, in return for which I'm buying a share in the production if you go on to commission a script and make a movie. With an option to go in deeper if I want. Is that O.K.?"

They were mirror images of each other's shrugs. Then Prackup stood over me and became what I was destined to see a good deal of later: a director quizzing an actor about motivation. "Why are you doing this?"

"I said my boy was working like a dog. That's not quite true. He was, but now he's slacked off because there's nothing firm between you. This would put steam back in his engine, make him get his teeth into the job."

They agreed. Why not? What could they lose? The check made out to B. and P. Productions, we settled on preliminary arrangements to be incorporated in a letter of agreement which their lawyer would draw up and send to mine. "What's so funny?" asked Bogomil, seeing me smile. "Nothing." I just had a picture of "mine" sitting in shirtsleeves in his Appleton office reading what "theirs" had sent him, for I had decided to make it a surprise. When this thing actually began to cook and these birds got a load of Will Gerstenslager, a whole nother mixup got started in their heads. From thinking I was an actress, or would-be one, they got the idea that I was some business-woman from the sticks who had made her pile in a line of home-style relishes, or fruit preserves, on whose bottle labels they even swore they had seen my picture, complete with lace choker and hexagonal specs.

"Well, fine," I said at the door. "But remember, I'm the silent partner. Not a word of my coming here. Or of any future involvement. You break your promise and we'll see who's not the battleaxe type. Goodbye for now, then."

Osgood was working already when I got home. All he'd needed was the telephone call from Bogomil, put in the minute I left the office.

My problem at this point was twofold. Getting Osgood out evenings with Virgie was easy now that she spotted in him a possible winner in a field in which he might give her her Big Break. Keeping this Pilsudski cat away from him during the day so he could work was tougher. You will remember Bunk's collaboration with Warshawski in the piece we were adapting. That too was quite based on fact. Ozzie and Pilsudski had been batting away at a play, now put by as far as the one was concerned but still very much on the other's mind. I personally assigned myself the task of getting him out of the house when he showed up. By the time his rap sounded on the door after being buzzed in off the street, I would be fully dressed and waiting, my bag slung over my arm, to take him down to some bar or chili parlor to regale him with tales drawn from my rich background in human misery, as material for the comedies we both knew he had it in him to write. I have always wanted to say to these black humorists (not racially black but the other kind now in vogue), "Shucks, son, you don't have to empty a bucket of slops on my head, beat me about the ears with bags of garbage, and set off a stink bomb under my chair to show me life can be nasty. Just tear up my ticket to the garden show and blow the pieces in my face'll be enough." But I guess I got carried away, knowing that I'm no judge and styles in humor do change.

"There were these poor people, that the father was a known drunk and a suspected syphilitic, and the mother had varicose veins so bad she could hardly walk," I related as we slumped cozily facing one another in the booth of a joint where we had gone for a bowl of chili and a few beers, "living in a trailer camp on the outskirts of a little town near Appleton. One day their house caught fire. Some sort of explosion with bottled gas while the father was smoking a cigar in a drunken stupor. Luckily their daughter was in the hospital at the time with tonsilitis. Well, when the mother telephoned the fire department, she was told that one of their two pieces of equipment was out on an alarm in a nearby village while the other was stalled. They couldn't get the truck started. But learning that the "house" in question was a mobile home, they had a bright idea. Why didn't this party just drive this particular fire to the firehouse? Which they did, tearing down the highway sixty miles an hour — 'like a house afire' indeed. Now, the father being sprawled out blotto behind, the mother did the driving, and found she had a choice. A dilemma. If she maintained this speed, the wind would fan the flames to a degree where the trailer would be gone by the time they got there anyway, while to slow down to a crawl, eliminating that hazard, would, contrariwise, give the fire that much more time to spread. It was six of one and half a dozen of the other, with one's natural instinct winning the day: floor it. By the time the poor old woman got there her mobile home was gone, and so was her husband — incinerated on his cot."

Pilsudski nodded, sitting back for a suck on his beer. He seemed to like this, as far as I could tell. He seemed pleased by what he heard, and hungry for more. I was encouraged to go on.

"Here's another story about fire," I said, licking the foam from my lips after a gulp of my own beer. "Friend of mine — and Ozzie's, you can ask him if this isn't true — had a cottage on a lake in northern Michigan. He used it only as a summer resort. A friend of his wanted a place to stay during the fall and winter where he could start all over again with his wife. They were trying to save their marriage by fishing through the ice, walking five miles for their mail, and visiting local sawmills. All right. So, 'Go ahead, take it,' my friend says to his, with a casual laugh. 'All you can do is burn it down.' " I took a pull on my beer and looked around the bar. "He burned it down."

Pilsudski, as I say, seemed to like this material. Whether any of it could be worked into his purposes remained to be seen, of course. It was in any event not my problem. Mine was to relate things from my past life as they came to me. I usually tried to string these sessions out till four or five o'clock, when Ozzie would be through with his day's work and could be safely interrupted — if indeed Pilsudski wanted to come back to the apartment. Often he went straight home. But the next day there would be another rap on the door. "Let me in! I am a poet seeking his vision of eternal beauty. My clothes are in rags, my feet are bleeding, and I haven't eaten in seven languages. I mean I speak three days. Let me in, that I may sing you my verses in return for a crust of bread." Osgood would remain quiet as a mouse till I had got into my coat and plucked my bag off the chair, ready to pop into the hall and bundle the crazy nut down the stairs and into the street. Sometimes he would be on his Old Testament kick, mouthing dire prophecies in the manner of Isaiah and Jeremiah. "Ye wastrels and libertines, riding to and fro in cars of a hundred and fifty horsepower, even the horses of the Lord. His steeds shall tread thee down, yea the mighty stallions of his vengeance. Ye pollute the firmament therewith, and with noisome gases defile ye the air. From the proud chimneys ye have in your arrogance

251

reared high doth belch smoke as black as the wickedness of my people, yea a smoke that stinketh. Therefore, and because thy works too have been a stench in my nostrils, I shall hear ye not when ye pray. Wheezing and gasping will ye say, Wherewith shall we be saved, who shall redeem us now that we have befouled his holy firmament from the cities of the east to the valleys of the west? Where shall be found unguents to sweeten us now, yea sacrificial incense that shall arise through this pall and make our prayers acceptable unto the Most High? None, saith the Lord. Wheeze, gasp, and stink away. I am phasing you out."

Pilsudski often looked the part when he jabbered away in this vein, a regular Lamentations of Jeremiah. Once in particular I sensed he was lower than a snake's belly, as we use to say, the instant I stepped into the hall and saw him waiting there for me in a Navy blue pea jacket, turtleneck sweater and knit cap. Negroes generally to my knowledge aren't guilty of the perverse practice of making you depressed just because they are, but I guess today his white blood came out. He was going to give me a hard time, I could see that as we walked down the street. A light snow was falling, and once or twice he rolled his eyes heavenward, as though to remind the powers that be that he knew it was all a swindle, and he was not going to be bought off with a few flakes uniformly dissolving in the muck of the pavements, however unlike they were as they fluttered briefly down to earth. I abandoned the "material" angle, and just tried to cheer him up.

"You and Ralph spoke of hoping to get up to New England for some skiing," I said. "Would you believe I did some skiing once?"

"Oh, yeah?"

"Fact. Broke my leg in two places."

"Yeah?"

"Yeah. Stowe and Kitzbewl."

At last the screen treatment was finished, and high time I'd say, what with Noel Coward needing only four days to toss off *Private Lives*.

Well, Bogomil and Prackup liked it, and would authorize a script for the venture immediately — had they the money. Independent production companies all have to borrow from the banks, or from the larger studios who in turn have to borrow from the banks, at steep interest rates, movies all being risk investments. They were in conference and on the phone about it for several days, with no luck. Finally I went back to their office and asked them point-blank: "How much do you need?"

"Not much," said Bogomil. "It takes very few sets, and a lot of it can be shot outside in town here. Prackup has some friends on Long Island who'd let us have their house and their garage guest apartment for interior shots, and their grounds and beach for the water stuff. You're familiar with that new angle?" Osgood's treatment now had the flashbacks all done as scenes in the boy's life flashing through his mind while drowning, or nearly drowning until his mother jumps in and saves him. The death is turned to birth: he is literally born again, water being a birth symbol and the sea of course the original life matrix, since everything began there. Hauling the hero half-conscious back to shore offered a chance to use surrealist techniques such as even far-out films had hardly scratched. Bogomil especially could scarcely contain his excitement at the wedding of photography, color and sound that might here be realized. Dubbing in "subaqueous Debussy-like music" to semi-abstract full-color negatives that had been marinated, baked and fried in special laboratory equipment would produce delirious effects that would send the customers reeling through the lobby into the streets like bats into the dusk. "This can be goo, these special effects, or they can be the glories you saw in 2001. But to go on answering your question. Movies are expensive, but they don't all cost three million dollars. *Lions Love* was shot for under a quarter of a million. We might do even better. Say — oh, maybe two hundred thousand."

There was considerable ocean spray connected with this explanation, and I moved to another chair as was my right under marine law. "I think I can put up the capital," I said. "Under two or three slight conditions. One. You've given Miss Quilty a screen test. She's pretty, but can she act?"

Bogomil shook his head compassionately. "No."

I concealed my relief at this fact. So far so good. She would remain dependent on Ozzie's good graces for any breaks. The next question was also important since I wanted her embedded in the project somehow. "But she'd be O.K. for a bit part? Somewhere?"

"I suppose so." Bogomil was beginning to look at me a little skeptically. "What next?"

"Osgood is to write the script — with collaboration if you decide to call that in. We won't meddle there. I'll leave all that to your judgment. But I want to stay with the production as technical adviser."

"Technical adviser?" he asked, quite baffled now. "On what?"

"I'm a mother." I leaned back and shook out my furs. "I don't want credit or anything like that. I just want to be associated with this production. Which I'm financing. I cannot be absolutely certain of this until I've had a discussion with my lawyer, who is also my financial adviser, about my assets. But I'll call him tonight, and I think I can have him flown out here tomorrow, or the next day at the latest."

Will looked awful when he stepped off the plane. Worse than the morning on the train. Than the time he picked up the tab at the Niçoise, a month or so before.

"Emma, what in the Sam Hill has gotten into you? That nest egg Frank left you for your — Let's get my luggage."

He was neat enough in the everlasting gray-blue suits favored by middle-aged men from the Midwest, but an overcoat always tended to dishevel him a little. A slight stoop made a gap between the collar and his thin shoulder-blades, and there was always a stray muffler-end coming out of the lapels. The apple cheeks were pale green rather than rosy Jonathan now, and his fedora had more than the customary two dents in it. As we stood waiting for his luggage he puffed out his cheeks and blew like somebody extinguishing a birthday cake. He rocked on his heels and said to the ceiling, "Sell her Bailey Instruments to sink the money in a picture show."

"We'll talk in the bus."

But the bus was so crowded that when he started in there I insisted we wait till we got to his hotel. With the head of steam built up inside him, though, I saw that this was impossible if not unwise, so I merely drew the line on money matters, and let him get off his chest, in as quiet a voice as he was able, a lot of things he had been saving up to say about my present "shenanigans and gyrations" of which this contemplated financial folly was only one aspect, of a piece with the "ways I had fallen into." He criticized the intellectual click I was hanging around with, the jet setters who could leave me without the price of a subway token. Coming from an old friend known for liking to cut a swathe, at least by back-home standards, this gave me pause. I wondered if I hadn't been going too far and getting in too deep (the resolve to help Osgood over a stile aside). I was momentarily sobered. Then something got my back up.

"I talked to Nellie Outfatten — she telephoned me about some business matter," Will remarked, "and in the course of the conversation she said everybody in town knows and is talking about the colored fellow you've been seen running around with."

256

"Nellie's got one hangup. She can't hang up. Which ear is cauliflowered again, the right?"

"Now Em —"

"Will, you're the salt of the earth, but you've got a lot to learn. You're naïve in many ways."

"Oh, God." He swiveled wretchedly about on his seat and looked out the window. "I don't even understand what you're doing half the time. Like now. What is that kind of clawing the air with two fingers of each hand? I see Ralph and them doing it at the dinner at the Niçoise."

"It's putting things in quotes. I put them around 'the salt of the earth,' just now. It means the same as saying 'quote unquote.' Everyone's doing it this year."

"I'm taking you back to Appleton with me. In time for Christmas!"

"Tell me, how are things in Appleton? Is the Christo-rama up yet? Have you been skating in the park? Is this the first Nellie Outfatten has heard of salt and pepper?"

"Salt and pepper?"

"Mixed dating."

"Will we *ever* get to the Biltmore?"

New York's normal congestion becomes impossible at Holiday time. The driver kept barking at cabbies and pedestrians who barked back at him. There are simply too many people. Man is not a species intended by Nature to swarm. We're not bees. So when we are forced to swarm, we sting.

But at last we were in his quarters at the Biltmore where,

257

having called room service to send up two chicken sandwiches, and a little something from the bar to oil our
hinges, we had it out. I led off with a sizeable beef of my
own.

"Why did you let me think over the telephone that
Bailey Instruments had dropped from 82 to 56? When in
fact it split in my absence, naturally dropping to 41 as a
result, but climbing right back up to 56 again. Why did
you let me worry all this time, till a broker I called here
about it straightened me out, that it had split two for one
again? Huh, Will?"

"I'm trying to save you from yourself." He heaved himself out of his armchair with a force that propelled him halfway across the room. "Emma, Frank bought you those
shares at 2½, a gamble even at that price for a new growth
company like that in an industry still untried. But he
wanted to leave them to you for your old age, and I'm not
going to see you shoot craps with them on a damned
movie!"

"Frank shot craps with the money, which is what you
just as much as said. The one gamble paid off, why not
the other?"

"Odds double themselves when you take a chance on
them twice in a row. And stop twisting my words! If
you want to re-invest your money, fine. Take it out of
Bailey and put it into the integrated garden apartments
they're going to put up in Appleton. If you're so interested
in salt and pepper."

"I'll put the profits from the movie into the apartments."

"Ach!" He stood at the window flapping his arms, as though he might try at any moment to take off and fly away. Seeing my mind was made up, he finally turned and said, "All right. But I won't let you sell the stock — at least not unless you have to. Here's my idea. You borrow the money from the bank with the stock put up as collateral. If it should drop to where the bank has to close you out, or nibble into you, well, you've still got this maybe investment. If it keeps going up, fine, and we'll in any case pray you break close enough to even on the movie to repay the loan. Say after a year." He lit a cigar which he began to wave threateningly at me like a weapon. "But you're not borrowing the full two hundred and forty thousand the stock is worth. No siree, Bob. Two hundred thousand is the limit. I insist. That'll allow a rough forty-thousand-dollar leeway for temporary fluctations, and interest. And may God have mercy on your soul."

There was a rap on the door just then — four knocks like the opening notes of Beethoven's Fifth that are said to represent Fate beating on the door. But it was only room service with our chicken sandwiches. As we fell to, I seemed to sense that Will and I, now that the decision had been made and the roulette wheel was spinning, had produced a kind of emotional exchange. I became infected with his apprehension and he with my excitement. "The day of the high-budget picture is on the wane," I said. "Lots of movies are now made on a shoelace, and some of them are winners." He nodded, his mouth full of food and a glass of beer at his lips. His spirits rose even more when

I said, "Oh, by the way, you're invited to a dinner tonight with the whole crowd. Osgood's taking us out. We're celebrating."

Osgood threw his party at an Upper West Side place called Basil's. I naturally watched Virgie closely all evening, and was interested to note a kind of bossiness had crept into her attitude toward Osgood. At one point, when he thought he would have a coquille for an appetizer after having said he wanted the trout amandine for a main course, she said, "Oh, Ozzie, don't order fish for an an appetizer if you're going to have it later." He nodded compliantly, and studied the menu some more. It was the same way in the general discussions. Once the talk got around to a new book by a young friend of some of them, which everybody knocked (evidently another novel of the more-multilevel-than-thou school) except for Ozzie. "I rather liked it," he said, and Virgie, "Oh, for God's sake, Ozzie." This struck me as a good sign. She was becoming possessive. At such times he might grin sheepishly, but there was more than sheepishness there; mainly you detected a boyish pride in having such a smasher think enough of him to treat him like her property. She was stuck on him. For what reason I didn't care, not caring to look a gift horse in the mouth. She was stuck on him like a label on a bottle. That was all that mattered. Randy, who was with us, frowned at this development. He was so morose that everyone tried to cheer him up, being in the general fallout from his mood. "What are you doing these days, Randy?" someone asked, and he said, "Trying to hit the right keys," and finished off his martini. He hadn't really been interested in Virgie as a permanent connection. But his ego required that he call the tune. We've all got a little of the "You can't fire me, I quit," in us. It's only human. Randy was especially that way, if I knew him. He was furious with Virgie, and in his anger lashed out at Marshall McLuhan.

"Television 'tactile'! It's not even *visual*." He glared around the table as though defying anyone to disagree with him. "That is our quarrel with television, is it not? That it isn't visual enough? It cannot make us *see* Jeeves entering the drawing room, 'a procession of one.' It cannot make us see the woman in *Dorian Gray* whose dresses always looked as though they had been designed in a rage and put on in a tempest. It cannot make us see Dickens's Mrs. Gamp whose neck is so short that she has trouble looking over herself, or the woman in Henry James who appeared to have developed her character as she had her figure, by riding cross-country. Much less can it begin to make us see the old man in Faulkner's *Sanctuary* with eyes like clots of phlegm, or certainly, God knows, Temple Drake at the end of the book in the Luxembourg Gardens, seeming to follow with her eyes the waves of band music — how does that marvelous last sentence go again? — 'across the pool and the opposite semicircle of trees where at sombre intervals the dead tranquil queens in stained marble mused, and on into the sky lying prone and vanquished in the embrace of the season of rain and death.' Never, never, never can television make us see the

261

character in Ring Lardner who served 'what he thought was good Scotch, though he may have been deceived by some flavor lurking in his beard,' or the poor egg in Max Beerbohm whose black hat and cloak were Bohemian in intention though clerical in effect."

There was a silence following this brisk and telling spiel (which I thought it was a pity they had missed in Appleton!) during which we all sat awed, even a little cowed. Then Osgood leaned across the table and said:

"Or the father in *Don't Look Now, Medusa*, with the single tuft of hair left on his head, 'like the divots he hacked up with his clubs on the local golf course.' I see what you mean, Randy. That kind of seeing requires transmission from one mind to another via the printed page. Linear type is not dead!"

I chimed in with my own bit. "Much less can it make us see the woman, also in *Medusa*, whose husband bought her a new car so annually that she even came to have a new-car smell, my dear Randy."

The compliments restored his mood. A gracious feeling spread among us. The party percolated along beautifully. Virgie was in her element. The Best Restaurants, sum it up in that phrase, but with all that it implies in a general way of life. Other proofs of her influence did not pass unnoticed. She had got Ozzie to shave off his beard and at least landscape his hair. Now only the mustache remained — and of course the dense sideburns, but they were common on men just then. Like pillars. Supporting the temples, ha. Even Will Gerstenslager had them, though with his hoary locks they looked like side orders of coldslaw. In Ozzie's case they helped confer the authority with which he played host. To a party everyone hated to break up. But disband we did around midnight, and finding myself momentarily alone with Virgie Quilty in the foyer I took the opportunity to drive in another nail.

"Look," I whispered, drawing her to one side, "we must have another heart-to-heart talk, but right now I wish somebody would tell Osgood not to throw his money around. Oh, not this thing tonight. This is nothing. But things like backing the production."

She opened her mouth in the soundless gasp women have (and some confusing spring warblers). "He's *financing* it?"

I shrugged. "It's his money. Family money is family money, and after sitting on it like a miser all your life you expect your offspring to get lavish with it. Maybe that's better. We're here to live our lives. And if he wants to put his money into pictures and then help people into them he's personally interested — Oh, my goodness, I've made a booboo. This is news to you. Then that means he doesn't *want* you to know, or anybody, he's the power behind the — Oh, Lord, I've done it now. You must forget I ever mentioned this. Mum's the word. Here come the men now. You don't know a thing. We'll talk later. That's a stunning outfit."

It consisted of a muskrat greatcoat slung over a pants suit of tartan plaid, crinkle patent boots with a side zipper, and a white knitted wool ragamuffin cap in a crunchy open

263

stitch, from either side of which her gold hair streamed. A patent-leather feedbag on one shoulder completed the ensemble — the bag of the year to keep milady's purse and compact in. I could remember my father's horse eating out of one. Even Will Gerstenslager's striped shirts and wide election-bet ties were once again where it was at.

Snow was falling as we sauntered down the street.

"This won't amount to anything," Will said, sniffing the air with his weather-wary nose. "Just dandruff."

"No," I remarked, "we don't get blizzards like we use to." As we strolled along, a gay group putting out our tongues to catch the flakes, sophisticates having fun that others turned to glance at, I remembered a favorite poem of Randy's from the old days on 312 Crown. "Like Villon says, 'Where are the snows of yesteryear?'"

"That's not what he means, Mother," Osgood called from behind, where he was walking arm in arm with Virgie. I thought I caught the sound of Virgie shushing him, and with it I imagined her jerking on his sleeve. But he went right on. "He's expressing the ephemeralness of everything. Not bragging about the size of the blizzards they once had, for God's sake."

"*Oz.*" It was faint but audible, and its meaning was unmistakable. Virgie's bossing whisper, jumping on him for correcting his mother. Good for her. We would make a man of him yet.

nine

Osgood's screen treatment, if you will remember, let creep into the story line elements not present in the book. Hostility toward the mother was made to conceal affection for her, evinced by letting her jump into the water to save her drowning son. The actual scenario went a step further. The movie would show, for the first time anywhere, they said it couldn't be done, incest on the screen. In a dream sequence, but incest, not sibling incest — that's old hat — but Oedipal. Mother and son would be portrayed naked, making love, in bed.

I was back home in Appleton when the script reached me, flown out by Bogomil. I dropped what I was doing at the time, planning a tea at the church Ladies Aid for the benefit of our missionary society, and boarded the first plane I could catch for New York.

"Well, I thought you'd be in Sweden by this time, shooting this compost heap," I says, dropping the script on his desk. "This is out. I was all for him loving his mother — it was my idea — but not on this scale. We're scrubbing the project."

"You don't have script approval," Bogomil smiled. (Conrad Veidt, remember him?) "I just extended you the courtesy of showing you a copy."

"It's not script approval I'm exercising. It's script disapproval."

He turned for support to Prackup, who sat in a corner of the office with his head in his hands. Prackup emitted a muffled groan, as much as to say he wasn't up to handling newances today.

"All right. It comes to the same thing," said Bogomil. "But we as producers have to have artistic say or it's chaos. This picture is not for the whole family."

"Have you read the script!"

"We're participating in a contemporary trend in order to travesty it. This is satire. We disapprove of what we're doing."

"Oh, if I could believe that."

"You can. Can't she?" Prackup raised his head long enough to nod it, without actually taking his hands away from his face. They disapproved of what they were doing.

"Including when he mounts his mother from behind?"

"Especially when he mounts his mother from behind. There is no excuse for that. We're all in this up to our necks, but we have to be outrageous or we will outrage.

In order not to offend, *we must go too far*. It's a fine point. Did you by any chance see an English movie about an aviator breaking the sound barrier? Ralph Richardson keeps sending his son-in-law up on test flights. Each time, as he approaches the sound barrier, the ship vibrates and shudders as though it's going to fall apart. So each time he exercises caution and pulls the speed stick back. Then he thinks, 'Maybe I should push it all the way *forward*. Take a chance.' He does and wins — breaks the sound barrier, and all is well. So it is with this. Pussyfoot and we're lost. Get gingerly about it and we're sunk before we dive in. *Doctor Strangelove* gambled on so unlikely a themo for laughter as atomic holocaust, and won. Only because they were bold and went all the way. So must we. No hedging, no apologies. Blithely lay it in their laps. Tell me, have you read the *Odyssey*? Homer?"

"Yes."

"What did you think of it?"

"I thought it excellent."

"There's a line in it, 'An honest business never blush to tell.' I nail my flag to that mast. Have you had lunch? I want to hear all about the pickling business."

Osgood of course got the idea from our visit to the marriage counselor, the klutz who thought we were having an affair. He simply developed it from there. He had Bunk, in the script now, feel edgier than ever toward his mother after such a session, but with new overtones. They go home and start picking at each other. He senses it is like a lovers' quarrel, and in the hostility begins to feel the flickerings of actual erotic desire, as in a normal bond. When they kiss and make up, there goes the ball game. Or it's a whole new ball game, as I believe the term goes. They share a bottle of wine, talk of the things he's learned at her knee, and before they know it he has his hand *on* her knee. They doze by the fire, and — in his dream at least, which merges surrealistically with hers, you're never quite sure — they become lovers. They stand naked before each other and know it is to be. The Phaedra legend in modern dress. You will recall from your classic mythology that the son, Hippolytus, was falsely accused by his stepmother, Phaedra, of ravishing her. All right. Theseus the father, understandably peeved, called upon Poseidon for revenge, and that god sent a sea monster which so terrified Hippolytus's horses that they dragged him to death. That ties in with our sea motif — the mother rescuing the drowning son to kick off the movie in the series of flashbacks in which the hero's life unreels in his mind. The mother has a child, who is of course her own grandson, the father, Bunk, siring his own half-brother and one thing and another, with a few other complications not covered by Homer etc., but never mind. We have all got to go on trying to find *the usable myth for our time.* Our best writers are trying to help us do that, from Randy Rivers to James Joyce, passing on their best intuitions in this area to we readers, who continue to cheer them on while pursuing the quest on our own. Of which more later. The breakthrough with the mother enables the son in our story to resolve the hangup that has been impeding his relationships with other women and in particular with the girl, with whom in the final fadeout he is seen running naked, hand in hand, into the sea — our first mother again, and the eternal generative principle — against a musical background that our composer said he wanted to make "purposely reminiscent" of Debussy, something of his called *La Mare*, as I caught it. Something like that.

So that is how, one bright morning in early July, we were all gathered for the first day of shooting around a swimming pool on Long Island.

It was the private estate of these friends of Prackup's, with this wonderful pool only a few hundred feet from the ocean. This made it economically convenient to shoot water sequences in either place, for we found some of the closeups were better handled in the pool. In the guest apartment over the garage we very easily simulated the grubby-Village-flat interior in which Bunk holes up with the child, though for some actual street scenes we would have to truck back to New York, as well as for sets requiring the studio we rented there. We stayed on location in Long Island three weeks, always with onlookers gaping at us through the windows of the house, friends of the owners, or neighborhood people rubbering from the road, where a local cop was finally posted to keep traffic moving. Movies and movie-making are inevitably glamorous, and I suppose we were a rather fabulous little group, both when we were shooting and when we could relax between or after takes. It was the summer we were all drinking Madeira on the rocks and playing Chinese checkers, lying on our stomachs around the pool or on the beach. There would always be a gay crowd coming up from the Hamptons or somewhere to join us after work, when we would push on to Emile's or the Seven Rocks or another of the restaurants having a vogue there at the moment. This together with the rich lunches catered to us by truck each day had a lot of us wearing those Slim-O-Matic belts around our middles. Their leatherette pockets filled with lead pellets weigh a good ten pounds, so it's no wonder they reduce your waistline by strengthening your abdominal muscles. Bogie and Prackup wore them all day long, as did several of the crew and some of the cast. Sashaying around there with these belts on we looked like we were shooting a Western. The fad in the company was started by Lena Bascombe, the actress who was playing me.

I did not like this woman. Too much of a tartar for my taste. I immediately didn't cotton to her. She didn't get along with anybody but the pickets — for we were picketed over some slight jurisdictional thing, nothing to worry a liberal. The girl playing Mary Hackney was a delight, and I was glad to see Virgie Quilty's eyes turn green at the sight of Osgood hitting it off with her. Virgie had this bit part, but was used as a stand-in for the actress playing Mary. This practice is unusual, and probably even a little irregular, but the producers were keeping their promise to cut corners wherever possible. Ralph Frawley dressed everyone for a very small fee, and everyone took his costumes, or his advice about what to wear from private wardrobes, cheerfully, except for Lena Bascombe. She tried to doll up, forgetting she was playing a frump. Not that her own tastes in clothes were so far off the mark! And as for perfumes, lucky that scent she wore didn't photograph. It knocked me over every time I got within noseshot of her. When it came to her performance, she was not going to capsize anybody, but she was adequate. She was adequate.

I was interested to note that this number also graveled our poor Prackup. Every time I approached him on a scene with her, with a suggestion as technical adviser on how a mother would react, or to explain a woman's motivation, he would seem to be grinding his teeth and saying under his breath, "Get that woman —" as though the rest would be "out of my hair" or "off my back." I had to guess it, because he lowered his voice when I drew near, obviously not wanting it to get around that there was friction between him and a featured player. That sort of thing is bad for morale among a company. He told me at last that suggestions should come before shooting, certainly no later than line rehearsal from script, and I agreed, but said that sometimes faults or fallacies in the way actors were doing something didn't appear till the cameras were rolling — and there were almost inevitably retakes into which changes could be tucked. That was the case in a scene in which the mother was telling someone, "We have a boy and two girls." Something didn't ring right, especially for that character, and between the eighth and ninth take (Lena Bascombe was always blowing her lines) I started forward into the set to tell Prackup that the light had dawned,

271

tripping over wires as I did so. He sat in his canvas chair and listened to me with bowed head, a hand to his brow. "Most women will say, 'I have such and such children,' rather than 'We,' even with a husband sitting right there. Mine remarked on it once at a party — well, party, just a few friends we had in for coffee and dessert and an evening of gibble-gabble — and it was the oddest thing, all the men laughed and nodded agreement. Their wives did it too, come to think of it. Women do say that. They're the custodians of life, brought it into the world, often with pain and travail, and so why shouldn't they be proprietorial about it. But the point is, it certainly should be a character touch for one as possessive as her."

I turned and picked my way among the cameras and lighting and sound equipment back to my own canvas chair, hearing whispered snatches of the old refrain, Prackup hissing, on the remains of his sanity, "If somebody doesn't . . . that woman . . ." The cause of this conniption fit returned from the washroom to which she had briefly excused herself to go, and was given the line change, which she managed to master. But my patience with her fell as my sympathy for Prackup rose, poor devil, with everything a director has on his mind under shooting-schedule pressure, to say nothing of the paper work to be done evenings in preparation for the next day.

Prackup had a novel way of keeping fit.

There was a nearby golf course where he jogged eighteen holes every day. A wedding of two forms, you might say. Golfing is a bore and so is jogging, but running around a links has a certain flavor to it, with a sense of progress from flag to flag, whilst affording pleasant scenery as well. So he ran eighteen holes. When I heard about this I watched him through binoculars to see if he jogged them without stopping, and of course he didn't. Or always run the full eighteen, for that matter. It was a good two miles around even this small course. But there he was every day when he could get a break, chugging from hole to hole in sweat pants and sweat shirt, heading for a cool destination in the clubhouse shower, to which he was given special privileges as a friend of our host, who was a member there. He would stop every four or five holes for a rest, sometimes bypassing a few to keep out of the way "of halfwits knocking balls around in what they delude themselves into regarding as exercise," but after only a very short break he would be up and steaming along again. He claimed that in addition to the physical workout it shook up his brains, and gave him lots of his best ideas. I decided to try it myself.

I made no bones about needing more than a Slim-O-Matic belt, hardly a form of exercise. I was indeed taking off a little girth, but no weight. Such a rig only turns flab into muscle. So I too would slip away from location when there was a lull in the shooting for the lighting technicians to set up a new scene or something, and run at least nine holes. It was a very pretty course, with some especially idyllic spots in the first few holes, such as a spur of beeches to form a dogleg in the second, and just beyond that a stream with a charming wooden bridge across it.

I liked to steam around the dogleg and head along that fairway toward the bridge, cross it and sit down for a bit.

I was taking five there when, looking up, I see a familiar figure in sweat suit and sneakers tooling toward me. He gave no sign of recognizing me, behind his thick sunglasses, but as he dogtrotted past where I was I thought it only sociable to fall in beside him. Which I did. He was gnashing his teeth and groaning, so I figured he must be having his troubles again with La Bascombe, that burdensome old bag. Some muttering here about "kill me yet" and "the death of me."

"I had an idea for that P.O.V. shot of the boy in the kitchen," I said, settling into my stride beside the tomato-faced Prackup. Some sequences are photographed from a certain set point of view, usually that of a character. We call that a P.O.V. shot. "Bunk is in bed, made impotent by the thought of his mother. Fine. So far so good. Mary Hackney gets up to poke around the room, and as he watches her arrange some flowers in a vase we fade back to a boyhood memory of the time when from the kitchen window he saw his mother make his father plant a whole iris bed over again because he's done it wrong. Buried the rhizomes instead of leaving them exposed on the surface. I don't think that's de-balling enough, Prackup, even allowing for the phallic symbol you get in there with the horizontal stems of the rhizomes. Even with your idea the boy only sees the scene in pantomime and we don't hear the dialogue outside there in the yard. Would you like to hear my idea for a memory shot that's more castrating?"

Prackup made a strangled sound in his throat, which I took to be a grunt of affirmation. But I sensed that he was letting his problems give him too hard a time. I let him have my thinking on the subject.

The reason the scene wasn't moving, and you can feel these things in your bones while they're being shot, you don't have to look at the rushes — or "dailies" as we now call them — the reason it was laying there was because Lena Bascombe wasn't communicating enough sly malice in making the husband do something all over again as punishment for his incompetence. Osgood had drew on his memory in recalling the scene, but now I drew on mine in roughly outlining a substitute. We had a tomcat who was so vicious that when my husband, Frank, put him out for the night, he would always draw on leather gloves so the beast wouldn't claw him to shreds. Gauntlets yet, covering him to the wrists. I said the damned cat wouldn't scratch me, I'd fix him if he did, and with that scooped the animal up and set him outside with no trouble at all. You had to let them know who was boss.

"Let this be the castrating memory," I suggested as we puffed along. Prackup had fallen back a step, and I eased my stride to accommodate him. We were both sweating like Swiss cheeses, for the day was warm. "That a neat tie-in? That emasculating? Because she can then cast a sly grin around at both husband and son, which he now remembers as a grown adult and confuses all women with. You can trip it off by having him watch Mary give her kitty milk, rather than arrange flowers. That way you can have both the establishing shot and the memory flashback in the kitchen. That gives you more consistency. What do you think? The cat is an unaltered male."

Prackup staggered a few more steps and fell face forward into a sand bunker. He resembled the delirious desert travelers who pitch downward and scoop up sand thinking it's water. I didn't like the looks of this at all. He kind of moved his palms around in it in little circles, making little sounds in his throat for all the world like death rattles. Lucky thing I was around, in case there was an occurrence. Why did men always seem to be dying in my arms, dropping like flies? He laid there heaving away, with his brow on his forearm. Some people overdo the health kick. Unevenly sunburnt and peeled, he looked like scraped toast. "Why do you run eighteen holes?" I said, settling down beside him to get my own wind. "What are you trying to prove? Do you want to kill yourself?" He nodded dumbly into the crook of his elbow. We were both pretty much out of breath, and the conversational ball wasn't exactly rolling. He did finally sit up, swinging around, and, mopping the sweat from his face with the sleeve of his shirt, he said he tried to keep up his jog daily because otherwise there was no point to it. Taking this break, we looked around the links, our attention presently brought to a hole where a party watched a man sink a long putt and then dance around the flag when he made it. When we got our breath back, Prackup said he would bear my suggestion in mind, and perhaps take it up with the others. He gazed up at the sky, his teeth bared in a grimace. Thin high cirrus clouds hung in otherwise clear blue, making the dome of heaven resemble veined marble.

"There's something else I want to talk about," I said.

He flopped over backward with his arms outspread, like someone crucified.

"It's the opening scene. I hear you're not satisfied with it."

He became serious.

"No, I'm not. It needs a more wildly ironic — oh, crazy kind of kickoff. Something . . ." He paused for the right word, and even when he had it he wanted to qualify it. "Existential, call it that. An insanely apt commentary on life that at the same time outdoes and satirizes all the commentaries that have become part *of* that life today. It's a fine point." He paused to look up at the sky, making a pillow under his head with his fist. "When you are taking something off you are artistically obliged to produce a good example of what you are taking off. The sooner you do that in a movie the better, and I would like the very opening shot to kick us wildly into orbit."

"I'll think about it," I said. "Come on, last one to the eighteenth is a rotten egg."

We settled into our dogtrot again. "A dramatic device, but not a mere gimmick," Prackup said as we galloped down the fairway. "A gag if necessary, fine. But not merely that. A kind of parable of our time."

"A gag but not merely that," I repeated, as my homework. "A gag that is a parable of our time."

"Preferably a sight laugh."

"A sight laugh."

We pounded steadily along over the summer turf.

Ah, the memories of that summer. The bright particular moments. Of Virgie so happy as a clam to be doing her bit before the camera, a mere walk-on, but never mind. Fetching in her Bikini on the beach or around the pool. Or in it, swimming into your ken, as the poet says. She had a walk as begiling as the Renault. Remember her from the scholars I granted the interview that time, when all this got started? The girl with the motor in back? Virgie was no slouch for sexiness either, if it came to that. One look gave you the minimum daily requirement. I had to laugh at the extremes to which she went to stay slim though. I have one impression of her eating a hot dog the day the catering truck served them for lunch. She nibbled it from side to side so as to eat only the weiner, leaving the bread. She looked like somebody playing a mouth organ.

Pilsudski kept turning up, spouting dire Old Testament prophecies.

"And thy money shall dwindle even as it increaseth. As it now taketh a quarter to buy what a nickel once did, so shall the day be not far hence, saith the Lord, when it will require of thee a dollar. And at last even that shall be of none effect, yea avail thee nought. Ye shall wave your bills and say to the merchants, Give us bread and meat herewith for ourselves and our children, and oil for our lamps. But the merchants shall turn away, each unto his own way. Neither shall the merchants themselves lay up meat and fine raiment. For there shall be no more furs in the stores where once ye bedecked your women, that each might stroke the skins of beasts slain for her vanity and

278

say to her neighbor, See, I am better bedizened than thee, and me shall the eyes ogle and not thee. For the fox and the marten shall inhabit these stores, yea come down from the wilderness and the woods to whelp freely among their ruins, in the day of the desolation of my people, saith the Lord. Among their walls where the wind whistleth shall the mink and the leopard freely roam, even the otter that slideth down into the water, as my people hath slidden down into their iniquity. From the sleek boulevards of the east shall ye no longer obtain fine raiment; nay, ye shall go humbly again to the heartland, to the southland, yea to the corny places, and there obtain thy raiment in stores open Thursday evenings until nine.

"Oh, why could ye not be worthy of your heritage! For now must the coon too stalk the land, seeking his own and crying out against the oppressor, smiting him with sticks and stones, and putting to the torch those stores in whose windows yet hang the few furs that remain, only the rabbit and the skunk that even none can buy. For I shall surely bloat thy currency, saith the Lord. Then shalt thou know that I am Almighty, and not the dollar."

He was immediately taken up by the fashionable set.

Then Will Gerstenslager flew out for a weekend, dressed in one of the suits that showed every sign of having been bought in stores open Thursday evenings until nine. He did nothing to spike the rumor that I owned a canning factory where I put out a line of Ma Wallop's cottage preserves. It might be a good thing to go into on the profits from this flick, if any. It gave me intense personal pleasure to see how tickled he was to be part of the group, especially that Sunday when, unwinding from a tense week of shooting, we plumped down with picnic hampers on the beach. A gay bunch from the Hamptons choppered over, setting their helicopter down in a nearby field, something they couldn't do on shooting days because of the sound. Many's the take killed by airplanes overhead, or passing cars. We had seen the dailies of a speedboat chase scene shot the week before. I had just had to tell Prackup what I felt. "I thought the chase scene static," I said. He looked at me with a blank expression. Then his eyes seemed to go glazed. "Chase scene static," he muttered to himself. He walked around in circles, staring at the ground, and re- peating it to himself, interpolating things like "unprece- dented" and "ought to be a first." It was very odd. I be- came alarmed about him again, and to encourage him said, "Maybe we ought to skip-frame it." That's a technique we have for speeding things up by cutting out every other frame in the reel for that sequence. But he didn't listen, but wandered off along the beach, staring down at the sand and babbling about Oscars and achieving the impos- sible and other like curious things. I shook my head and re- joined my group.

There were seven or eight there breaking out the fried chicken and deviled eggs and uncorking bottles of chilled rosé. We didn't watch our diets on weekends, though some of us hitched on our Slim-O-Matic belts. I was about to have more important things to worry about than my figure; for in a very few minutes an incident developed that nearly cost me my life, though it saved the picture.

One in our party was Lena Bascombe. I decided I should be more tolerant of her, more charitable toward her. She had lost a lot of the looks for which she had been famous as a juvenile, and was going to muscle certainly, if not fat. She fussed constantly with her makeup and could not pass a mirror without glancing nervously into it. "Don't worry about the lines in your face," I said. "Gray hairs will come to soften them. Nature is wonderful that way." But all the good my assurances did. Concern about the very things that suited her to this first mother's role in her career made her turn in a pretty average performance. She would start the day's work with a bang, then about two, two-thirty, begin getting insecure. To offset blowing lines and being ordered around, she would order around the current stud, of which she was said to always have one in tow. "Dan! Get the aspirin from my bag there, will you? *There*, for God's sake." Or, "Danny, run into town and mail this letter for me, like a good boy." Today he moved around straightening the beach towel she was lying on, brushing sand from it, lighting her cigarettes and refilling her wineglass. The various ministrations offered a chance to show off the rocks in his slingshot, which threatened to burst with every move. All this while a parallel flirtation was going on between Lena Bascombe and the lifeguard, a handsome blond Adonis who had jollied it up with our groups from the first. He had joined our particular picnic, and from the way things looked, Lena might be grooming him for the next stud. He lacked the rocks in his slingshot the present incumbent sported, but his physique was magnificent. His chest and shoulder muscles rippled like serpents under skin tanned mahogany. Lena had been bugging Bogomil and Prackup to put him in one of the scenes for background. There were other matters of interest to me at the moment.

"Should you be eating this much?" I asked. "On duty?"

"It's my lunch hour," he smiled.

I had spotted him an hour before tucking in his share of fried chicken with another group, but let it pass. He was a fop. A naked fop. There are those.

"And I didn't have any breakfast," he said, his teeth still bared around a drumstick. "Besides, nothing ever happens here."

He fixed that himself personally. Stretching out beside the ever appreciative Lena, he rolled over on his tummy for a snooze. There was nobody in the water at the moment. By now we had capsized three or four bottles of Tavel and were all pretty glutted. Some of us dozed off. Cries and splashes indicated several bathers had entered the water, and the lifeguard instinctively came to. He sat up, gazing out across the sparkling surface of the Sound. For I should add that this was the northern shore of Long Island with its relatively placid waters, not the oceanside where the surf pounded. He rose.

"Think I'll go in for a dip," he said down to Lena. "Coming?"

"Later," she murmured, flicking his heel with a downward dawdling hand.

We all watched Adonis walk into the sea, dive in and melt among the bathers. We settled down to our conversation or our naps. The afternoon had a lazy, droning, siesta air about it.

I don't know when I became aware of a faint hubbub at the water's edge. It was suddenly split by a voice shouting, "Somebody's in trouble out there!" There were other voices, "I can't — Where — Can't anyone . . . Hey! Where's the lifeguard!"

I'm a pretty good swimmer, which, combined with a woman's natural instinct to save life, sent me dashing across the sand before the others. A small girl in a red swimming suit was pointing. "Out there!" she said, indicating a figure bobbing and threshing on the surface a hundred yards out. The distance is only guesswork but there was no guesswork about the swimmer being in trouble. His arms appeared and reappeared in a series of gesticulations as he called out "Help!" Not pausing to curse the lifeguard I bolted forward into the water and made for him as fast as I could. The slope was very gradual just there, and I ran halfway to Connecticut before the water was deep enough for me to swim. There the bottom dropped away abruptly, and so did I — for I had forgotten to take off my Slim-O-Matic belt.

I sank like a stone. There were also stones in quantity under my feet. I twisted an ankle on one nasty little boulder, and in my confusion went in over my head, clawing at the belt. This was not the now popular Tone-O-Matic sash with the magnetic adhesive Velcro fasteners that lock

283

automatically and that you just have to rip apart to undo. This was a predecessor of that, with a huge buckle having two prongs. The extra ten pounds nearly did me in, to say nothing of the time lost getting them off. Thank God I had presence of mind enough to scramble back a few feet to where I could stand up with my nose just above water level and, making haste slowly, draw the buckle tongues out of the binding strap and let the whole load drop. I kicked off and resumed what I can boast is a powerful overhead stroke toward the bather in distress.

My amateur life-saving techniques were a little rusty after all the years since I had practiced and even taught them as a camp counselor to young girls, and what presence of mind the unexpected crisis left me was further jeopardized when I drew close enough to recognize the object of my efforts. It was the lifeguard, going down for the third and last time.

"Cramp," he gasped as, treading into position, I slung an arm around him and started to tow him back to shore.

"I'll bet, Mr. Epicure," I thought, but certainly didn't waste any breath saying. Not just then anyway.

At least *his* training as a lifeguard stood him in good stead so far as cooperating as a subject of salvation was concerned. He knew enough not to fight me. I settled into the one-armed-paperhanger job of getting us both back to dry land. Once we had established an orderly rhythm, and with safety close at last in view, I couldn't help panting out an observation or two.

"So. Quite the . . . party boy."

"Sorry. Ate too . . ."

"And . . . how! Not to . . . mention drink." Save your wind, I told myself. I tried to maintain a calm, steady rhythm of stroking, kicking and breathing. But this citizen had my goat. "No . . . moral fiber . . . Sense of resp . . ."

"Oh, I know, I know."

"Hush! I'll do the . . . talking around . . . here, Buster."

Willing helpers had by now swum or run out to meet us, permitting me to turn my burden over to stronger hands. These also aided and ushered me to shore. I had perceived by now that Dream Boy had not been at the end of his rope, or "going down for the third and last time," which is really a kind of popular superstition anyway. But we were both pretty tuckered out as we waded ashore and dropped, gasping and snorting and spluttering, on the sand. My nonesuch coughed up some more apologies along with the salt water, and I told him to save it for the Park Commissioners or the Bureau of Recreations or whoever the authorities were that were going to be apprised of the sybarite in their employ. A regular Diamond Jim Brady. By this time Osgood had appeared from somewhere and anxiously knelt over me.

"Mom, are you all right, Mom? Oh, Mom!"

I had something else on my mind. What had flashed into it out there in Neptune's realm was not my past life at all, but the gimmick for the script we were all digging for. The opening kicker.

"I've got it," I said. "The first shot. A lifeguard yelling 'Help!' That rich? That existential? Easy to do. Just make the boy, the main character, Bunk, make him a lifeguard. One of his temporary jobs, that he flubs all the time, a schlep even there. Then you can pick it right up from there as is, with the flashbacks. Easy. But what a gag that's at the same time a parable of our confused times. There's your Absurd for you. A drowning lifeguard. Oh, it's rich. We see him calling 'Help!' above the designation on his chest, in a closeup. Himself he cannot heal. Go tell Prackup. Hurry. He needs this."

ten

We have on the outskirts of Appleton a country club with a very pleasant golf course. When originally laid out it was so easy to go around in, in pars they had to keep lowering, that they had to blast a couple of ponds and gouge out a few more bunkers for hazards, all of which make it additionally picturesque and suitable for jogging too. I try to run at least nine holes a day on it, when the weather permits. Spring and fall are far and away the most exhilarating times for outdoor workouts of this sort, especially fall.

For I am back home in Appleton now, in late autumn of the following year. I tell myself I have to get into shape to enter the rest home where apparently I will have to spend my penniless old age. For the picture was unprofitable financially, though it got a good critical reception and is, on balance, an artistic success launching all connected with it further up the road to professional achievement. But I lost my shirt, and have as my own reward for the risk I took the satisfaction of seeing Osgood in demand among the independent producers and married to that pretty little Virgie, who had her eye out for the main chance just as I suspected. I pride myself on having spotted it right from the start. The money I don't for a minute regret. I was only letting it pile up for my sunset years anyway, not using it, so there is little outward change in my life style. Except the habit of running nine or eighteen holes a day in order to keep fit enough to go on working. I take a few private cases, seasonal jobs in local stores at Christmastime, and so on. But I also fancy I must get toughened up for them golden years, for possible enrollment in one of them convalescent homes where I know from brief professional stints the life inside can be such that you are well advised to get into shape to *enter* one, let alone stay out of them.

Ah, how I prize the memories of that summer, a little over a year ago. The summer we worked and played in the sun, all caught up and consolidated into the separate, enchanted community every new movie (and I'm sure play) forges anew out of all those connected with it, from the actors and producers to the technical crews. The summer we all wore signed scarfs, it was the fad then, and finally switched to bullshots from Madeira on the rocks. Gay groups choppering over from the Hamptons. Cries of

"Quiet!" and "Roll 'em!" Then the absolute hush as everyone watched the scene being done. The often ghastly suspense of innumerable retakes when somebody went up in their lines, or a plane rumbled overhead, or some other noise spoiled an otherwise good one. Then the relief of a perfect take followed by Prackup's "Couldn't be better, cut and print!" I have a chest of momentoes such as autographs, mimeographed shooting schedules for the day, business and personal correspondence, seashells, tavern coasters, and God knows what all. But my most cherished souvenir is the new Tone-O-Matic waistline belt Osgood bought me at Abercrombie's, white, so the whole bunch could autograph it, and set, so help me, with a couple of cabochon rubies over the fastening flap. We never did recover the other one. It lies somewhere in Poseidon's watery realm, reposing in peace. I'm not wearing the new one now, on my rounds over the hardening turf of Burnley Wood. I only use it around the house.

Running — or even a good brisk walk — does shake up the mind as well as the frame. My thoughts are like an old deck of cards newly shuffled, hands dealt and coming up different each time. As I take a dogleg in the fourth hole, rounding a clump of poplars beside a pond, I feel that perhaps I should revise my estimate of the world as a madhouse. There after all had been order unperceived in the chaos of my affairs. Still the nuthouse metaphor is valuable as such. A further application of it might liken revolutions, whether political or social, to uprisings by patients who have trussed and gagged their erstwhile keepers after herding them successfully into the head administrator's office. The ruckus today is generational. It remains to be seen which of the two generations is more crackers.

The fancy is driven out of my head by a cry of "Fore!" and the accompanying threat of a ball bounced off of it from behind, courtesy of some clown with a bag of sticks who is out smacking little teeny spheres around the terrain when he could be using it for exercise really meaningful. You are familiar with Mark Twain's remark about golf as a way of spoiling a good walk. How much more a good run. Jogging eighteen holes gives a man a solid sense of itinerary, across stretches delectably combining the natural and the man-made, manicured landscapes so much more pleasing to the eye than the average roadsides up which your joggers more conventionally steam, their faces always looking unhappy, as at a task to be gotten through. This is so much more fun, especially when committees from the country club await me at the nineteenth hole, or, as was once the case, pursue me around the fairways to tell me I am misusing the links in a manner not envisioned by its creators from the greens architect down to the club administrators. But they can't bar me. This club happens to be owned by the town, which bought it when it went into receivership following the migration of members to suburbs farther out with their own club, and the influx, into this area, of Slobkins and other parvenews not interested in golf and martinis but in bowling and beer. So all I have to do to trot its gentle osculations is pay a greens fee of one buck, or an annual municipal membership of ten, which of course is what I choose.

If the canters over the hardening sod stimulate thought, the resting places I have come to favor are ideal to reflect on my current problems, or reminisce on what I've just been through — that segment of my private time in which so much novel to me has occurred in so short a span. A certain covert behind a clump of firs gives on a bird's-eye view of the town, and a road winding toward it from nearby woods. Sitting here a moment, I recall the premier at the New York movie house. The tabulated audience responses on ballots handed out at a sneak preview two weeks before had left the fate of the picture quite uncertain. Of a total of 156 making out the cards, 12 thought it Outstanding (with one adding "outstandingly bad," that is, which I suppose leaves 11); 28 considered it Excellent; 12 Very Good; 9 Good; 58 Fair; and 37 rated it Poor, one of this last category penciling in a curt "Pew," and another, "Oh, brother, where's the Airwick!" The quality levels were divided about the same for the performances of all the leading actors, except for the girl who played Mary Hackney. She made quite a splash and is off on what seems like certain stardom, or at least success. Some disliked Lena Bascombe as the mother, but one said the part was no good. "This bitch was not well realized," the writer said. "Sez you," I thought. 60 would recommend it to their friends, 80 wouldn't, and 16 were undecided. "Which scenes did you like best?" drew some interesting responses. One man (there was an M-F box in which to specify your sex) wrote: "The scenes of blank water, far and away. This is satire at its keenest. I have never thought water quite comes off. This spoof of an element was long overdue.

Especially as a symbol of pre-sensate nugation. Nature will evolve something better (See my book, *Is There an Unconscious After Death?*)." One General Comment was: "All very well, but where the hell is the sunset and the laughter of children? I'm fed up with adult movies." But the one arresting thing about the tallies, and the significant fruit of the venture for many connected with it, was that *everybody* liked the scenes having to do with Bunk's masquerading as a working mother in order to stash the child at the day-care center. Which weren't "scenes" at all, but the whole middle section of the film. You didn't have to see the cards to know that all just rolled like a dream. The laughter in the theatre was enough. The humor had nothing to do with "transvestitism" or any of that sticky stuff. It was simple human, you might say folk, response to a *Charley's Aunt* situation. But the notations on the cards bore it out. "Beautifully written, directed, and acted," was the composite sum of it. So anyway, *Duchess* is having a moderate success among the art houses, but even before it started its run a producer was on the phone asking Osgood to do the screen treatment of some novel he had just bought, dealing with the same sex scrambles among we moderns. Things are getting pretty kinky, aren't they? Three of the notes after "Sex" on the opinion cards were penciled in "Undecided," and somebody X'd out both the M and the F. So Osgood is now hot, and our Virgie had the sense to spot it and bag her catch. Thus he is out of his own "Undecided" category.

And that is all I care about as a mother. The two hundred

thousand dollars' nest egg has been well spent, for all of me. As I rise and resume my workout, the old gray matter bounces along with its speculations on a suitable myth for our time, for my time, that obsession we can't get rid of. Medusa, Phaedra, Hippolytus, Poseidon (who damn near got me by posting an incompetent in his waters!), Samson and Delilah, all have been gone through and discarded. Pending the next candidate for our patron deity, I begin to be fascinated by the whole general concept of the gods coming down to earth in the guise of mortals and not being recognized. Want to know what's tested my mind along that track? The New York premier. I must tell you about that.

What happens at such a glamor event is this. Take it from the point of view of the people arriving. Your cab, or limousine owned or rented, draws up to this blazing theatre front, and as you alight, holding up your skirt or handing your lady from the vehicle onto the red-carpeted sidewalk, all the cameras wielded by newspaper and magazine photographers, but *all* of them, go up, in a reflex, simultaneously, a solid battery ready to snap you if you're somebody. You are given a fast once-over by the entire phalanx, and if you're a nobody, down they come again, to await the next arrivals. They flash and click in that mass salute only if you're somebody — and not always then. Which is what made me think of this theme of immortals moving among us unrecognized. I got there early and stood outside rubbering with the mob, but in the five seconds it took me to step out of the cab and move over with the sheep, I got a glimpse of the terrible ordeal this could be for people who think they *are* somebody (and maybe even are in some field or way unbeknownst to that cruel jury), and then aren't snapped. The pain must be doubled if you're with somebody you're trying to impress, and then get relegated to the masses by the cameras coming down as one, the way they went up, exploding your hopes instead of their bulbs. You could see it in the faces of some of the hopefuls climbing out of limousines and even cabs. Those faces fell apart above the white ties and the sable wraps. It was funny — until it became too sad. I had been watching for about ten minutes when a cab drew up to the curb and Ralph got out. When his face collapsed at the blank he drew, what remained of my amusement vanished, and I felt a twinge. "This is Ralph Frawley, the noted stage designer," I scolded, pointing, and several bulbs flashed. He was in dinner fig, with a foxpaw cummerbund under his tuxedo, and Pilsudski had on a white turtleneck shirt under his. They smiled and came over to shake my hand, and I suddenly had a warm feeling for them, mixed with gratitude, because they represented the woods Osgood was out of, or at least seemed to be. He and Virgie were safe inside that auditorium filling up with swells who had paid twenty-five and fifty dollars a seat for the benefit of the Society for the Prevention of Blindness. I had refused absolutely to let the figure they cut be spoiled by the likes of me. Whether the cameras had flashed for them I didn't know, or care. Most likely not. It was not important . . . just yet . . .

My thoughts are abruptly interrupted. Who is this galloping towards me from the left, cutting straight across the grass with no regard for the numerical succession of flags? His mackinaw collar askew, his checked tweed cap no more horizontal than vertical, and no more on his head than off? It seems precariously pasted to one side. A grin splits his rosy face like a crack in a baked apple. "Hi, Em." I suddenly feel that we ought to stop giving ourselves airs by trying to hew out classic myths for ourselves, because we are not gods or even heroes, but comic-strip characters. Characters in an eternal comic strip. What inspires this fancy is the cloud of breath around Will's panted greeting, like a speech balloon above a figure in the funnies. A similar balloon accompanies my own cold-weather "Morning, Will."

This is the third time in as many weeks that Will has joined me, and again I must slow my pace a little to favor his. We trot easily along for a bit, not talking much. But this morning he has something on his mind.

"Em, as you know I'm on the greens committee."

"So whip us up a nice salad for lunch, Will."

"Em, they don't think this is a proper use for a golf course. Your running shoes don't cut up the turf as much as a club digging a divot out of it, I know. We been through that. But they think it doesn't look right. Just — puff — plain doesn't look right. It gives the place a bad name. All right, an odd look. I've been asked to speak to you about it."

"And you have, and I appreciate it, Will. Now you've done your duty. Let's enjoy the morning."

295

"They're commencing to feel — some of the others, Al Henshaw and Fess Dalton — that this is a put-on. New ways you've brought from the city. Well, you're not getting a rise out of me. Except to say that I think maybe you do the things you do — not just this, other things — because you're at loose ends. You need a man in the house. A woman plain and simple needs a man in the house."

"I've got one."

"Who?"

"Pilsudski."

Will slowed, seemed to stumble. Then he staggered forward a few more steps and fell facedown in a sandtrap. What, another one! Were men going on dying in my arms, dropping like flies? I thought I better take a little breather with him, so I sat down on the ground beside where he did, trying to pull himself together. I ran some sand through my fist.

"Pilsudski wanted some place to lie fallow for a while."

"Now what, he in some kind of trouble? Riots or something?"

"No, no. It doesn't mean lying low. It's a term artists have, for relaxing after a period of work, so their soil can regenerate. Recharge their batteries. He's been working like a dog on a book and needs to get away from the distractions of New York and knock off. A change of scene too. All that. So I invited him to hole in at old 312 Crown."

A light come into Will's eyes, as he pointed a finger at me. "Aha! You're broke and taking in roomers again."

"Yes, it may come to that, life may waltz me around that

296

way once more. But not in this case. No, Pilsudski just wants a place to hole in and pull the hole in after him. I'm not charging him."

Will shook his head, not in disapproval, but more an air of concern on my behalf. "You've got yourself into a bind, or you're heading for one, Em. And I can't honestly say I'm not secretly glad. Because it boosts my hopes you'll *have* to marry me and let me take care of you. So let's leave it that way. I'll kind of stay on the sidelines, like that bird in *Strange Interlude* who got what's-her-name in the end. Shall we dance?"

We're off again, Will giving the slipping cap a corrective shove. We pounded along, hitting our stride together.

"So you've become a patron of the arts."

"Or matron." Edging a little ahead of him, only an inch or two, not to be hairy about it, just make a point. A break in the trees ahead opens up a wider vista of the town. A long stretch of Main Street with its current rash of 'n' shops. Bill 'n' Lill's Bootery, the Wash 'n' Dry coin laundry, Harry 'n' Myrtle's café, a lunch counter called the Chew 'n' Chat, as God is my judge. Pilsudski likes that, but I wonder how long Appleton will keep him amused. I imagine him slugging away up there in Randy's old room, getting heaven knows what demons out of his Black American system after this fallow period, in which nevertheless some poetry keeps coming out. Lines like "Miraculous suppositions that the dawn shall pose," which he says is reminiscent of somebody named Hart Crane, who I don't know. He has abandoned the play where the colored maid comes in and runs her finger over the old white man in the chair to see if there is any dust on him. He says he doesn't sleep very well, might do better if he was working. The sheep he tries to count behaving more perversely than ever, he relates at breakfast, backing through the fence, crawling under it, digging with their forepaws like dogs, even barking viciously. *He* drinks moderately, beginning at eleven in the morning. Lord, am I to go through that again? A lot of shopping at the Grape 'n' Grain — another one. Probably related to his sexual problem. Always gives you a start to see a Negro one of them, or one of them a Negro. Grotesque, since one thinks of them as primitive so hence normal. Yet New York is full of them, floating along with two feet off the ground. He's very nice around the house, pleasant to live with save for a few irritating habits. He'll keep chewing gum while drinking a highball, worrying the pellet around in his front teeth in a manner scarcely envisioned by the mfr. But his clowning is Grade-A.

"Were you ever born in Georgia?"

"Can't say as I have." (Dutifully feeding him the straight lines.)

"Well, I have, and it's not a happy thing. And then to have a father trying to pull himself up by his bootstraps but failing in everything, because he simply antagonized everybody. Opened a hardware store, then when that didn't work out, a haberdashery, then he tried landscape gardening. But in each case he fizzled because he just couldn't get along with the public. Finally, after working

298

for a spell in a club gymnasium, he thought he'd picked up enough knowledge of massage to open a place of his own as a masseur. Which he did."

Pause. A put-on I know. But I feed him the straight line. "And did he make a go of that?"

"No. He rubbed people the wrong way."

When Will and I take another rest it is again where we have a nice topographical view of the town, and as we sit there together, breathing heavily but for the moment happily, I note something. The thing of which we are most aware in our suburbs and our rapidly changing American towns in general is not the shopping centers and factory chimneys which are everywhere, but the church steeples, precisely because they are so outnumbered. I noticed it in a trip through Connecticut. There, the white church steeple is practically all that remains of the traditional New England landscape. And one is haunted by it as one, oblivious to the tenants in a house, will be haunted by its ghost. The less you believe what it proclaims, the more you cherish what it recalls.

It's reason enough, I decided as I sat there beside Forever Panting Though No Longer Young, to go to church and stay on the parish committees. That and a chance to ram integration down a few holdout throats. Both Will and Osgood chide me about my motivation for working on behalf of the proposed new housing project. They claim I do it more to irritate certain pillars of society, mostly females I could never stand, than to champion the cause of the oppressed. Maybe so. But if we can't put our vices to some good use, where are we? Pilsudski, who doesn't seem to care where he lives, says integration is old hat; the Blacks now *want* segregation. And I may have the Black Panthers to contend with. Well, I've handled worse than them in my day, so bring them on.

"Come on," I says to Forever Panting. "We've miles to go before we sleep."

"Say, that was well put, Em," he said, rising and slapping dirt from his jeans. "You certainly have a way with words."

Late afternoon now, of a winter's day. Dusk has slipped like a ghost between my lace curtains and now softly obliterates the furniture in my parlor, except for the antimacassars whose white circles resist him to the last. And, of course, the curtains themselves. In a moment I will light the lamps, and their warm glow will in turn extinguish the phantom of December darkness, in which, outside, the oak leaves rustle like empty brown cups in an all but plundered candy box. I hear the radiators softly hiss, between machine-gun bursts of the typewriter overhead. For Pilsudski is off and running again, not lying fallow at all. We may not be able to pry him loose when Will Gerstenslager comes, to take us out to dinner. I have not yet cleared away the tea with which I have at least briefly lured him down, a break in the toil that has continued since early morning. He was abstracted at breakfast. The pot is cold, the gray caracul Cossack hat Pilsudski has plumped down over it for a cozy still there where the buffoon put it. He got a letter today from Ralph Frawley. Ralph is living with an actor often in the news with didoes of substance to the jet set. I leave it there, the cozy, for I know Will Gerstenslager will get a bang out of it. He'll give his familiar adenoidal chuckle and that headshake, meant to convey that "We're a blast. What a riot we are."

I have got to think about Will. A man of the world by rustic standards, but something of a yokel by worldly. He exposed himself, or I exposed him, to a completely alien environment. The result was bound to be inevitable. Many's the time in New York I had to explain the various wrinkles and specialties of New York types. Or merely some term that cropped up, such as S.M. "It means sado-masochistic," I said, and you can imagine I wasn't through with it then by a long shot! The sadists he understood, of course, but I had to go into what masochists like. "They derive pleasure from pain. Even whipping and beating." And Will: "They need a good kick in the pants." Still he thinks he's with it, as you can tell by the way he'll lean back and ask a waiter how the veal is done, or order a bottle of Chateauneuf-du-Pop. You've got to love him for it. And he is in his own way a bit of all right, as we say. It's all we can ask. But the honeymoon, if any, can be imagined.

Best hotel in some tropical paradise, and the bed's been pied. One of us at least in stitches. The faked voice in the hall saying it's the house dick, and can I show my license. And objects coming through the bathroom door the way they did into my berth that night we took the train to

New York, landing in the washbasin over which I'm making up: a teaspoon from room service, ice cubes, followed by a dill pickle spear or a couple olives. We're full of the old Nick. But he's absolutely loyal and affectionate, yea unto the end. Bubbles had three kitchen sinks when she died. He's also good to his single child, a daughter who lives in San Francisco, a swinger but getting nowhere fast. I often tell her, "What good is all your sexual emancipation getting you, since you're still not married at the age of twenty-seven?" Pilsudski believes he's met her once in New York but can't be sure, so she must of made one of her delible impressions. He was a little catty about what I *told* him about her — as he can be about me too. Once he hinted some woman in town dropped a rather slurring remark about my present mode of life. "Her opinion is a matter of complete indifference to me," I replied with some heat. These confusing spring warblers have odd quirks. Like Charles Pilsudski signs his name on two lines, the first name above the last. But he's a good listener, for whom I must polish off some more of my tales. He might make something out of that picture hassle in the hospital that time.

I once had an appendectomy and a diverticulum in a double. I speak of having both though I was only working for the appendectomy, because the diverticulum couldn't afford a private and would keep calling on me for the innumerable little things floor care can't give you. We often do that. Nurse, another glass of water please. A newspaper. A couple aspirin. Once I hear him calling for a

Utrillo. Now days we don't arbitrarily hang a picture on a wall and that's it. No, we keep changing the prints to suit your taste, or mood. Your Bluebird, or whatever the volunteers may call themselves there, will come in with an armload of masterpieces for you to make your selection from. "Nice Van Gogh this morning? No? How about this Matisse then? Jackson Pollock, Braque? Do we like this abstract?" My appendectomy selected the abstract, which the Bluebird then slipped into the frame, removing the old print. But when the diverticulum woke up from a snooze, oy, did we have a little art criticism. "Get those bleeding ulcers off the wall! I have some rights here too, and I don't want to look at that garbage for $22.50 a day. Nurse! Get me a Utrillo or something. A Monet, a Renoir, even a Paul Clay. Anything but that." My appendectomy was nice about it, laughing as he told me to get the Bluebird back with her stock. I don't remember what selection we finally stuck in the frame. The other guy was on the borderline of being a mental case, and we felt sorry for him. He claimed to be in a long physical decline beginning one day when he caught a terrible cold from a faith healer.

Pilsudski may be able to make something of these raw materials. He seems to dig complicated and mixed-up characters, of which he is certainly one! He toys with the idea of a protagonist who is a study in contradictions. "The town's worst bitch is its best saint," he says to himself, trying something or other on for size, an anti-heroine I suppose. In any case she's not my problem. He spends a lot of time in his room listening to good music, just like Osgood and Randy did. Naturally a lot of rock and roll too. He fancies a group called the Electric Gas Stove, whereof the vocalist seems to pursue a technique of singing the words of a song other than that being played by the instrumentalists. And if you can call them words. "Thruss muh baby, liss muh honey, lemme plop yuh thrucks!" Or some such. A maid would quit. He appreciates another bunch known as The Single Girl and Red China. Honestly. Will anything be deader than that vogue when it's dead — odd names? The pictures on the albums inspire brisk discussions about hippies. Don't I think at their purest they resemble the early Christians? I do indeed, and I would like to see the parallel completed by having them thrown to the lions. If not the Kiwanians, ha. Serve 'em both right. But somehow the memory of Pilsudski that comes oftenest to mind is the time we're picnicking on the sand at Long Island and look up to see the black screwball running erratically around the beach holding a forked stick he has found before him like a dowser's wand, then suddenly veering to the right and plunging wildly into the sea.

As for Oz and Virgie, I went into that marriage with my eyes wide open. There'll be no disillusionments there, as the faults of both have been squarely faced and charitably accepted. She comes of people who say "means" for money, and God knows they're the graspingest of all. That first night at the house when Will and me come home and found her cozied up with Randy, she regaled us by reciting some Shakespeare, a school play she'd had a part in. *The Merchant of Venice* I think. "How sweet the moonlight sleeps upon this bank," she sang, and I thought, yeah, the Chase Manhattan. But no regrets, or even misgivings, like I say. We must all be taken as we are. But the intellectual conversations that night! A person would bang their jaw and swallow to make their ears pop, such rarefied atmosphere.

The important thing is to put ourselves in other people's shoes, get inside their skin. My late Frank had a cheer about that. There were those who looked down on these "yoll" poems for dealing exclusively with objects such as fruits and vegetables, which is not quite true as we shall see. His more cerebral efforts dealt with abstract values. One for example is this peon of praise to decency and perspective in a world of jostling competition and rampant me-tooism:

> *We're neighbors miles apart*
> *Because the garden of our heart*
>   *Is something that we've simply got to weed.*
> *So let's belt it out for kindness*
> *And an end to petty blindness*
>   *Resulting in particular from greed.*
> *Oh, the other fellow's viewpoint*
> *May constitute a new point*
>   *For getting fresh perspective on your own!*

(A pause here while the cheerleader crouches in his locomotive stance, for a gradually but irresistibly building

tempo, throwing his megaphone away for the climactic
leap into the air with legs apart and both arms upflung
as he faces the audience, as a cheering section for the
Human Team.)

> *So ... let's ... hear it for perspective,*
> *Let's all make it our elective*
> *In the coming proper study of mankind!*

(He gets into position for the final yell.)

> *A per — per — per*
> *And a spec — spec — spec,*
> *Here a per, there a spec,*
> *Everywhere a perspec,*
> *A tivio, a tayvio,*
> *And a tiddleyo and away we go*
> *For PER ... SPEC ... TIVE!*

Some were devoted to evils rather than virtues, in which
case they became *Bronx* cheers, with the whole audience
putting out their tongues and fluttering their collective lip
to deliver the resounding "raspberry" for selfishness, nar-
rowness, corruption on both public and personal levels, or
going off half-cocked. One such raspberry was for gossip,
unfortunately not preserved in manuscript form, but of
which I recall a fragment:

> *Ibbity bibbity sibbity sab,*
> *I wish to God she'd shut her gab.*

It goes without saying that, like all artists, these out-
pourings arose as much from inner bitterness as from the

sunniness they celebrated. It is from the pain of limitation that the ideal is often best apprehended. That was one of Randy Rivers's pet notions, oft asserted. Frank even had a certain antisocial streak, fairly well repressed until we had to go out to parties or entertain, then whammo; a misanthropic strain that made him resent visitors, sometimes greeting them at the door as though he was going to punch them in the nose for having come, their having been invited being no excuse.

Oh, the years, where have they gone? Where is the little boy, name of Osgood Wallop, not the grown man, the little fellow who put a fever thermometer into a pot of mustard to see how hot it was? Will you tell me that? The little fellow I did all I could to help by being a den mother. The tricks I'd show him to entertain the Cub Scouts, to give him security? Status with the group? Here's a piece of rope two or three feet long. Can anybody take this rope, one end in each hand, and tie a knot in it without taking either hand off? No? You'll never figure it out. Flog not your brains. You pick the rope up off the table *with your arms folded*, and by unfolding your arms automatically tie a knot in it. Presto, a hit with the bunch. He also did some of his tricks at a birthday party to which he took his first girl. Marjorie something. Whipple. She couldn't stay because she had butter on her dress. They were what then — twelve. And not much after that they start sleeping together and taking things, now. Is this what's happening in the land where He gave us, as our poet sang, dominion over palm and pine? The other night Pilsudski went to a pot party for the benefit of a Synanon they're trying to start up in the neighborhood for drug addicts. Is there any rhyme or reason in that? Maybe, but I shake my head. It's getting too many for me. We have a new minister in our pulpit who preached a sermon in favor of legalizing marijuana. I give that Buster a piece of my mind coming out of church. Declining his outstretched hand, I pointed with mine to a sign on the church lawn reading "Keep Off the Grass." "That's a better sermon than yours!" I said. He may have second thoughts as a result of some parishioners whose boy was arrested for possession. I know them well. An only son, of eight children. I nursed the mother for three or four of them. The husband was dead set on a boy, so nothing for the woman to do but peel off one girl after another till she got one. Of course the minister's point was that punishment of any sort is too severe for mere marijuana, but that's the argument: who knows when they'll escalate from it into the hard stuff, as people don't from alcohol? The father was quite broken up. He cried like a baby, and him high up in the power-shovel game. The minister is one of those who say "spidit" for spirit and "spiditual" for spiritual. Who needs that?

But the thing is — are we to become a nation of Lotus Eaters? Well, you may take it from there, it's all yours, because I have reached a decision for myself about all this mythologizing. My homework is finished. I have decided that all quests for defining myths are vain, a pathetic attempt to give ourselves a scope and a glory we do not intrinsically possess, that we are comic-strip characters plain and simple. "Pull down that vanity," Randy would quote

308

some poet whose name I never got clear. I suddenly have for that reason a desire to read the funnies again, the way I once did long ago, right here in this very parlor, which when I was a little girl was my grandfather's. At home I read the daily paper, but here on Sunday visits there was always an out-of-town supplement to curl up with while the grownups drank coffee and talked around the kitchen table. I'm seized with a burning curiosity to see what the cartoonists are up to these days.

On another chair is the comic supplement from yesterday's local Sunday paper, where I have dropped it. I get it and settle down with it in mine, switching the lights on. I turn a few pages and then my eyebrows go up.

One of the leading features is a funnies version of Homer, drawn with epic and godlike heroes and heroines. Today's installment deals with Cronus, the youngest Titan, and Uranus, his father. Uranus was the Heaven, first ruler of the universe, and son of Gaea, the Earth. He was also the father of Gaea's children (some more incestuous mishmash here, apparently), the Titans, the Cyclops and the Hundred-handed ones. Fearing that his children would rebel against him, he imprisoned them, but Cronus (the youngest Titan son remember) castrated him with the help of Gaea, thereby taking away his power. Small wonder. It was from the blood of Uranus which fell on earth — tie this — that the three Furies sprang, the Erinyes, the goddesses of revenge. First cousins to me, you might say. I'm a Gorgon, another branch of the family, but we all have the same hairdo. If yours is in snarls by this time, forgive me. This is where you came in. According to some reliable sources, Aphrodite was born of Uranus's discarded giblets and the foaming sea. Showing that nothing goes permanently down the old Disposall.

I dropped the paper and threw my legs out with a long sigh, feeling that the top of my head was blowing off. Nor was that all. The front door chimes rang, which would be Will Gerstenslager calling at an unfashionably early hour. At the same time there was a violent volley of noises resumed overhead, a bolt from whoever was in charge of hurling those now. With a nervous laugh, a tingle of alarmed excitement, I glanced upward at the ceiling, where was to be heard, once again, the steady rumble of a typewriter, the sound of thunder gathering in my parlor sky.